radiant press

# THE
# ERRANT
# HUSBAND

## ELIZABETH HAYNES

Editor: Susan Musgrave
Cover art: Brandi Hofer
Book and cover design: Tania Wolk, Third Wolf Studio
Printed and bound in Canada at Friesens, Altona, MB

The publisher gratefully acknowledges the support of Creative Saskatchewan, the Canada Council for the Arts and SK Arts.

Library and Archives Canada Cataloguing in Publication

Title: The errant husband / Elizabeth Haynes.
Names: Haynes, Elizabeth, 1959- author.
Identifiers: Canadiana (print) 20210284072 | Canadiana (ebook) 20210284102 |
ISBN 9781989274583
(softcover) | ISBN 9781989274590 (PDF)
Classification: LCC PS8565.A934 E77 2021 | DDC C813/.54—dc23

radiant press
Box 33128 Cathedral PO
Regina, SK S4T 7X2
info@radiantpress.ca
www.radiantpress.ca

Expertly entwining present and past, ordinary and extraordinary, comedy and seriousness, this sparkling novel about a likably cranky Calgary parks manager in Cuba resounds with depth. A multi-faceted, satisfying read.

**ANNE FLEMING** author of *The Goat*

Part mystery, part history, part travelogue, Elizabeth Haynes introduces us to Thelma, a woman who, after being stood up by her husband at a Cuban airport asks the question, why are women always waiting for men? A curious note left by Wally has Thelma reframing and examining her marriage. Told in a quippy and fun manner, the book tips flawlessly between past and present when Thelma refuses to put her vacation on hold and instead goes on a quest for answers that lead to a personal journey of remembrance and intrigue. What and why we hold onto false ideals is at the heart of this book as we collectively discover that often being lost is key to allowing life to begin. This is a lovely and unforgettable novel.

**KATHERIN EDWARDS** author of *A Thin Band*

A funny, gripping mystery of the heart told with drop-dead timing and heart-stopping love. Nerdy missing husband, chatty stranger, flirtatiously artistic taxi driver, poetic potential husband thief—Haynes writes them all with full-fledged humanity and respect.

**ROBERTA REES** author of *Long After Fathers*

During a trip to Havana, Thelma Dangerfield gazes at a 16th century statue of Isabel de Bobadilla, governor of Cuba and wife of Hernando de Soto. The conquistador left his wife to govern the island while he attempted to conquer Florida. He never returned. As she waits for Wally, her errant husband, Thelma wonders about Isabel, a historic example of the waiting woman. Her husband has disappeared and she is determined to follow the clues to find him. Thus begins Elizabeth Haynes's compelling story of a woman who carries self- doubt, grief, and a heck of a lot more inside her. By turns funny, erudite, tense and quite moving, *The Errant Husband* introduces us to an intriguing new voice in Canadian writing.

**DAVID CARPENTER** author of *The Gold*

A travelogue with a literary twist, a mojito with an extra shot of lime, *The Errant Husband* is a wry, winsome adventure tale, ultimately revealing those secrets we dare not tell ourselves.

**MARGARET MACPHERSON** author of *Body Trade*

# THE
# ERRANT
# HUSBAND

For my father, Sterling Haynes,
and my dear friends Karin Herrero, Sophia Lang
and Sue Christensen-Wright.
You left too soon. You are with me always.

*Prologue*

IN THE CITY of Havana, where Avenida del Puerto meets Desemparado, stands El Castillo de la Real Fuerza, the first and oldest of four forts guarding Havana harbour. Built in 1558, it is surrounded by limestone walls six meters thick. Tourists can saunter inside the cannon studded courtyard, cross the moat by drawbridge, admire the suits of armour then climb to the top of a round tower for views of old Havana and the sea. On top of that tower is La Giraldilla, a bronze weathervane of a woman in a diaphanous gown holding a scepter, her crowned head held high, scanning the ocean. She is Isabel de Bobadilla, wife of conquistador Hernando De Soto. He sailed away to conquer Florida in 1539, leaving her to govern the island.

He did not return.

# 1

# CHAPTER 1

*Cuba, 2005*

ALL OF THE TOURISTS from Thelma's flight push their luggage carts through the glass doors of the International Airport into the brilliant Havana afternoon. Customs officials gather around a couple of expatriate Cubans, leaving a scowling young woman in a tight blue uniform to look after the rest of them. She stares at Thelma's new espadrilles for a few moments, then nods her past.

Outside, warm air caresses her. Men in starched white guayaberas and black pants wave signs: Mr. and Mrs. Marko, Familia Santa Cruz, Havanatour, Amistur, Hotel Melia Cohiba. Thelma pulls her suitcase over to a stone bench and searches for Wally. The waiting crowd surges forward with every whoosh of the glass doors, but Wally is nowhere to be seen. Maybe he's waiting further down the sidewalk where there are fewer people. She pulls her suitcase away from the entrance, stopping to smell some flowers. Jasmine? Heavenly.

A man appears at her side. "Taxi, Señora?" he whispers.

"No thanks."

Another man flanks her.

"Where are you going?" the second man asks.

"Nowhere."

"Nowhere. That is just outside of Havana. I can drive you there very cheap," he says, flashing a grin and stroking his moustache.

"I'm waiting for my husband."

"Your husband is Cuban?" asks the first man, who is thin and clean-shaven.

"Canadian," Thelma replies, looking past him to a guy in Bermuda shorts and wrinkled t-shirt who could be, but isn't Wally.

"He is working here?" asks the thin man.

"No, yes, he's doing some research. He's writing."

"What is he writing?"

"A novel based on Hernando De Soto."

"The first governor of Cuba."

"According to my husband, his wife, Isabel, did most of the governing."

"Es verdad," says the guy with the moustache. "Do you know that Isabel de Bobadilla is the weathervane La Giraldilla on top of el Castillo de la Real Fuerza? It is because she went to the tower every afternoon to see if Hernando was returning yet from La Florida. She is also the symbol on the Havana Club rum bottle."

"Yes, I do." Well, she didn't know about the rum.

"Ah, you are helping your husband in his researches?"

"No, I'm meeting him for a vacation." A marriage renewal holiday, actually, but he didn't need to know that. "And I don't need a taxi," says Thelma. With a dismissive smile, she returns to crowd scanning.

Wally probably went to the Museum of the Revolution and lost track of time in the Che room or at the Granma memorial, though how much time could one spend staring at a boat, even one as apparently illustrious as the one that transported Fidel and his fellow travelers to Cuba to start the revolution. Thelma slouches out of her sweater and takes a deep breath of the perfumed air. She can feel her winter-hard skin softening already.

"Long flight?" asks the thin man. He's still there?

"Yes."

"You are here for how long?"

"Two weeks."

"I hope you enjoy your stay. Many Canadians come here to escape your cold winter. I, myself, have seen snow when I studied in Leningrado," says the mustachioed man.

"Only thing that kept him warm was Russian girls."

"I bet." She smiles and turns back to the main entrance. Maybe she missed seeing Wally inside.

"I don't need a taxi," she repeats. "My husband is coming."

"I am Jorge," says the thin man, "and he is Tomás. If we can be of assistance, we...."

"Great. I'll keep you in mind."

4

THE SUN HAS disappeared behind the palms. The doors open only sporadically now, disgorging hassled looking Cubans and Cuban-foreigner pairs. She's been waiting for forty-eight minutes. The taxis and minibuses that were lined up against the curb have all filled up with happy vacationers and chugged off into the sunset. Where the hell is Wally?

The men appear beside her. Tomás leans against a pillar and lights a cigarette.

"Your husband is not here?"

"No. Listen, do you have a cell?"

"Sell?" he looks around, lowers his voice. "You would like to sell dollars? Buy pesos?"

"A cell for my husband."

Tomás wrinkles his forehead. "You have some tissues of your husband, for testing at one of our hospitals, Señora?"

"I need a cell phone."

"Cell. Phone," he says, as if trying to discover how the two words might go together.

"A cell phone. A mobile phone." She gestures opening one. "Para, uh, llevar...? (no, that's take-out), ?para llamar a mi esposa. Esposo."

"You need to call your husband?"

"Yes. He's a bit absentminded. He probably got the flight time wrong." The two men talk, then Tomás fires a burst of Spanish at her.

"Más despacio, please." Another volley from Jorge.

"Gentlemen, por favor. My Spanish is es, esta no bueno."

"You need a mobile phone, yes? Very small and very, uh, portátil?"

"Portable."

"Portable, yes. Our phone system here is, how do you say, un poco anticuado," adds Jorge.

"Right."

"How do you say it?"

"Antiquated."

"An-ti-qua-ted," repeats Jorge. "Is that correct?"

She's not an English teacher. "Yes."

"And cell phones, nobody has one," adds Tomás. "We have Cubacel company. But ordinary Cubans like us, we do not have even regular phones in our homes."

"Where can I find a public phone then?"

Tomás gestures inside the terminal and sighs. "Mostly our phones don't work so well. Hungarian equipment, you know."

Jorge frowns. "Yes. Hungarian. From before 1991 and the Special Period. Maybe you will get a line, maybe you won't. Maybe you have to wait, try many times."

Light is leeching from the sky. Where the hell is Wally? She wrote down her flight details and put them with his ticket so he wouldn't lose them.

"Señora, we will take you to your hotel. There are no more flights and there will be no more minibuses, no taxis. Maybe your husband is ill."

Thelma sighs. He better be. If he's not, she is going to kill him. Or injure him badly.

"Alright. Let's go."

They lead her across the parking lot to a side road with broken pavement where an orange Lada is parked. The tires look threadbare, one headlight is broken and the body is covered with scratches and dents.

"Hey, this isn't a cab. There's no sign. And where's your meter?"

"Not official taxi, Señora. But it will be cheaper for you, only fifteen dollars," Tomás says.

"Ten."

"Thirteen."

"Eleven."

"Okay, for you, Señora, special price of eleven dollars," says Tomás. "Because you are beautiful and have an unreliable husband."

She blushes. Gisela wasn't kidding about the men here. Beautiful? Her hair in the side mirror resembles a rat's nest. Not that she's ever seen one, Alberta being rat-free and all.

Rust tentacles the driver's side door and across the hood.

"Please, come in. It is good car," proclaims Jorge.

"Very safe," adds Tomás.

Sure, if you don't drive it.

Tomás yanks the passenger side door open, while Jorge tries to shove her suitcase into the toy trunk.

"If we are stopped, say you are my friend."

"Stopped by whom?"

"Police."

"What? Why?"

"Don't worry. It should not be a problem."

And she's always wanted to see the inside of a Cuban jail.

Wally had better be very sick. He better have something temporarily incapacitating from which he will recover by tomorrow. Unless he was in an accident. What if he is lying in a hospital, injured? No, Gisela said Cuba was a safe country.

"Where are you staying?"

"The Palco."

"It is a very nice hotel."

"New hotel," adds Jorge, tying the trunk closed with a piece of frayed rope. She reluctantly climbs into the front seat as Tomás tries to get the engine to turn over. On the fifth try, it catches. An errant spring pokes into her butt.

They bump down the potholed road and turn onto a large, dimly-lit road with multiple lanes, past groups of people standing at bus stops, concrete office blocks, and open-air snack bars. A pink bus pulled by a truck and packed with people briefly envelopes them in black smoke.

"Policia a la izquierda," calls Jorge.

"On the left? What should I do?"

"Pretend to be Tomás' girlfriend, put your hand on his thigh."

"I don't think so."

"Look they are beside us now." Jorge points. A boxy white car keeps pace.

"I don't see any siren."

"Please, trust us," says Tomás. He sounds sincere. Sighing, Thelma places her hand lightly on his knee.

The car pulls ahead and Thelma snatches back her hand just as Tomás careens onto an unlit road, spilling her sideways and sending the spring into her backside again. An illegal taxi and a taxista who can't drive. Great. Just look out the window, Thelm, she tells herself. The hotel and Wally can't be too far now.

A man leans against a small concrete house, smoking. Inside, she can see the flickering light of a black and white television, a small boy sitting alone in front of it. The houses are older, made of white stone. Limestone? She glimpses a crumbling Doric columned mansion behind a hedge of bougain-villea.

They lurch to a stop at the bottom of a circular driveway.

"The Palco, Señora," says Tomás.

She fishes eleven dollars from her purse and hands it to him.

"Thank you. I live in Arroyo Naranjo near the airport. This is the phone number of my aunt. Please, if you need a taxi or any help, call me. I am at your service. I am sorry but I cannot take you further."

"Fine, thanks a lot."

Tomás unloads her suitcase and hurries back into the rust bucket. Thelma pulls her bag up the hotel walkway, inhaling the fragrance coming from trees with delicate white blossoms. Maybe she shouldn't be too mad at Wally. This place is seductive, she can see how easy it would be to lose track of time and succumb to island lethargy.

At the glass entrance, Thelma turns to wave at Tomás and Jorge, but the car has disappeared into the night.

———

"VENACA," CALLS the woman at the desk. Thelma looks around for the Venacas. The lobby is empty. "Venaca," cries the woman again

My room, a shower, Wally. That's all I want, she thinks. Obviously the Venacas aren't here, can you just check me in?

The woman beckons toward Thelma. Right. Venaca. Come here.

"Dangerfield," she says. "Thelma. My husband, Wally, checked in two days ago. I'll just need a key to our room."

The woman, whose nametag reads Veronika, consults her computer. "Mr. Dangerfield has left but he's held the room for you. You're on the fifth floor. Eugenio will show you up. The pool is down the hall to the right. We have two restaurants and three bars, a poolside bar, by the pool, in the lobby and..."

"He's gone out for the evening?"

"He checked out."

"Checked out? No, that's impossible."

"At 11 AM"

"No, Veronika, he did not check out. Please look again."

"Perhaps he will call you, Señora. Passport please." Thelma fumbles in her purse, slides it over.

"Here is your key, Mrs. Dangerfield."

"Did he leave a message?"

Veronika turns and rummages through a pigeonhole behind her.

"Ah, yes, there is something." She hands Thelma a sealed envelope and nods at Eugenio.

Clutching it in sweating hands, she follows him to a glass elevator. He pushes number five. At two the elevator stops and a large family in swimming attire crowds in. A woman carries a sleeping baby boy, his little pink mouth pursed in sleep, his tiny fingers hanging limply.

He cannot have checked out.

They stop at three for a chambermaid and cart, at four for nothing.

In the room, Eugenio turns on the A.C., pours her a glass of water, opens the patio door, shows her how to work the TV.

"Yes, yes, thank you," she says, handing him a couple of dollars.

Thelma collapses on the bed. Stares at the painting of Mayan ruins, glyphs of tiny Gods and Goddesses. Maybe Wally found a better hotel—a fabulous place with a view of the ocean or the Morro Castle. What, one more fabulous than this one, with its marble floors and glass elevator, Thelma?

Ripping the envelope, she pulls out a piece of hotel stationary.

*Thelm*
*The opportunity of a lifetime came up. I was out walking in Old*
*Havana and ran into a professor, Dr Sánchez Portillo, an expert in*
*Spanish-Cuban history. We talked about my novel and the professor*
*invited me to meet a Hernando De Soto expert in Cienfuegos!*
*So I'm going there with the good doc. I'll be back in three days tops.*
*I'll call you.*
*W.*
*P.S. Try the puerco asado (roast pig) in the dining room.*
*It is fantastico!*

He's gone off with some professor he ran into? He'll return in three days? Is he serious? Cienfuegos is south of Havana, four, maybe five hours away!

She stuffs the note into her purse. I'll fucking 'puerco asado' you, Wally, she mutters. There are three bars in this place. She's going to visit each of them. She is going to get roaring, stinking drunk.

# CHAPTER 2

*Calgary, 2004*

THELMA LIES EXHAUSTED on the couch, wondering how much it would cost to hire a window décor person. Three hours shopping for new curtains for the den and nothing to show for it.

You'd think one could find a peach coloured natural fibre curtain somewhere in this town.

The doorbell rings.

"Can you get that?" calls Wally.

"But you're better with the Mormons than I am."

"How do you know it's..."

"I saw them earlier."

"I'm chopping."

Thelma struggles up from the couch, cautiously opens the door. It's Tim from Wally's writing group, his baby, Esme, dangling from a sling across his chest.

"Tim. I thought you were a Mormon."

"I am."

"Oh yeah, that's right. But you're, well, lapsed, aren't you?"

"Lapsed?"

"I mean you're not on a mission, not going door-to-door, not prac.... Forget it. Wall's just making lunch. Come in and join us."

"Sorry. Can't. Listen, Gina's shopping and I've got an interview. Would you guys mind watching Esme for a while, an hour. Two tops?"

"Sure."

"Thanks, Thelm, you're a lifesaver." He plops the diaper bag on the floor then takes the sleeping baby from the sling and hands her to Thelma.

Wally walks in, wiping his hands on his apron, a gift from her mother.

"Can you believe it, Wally? *Amber Durum!*" says Tim.

"You've got an interview with a bakery?" asks Thelma.

"No, it's a journal. The editorial collective read my story in *New Canadian Fiction*. They liked my 'prairie sensibility' and they're looking for an assistant editor."

"Great. Well, you better be off, don't want to be late for that," Wally says. Thelma detects a hint of bitterness, but Tim doesn't seem to notice.

"Thanks pal. See you at our next group. Hopefully I'll have some good news."

Thelma settles Esme on a blanket on the floor and stares down at the tiny thing. She's wearing white crocheted pants and a top with a pink lace ribbon at the throat. Esme's mouth is open, her cheek is hot. Thelma touches a finger to the corner of the little one's mouth.

"Do you want pesto mayo on your flatbread?"

"Sure. Hi there little Esme," Thelma coos, stroking the tiny wisps of blond hair from Esme's forehead then touches the crown of the baby's head, the soft spot, the fontanel.

Wally comes in and peers down at the little one's face. "Can I hold her?"

Thelma looks at Wally's outstretched palms, the pencil lead he accidentally jabbed into one as a kid.

"Later."

Thelma picks up the sleeping baby, lays Esme on her own chest. Feels Esme's tiny heart pounding against hers.

———

THEY'RE ENROUTE TO the Co-op for groceries. Thelma is driving. Wally is contemplating the grocery list, crossing out, adding.

"Put down olive oil, Wall."

"I get that super extra virgin stuff at Lina's, remember."

"Oh, right."

She switches on the radio. CKUA playing a jazzy version of Besame Mucho.

"How's it working out with Rosa in your writing group now?" Thelma asks.

"Fine."

"She adds some spice, does she?"

"Yeah, sprinkles cayenne in our coffee when we're not looking."

"Ha ha. You mentioned it was getting a little dull with just you and Alvin and Tim. A gorgeous Cuban woman should liven things up."

"Gorgeous? Is she? I hadn't noticed."

"Right. Is your group still meeting at The Masculine Boar?"

"The Wild Boar."

"Why do I always think it's called The Masculine Boar? Must be all those dead animal heads on the walls."

"No. We've started going to a Cuban place she knows in the North East. De Cuba con Amor."

"Is that so?" Thelma moves over to the right lane, cutting off a purple Tracker. The guy gives her the finger.

"Jerk."

"You cut him off, Thelm." The Tracker rides her bumper. "Jesus, what if he follows us home?"

"We're going to Co-op."

"I can hardly wait for the rumble in the middle of the parking lot."

"So do you think Rosa will be an interesting addition to your group?"

"Rosa's very intuitive."

"Is she?" Thelma asks, racing through a yellow and stranding the Tracker at the red. She turns onto Brentwood, deciding to go in the back way in case the guy is following her.

"Thelm?"

"Yeah."

"You know my Che beret?"

"Vaguely."

"Black with a red star in front."

"I know what a Che beret looks like. I just haven't seen yours."

"I bought it at the One World Film Festival, eight, nine years ago."

"Uh huh."

"I found it in the Sally Ann bag. You were going to throw it out." Busted.

"Not throw it out, re-purpose it."

"You seem to have a habit of re-purposing my things."

"Why do you want that old beret, anyway?"

"No reason."

"You haven't talked about Che in years."

"I'm re-interesting myself in him. You've got to admire the guy, Thelma. He sacrificed his personal dreams of being a doctor in pursuit of something bigger. A new country. A new man."

"Right," Thelma says, wheeling into a just vacated parking space. "I wonder who worked all week, who supported him while he was doing all that dreaming?"

Thelma sneaks a look at Wally, but if her comment bothers him he is choosing to ignore her.

# CHAPTER 3

*Cuba*

THREE MOJITOS HAVE taken the edge off Thelma's anger. She no longer feels like retreating to her room to throw glasses from the balcony and watch them smash on the cement below.

She grabs number four from the poolside table. Takes three big gulps and puts the glass beside a plate of chicken bones. Adjusts the chaise lounge to sitting position, tries to do those bloody calming breaths, or were they cleansing breaths, she learned in a long ago yoga class.

Twinkling lights frame the poolside bar; clouds scud across a starry sky. A pelican wheels across the moon. 'Feel this warm air surrounding you like a blanket,' she tells herself. 'Yeah—a blanket you could use to suffocate your husband.'

Calming breaths, Thelma, cleansing breaths.

He's gone off with a man he's just met, some sort of professor? That is not Wally-like behaviour. Why would he leave with a stranger? He is not a going-off-with-a-stranger type of person. He's shy. The only person he ever talks to at her office Christmas party is Norm from the city's Engineering department and only because Norm is also a De Soto enthusiast (man, not car). She pries the note from her purse, un-crumples it. Definitely Wally's writing. *I was out walking in Old Havana and ran into a professor, Dr Sánchez Portillo, an expert in Spanish-Cuban history.* How is it he just ran into a history professor? Accidentally bumped into him trying to negotiate the crowds in the Plaza de la Catedral? The professor was waiting outside the Museo de Armas for a De Soto enthusiast to happen along?

Something scrapes across the concrete to her right. A woman in a frilly pink dress is holding a drink in one hand and dragging a chaise lounge toward Thelma and the corner she deliberately chose for its distance from other people. There are chaises everywhere. Why does the woman have to sit beside her?

"Good evening," the woman says, plunking herself on the lounger and her drink on Thelma's table.

Thelma closes her eyes.

"Buenas noches," the woman tries in a louder voice. Thelma emits a small snore.

"Bonsoir," the woman practically yells. "Guten abend."

"Evening," she mutters.

"Beautiful night."

"Yes."

"It's a full moon."

"Is it?"

"Oh yes," says the woman breathlessly. "Look, you can see it over there just beyond that Royal Palm tree."

"Uh huh."

"If you watch long enough you can see the moon slipping behind the clouds, like a circle into an envelope, only, of course, it's not the moon that's moving. The clouds are traveling."

"Oh."

"I'm Cathy."

"Thelma."

"Nice to meet you, Thelm. I'm here on sabbatical. A self-imposed sabbatical. Actually, I was on a temporary teaching contract until Christmas and I was subbing until the end of February and decided to take March off. John, my ex-husband, wanted to take our daughter, Sara, to Hawaii and I said to myself, hey, you deserve a break, too, so here I am."

"I see."

"Last year, my grade twos did a unit on our solar system. I told them, 'ask your mom or dad to take you outside of town on a full moon night. Look for the rabbit in the moon'."

"The rabbit?"

"You have to look carefully to find him. His head is at twelve o'clock, his ears at one. His tail is at six and his two legs make eight and ten. Can you see him?"

Thelma nods.

"Really?"

"Yup."

The woman laughs. "But you're not even looking," she says, taking a sip of her drink.

The prof was going to Cienfuegos. Maybe this was Wally's only chance to get some crucial information for his novel. Why couldn't he have waited, she would have gone with him wherever he needed to go. They could have gone together. If she hadn't had to finish the damn budget, she would have been on the same flight as Wally and this would never have happened.

Thelma downs the rest of her mojito.

"So what do you do, Thelma?"

"Acting manager, city pools and arenas."

"That sounds interesting."

"Not so much."

The woman stops. Finally. Then...

"Isn't it lovely here? The frangipani trees, the jacarandas, the palms. There's something about the quality of the air that I can't get enough of. Where I live the winter air rubs your face raw. Here the air feels like a soft caress."

"Yup."

"Where are you from, Thelm?"

"Calgary."

"Me, too! Maybe we were on the same flight. When did you arrive?"

"Today."

"I've been here since Wednesday."

Wednesday. The day Wally left.

Thelma struggles to sit up. "Were you on the seven AM Air Canada flight by any chance?"

"Why yes, I was."

"Did you happen to notice a guy, mid-forties, wearing jeans, a red Che Guevara t-shirt and a grey Co-op baseball cap?"

"No, I don't recall seeing him. Is he a friend of yours?"

"Husband of mine."

Who abandoned her. What is she supposed to do for three days on her own? Wally has the guidebook, Wally has their planned itinerary. Gisela. She could call Gisela back in Calgary. Where would she be? At work, yes, she'd be in the office, maybe cleaning the fridge because today is Friday and Friday is fridge cleaning day. The day he left, Wally packed her lunch. She was too busy revising the budget, she didn't eat it, didn't check to see if he'd left her the usual post-it with a poem or quote for the day. If he did, it might provide a clue to his disappearance. She must call Gisela.

Planting her feet carefully on either side of the lounger, Thelma stands, loses her balance and falls, hitting the side of the chaise, which tips and lands her on her butt.

"God damn you, Wally!"

Cathy's pale face looms over her. "It's Cathy. Are you OK? Here, let me help you up."

"I'm fine."

"No, I'm serious, I think you need help."

Cathy may be a little younger, but Thelma is forty-four and perfectly capable of standing up by herself. Usually. When she hasn't had four mojitos. She flips on to her front, knees, feet. Just a few seconds to get her balance. There.

"Where are you going, Thelma?"

"Gotta make a call."

"Maybe you should sit down for a few minutes."

Thelma shakes her head. This Cathy doesn't seem to know when to shut up. Chatty Cathy, like the doll her dad gave her for her sixth birthday, you pulled the string and the doll said things like, change me, feed me, elemental things, elementary things, hey, she's an elementary school teacher, after all.

"Listen, Thelma, I'm going to the Gran Teatro tomorrow to see Carmen. Would you like to join me?"

"I'm not sure of my plans."

"What room are you in?"

"Five something."

"I'm in 352. Call me. And don't forget to check out the moon."

Thelma looks up. She knows all about the rabbit: the rabbit her father used to show her on camping trips, the conejo Professor Smythe described in Mayan cosmology class. She brushes against the flowery bush. She's smelled its heady fragrance before. Somewhere. In her own house.

# CHAPTER 4

*Calgary, 2004*

THE DINNER PARTY was her idea. To get Alvin and Rosa together outside Wally's writing group, ply them with good food and wine and wait for results. Though this isn't exactly how she explained it to Wally.

"We should have Alvin and Rosa over for dinner," she remarked one wintery night.

"Sure. Tim and Gina, too."

"Well, uh, honey, the table is a little crowded for six and I don't think Gina is comfortable going out at night with Esme yet."

Sweet little Esme. With her pink cheeks and baby powder smell. Last time they baby sat, Wally suggested trying again. Forgetting she was peri, practically post-menopausal.

The night of the dinner party, Thelma sits on the couch, surveying the smooth expanse of carpet, its vacuumed nap tidily upright, the table covered in the grape festooned linen tablecloth she bought from Lina's on Centre Street, and set with the sparkling silver flatware her mom and Peter gave them for their wedding, the tarnished versions of which she and Wally had dipped in a plastic container of silver polish and pulled out gleaming just that afternoon. Discovering their inner silver-ness, Wally called it. Had she known that the hours of tedious polishing she'd watched her mother undertake had been replaced by this new drip and dry system, she would have used the silver more. Even though its ornately whorled flower and leaf pattern isn't quite her style.

Too baroque. But who was she to look a gift mother and stepfather in the mouth?

"Thelma, hon, can you open the wine?"

"Sure."

She walks into the kitchen, just in time to see Wally tossing what looked like crostini rounds into the garbage.

"Too crosty?"

"Black crosty," he replies, wiping his hands on his apron.

The kitchen smells of roasting eggplant, rosemary and olive oil. Wally wears the barbeque apron Peter gave him last Christmas, heavy white canvas with the slogan, *bbqers do it with gas* written in red flame letters across the front.

"Smells delicious."

"Smells can be deceiving."

"It'll be wonderful", she says.

He hands her a bottle and the corkscrew.

"I hope so. I've never made this before."

She came home Monday night to find him with his old battered *Joy of Cooking*, perusing the chapter entitled "Stuffings, Dressings, Farces or Forcemeat."

He'd decided on roast pheasant with chestnut dressing, snail-stuffed mushrooms and dauphine potatoes.

By Tuesday it was paella, fresh chestnuts being non-existent in the city and snails too dear, he said.

On Wednesday, it turned out that the price of fresh seafood was out of this world. Thelma had argued he could use canned seafood and more sausage and chicken. He looked at her incredulously.

"You don't think Rosa could detect the difference between a real paella and an imitation."

Of course she could.

Thursday it was Italian, which it remained, with slight variations in the menu, the final one being triumphantly presented to her at noon on Saturday:

*Appetizer: roasted eggplant crostini Soup: Tuscan bean*
*Salad: roasted vegetable Meat: roast lamb*
*Pasta: tomato and basil risotto*
*Dessert: lemon semolina cake with strawberry coulis*

"Need any help?" she asks, taking in the smell of the Salt Spring Island lamb, sizzling in the oven, the red peppers sautéing on the stove.

"Don't think so. I just hope everything comes out at the same time. There's nothing worse than an overcooked lamb and undercooked risotto."

"You can say that again."

"There's nothing worse than an overcooked..."

Wally's cheek is streaked with something red. She licks her finger and rubs the spot like her dad used to do when she had a dirty face. She runs her wet finger around his lips and kisses him. He tastes lemony.

"What's up?" he asks, surprised.

"Nothing. How do you like my new perfume?"

He sniffs her neck. "Nice".

"*Eau de Temps.*"

"Water of time. Nice dress too."

She is wearing a new red slip dress and jacket that the clerk said brought out the rose tones of her skin and flattered her blond bob. She thought it was a little too tight, but the clerk had assured her that tight was the new loose (whatever that meant), and made her look ten years younger.

The doorbell.

Thelma rushes to answer it. Rosa has let her hair go curly. She wears a low-cut blue sweater and frilly skirt, gold hoop earrings, a sun pendant swinging above her cleavage, black leather stilettos. Rosa offers the multiple cheek kiss that Thelma can never seem to get the hang of (are you supposed to actually kiss the cheek or the air beside it?) and a bouquet of roses.

She closes the door and ushers Rosa into the living room. The bell again. Alvin. He's made an effort with his clothes, black jeans and a green corduroy dress shirt.

"For you," he says, thrusting a bottle at her.

"Thanks, Alvin, that's very sweet. Come on in, Rosa's here, in the living room."

Thelma offers a choice of a pinot blanc or noir. Alvin asks for a 'brewski,' then, catching Thelma's raised eyebrow, said he'd have whatever Rosa is having. Rosa chooses the noir.

"Thelma, I am wondering why you live in Alberta. Wally tells me you grew up in British Columbia, is that right?" asks Rosa.

"Yes. I'm from Kamloops and Wally's from Nanaimo. We both went to the University of Victoria then I decided to transfer to University of Calgary because they had a good archeology program."

"Why did you choose archeology?"

"My father was an exploration geologist so I was exposed to a lot of rocks as a kid. Also, I like digging things up. Anyway, Wally followed me here."

"Wally followed you?"

"Yup. Like a little puppy," says Thelma. "How long have you been in Calgary, Rosa?"

"Five years," Alvin answers, his mouth crammed with crostini.

Rosa crosses her long legs and smiles. "That's right. Soon it will be five years that I have been living in Canada."

"Did you move here on your own?" Thelma asks.

"No. I was married to a Canadian. Steve. I guess at first I was the exotic Cubana. But then I lost my allure. Or my looks."

"Oh no, you certainly didn't Rosa," enthuses Alvin.

"Didn't what?" asks Wally, coming in with a tray full of bowls.

"Didn't, uh, lose her looks. When she came here from Cuba. I mean I don't know what you looked like before you came but..."

"Crostini, Rosa?" Thelma suggests, cutting him off.

"Thank you, they look delicious. How wonderful to have a husband who can cook. You are a lucky woman, Thelma."

"Indeed I am."

"Soup is served."

"What kind, hombre?"

"Tuscan bean, Alvin."

"How delicious. You are a male Julia Child. Or the Italian equivalent. Thelma, how did you find such a man?"

"I did a house to house search."

"A house to house...?"

"Kidding. We met at a university party. On our first date, he told me the history of shoes. One of my obsessions, shoes. We've been married twenty-two years now. Alvin is also a good cook you know, Rosa."

"I am?"

"That wonderful cake you brought over last month?"

"My mother..."

"It was fabulous. Nothing like a good black forest cake with kirsch, real whipped cream and sour cherries, I always tell Wally. Shall we move to the table?"

Wally has removed his apron and is looking fetching in the new blue linen shirt she gave him last Christmas. He's run a comb through his hair, spiked it up the way the young guys do.

He could pass for someone ten years younger. Someone Rosa's age.

"DID YOU HEAR our idea for a new magazine?" Alvin asks Thelma, between soup slurps.

"No. What will it be about?"

"You know Calgary's *Avenue* magazine?"

She nods, thinking of the ads: funky eyewear, liposuction, smile specialists (also known as dentists), and upscale antique stores. Features on up-and-coming design companies, and avant-garde galleries.

"Well, we're thinking of starting a magazine along those lines."

"Is there room for two up-market yuppie mags in this town?"

"Nope. We're going down market," adds Wally. "What do you think of this for a name and slogan: *Cul-de-Sac—for smart people going nowhere?* We're thinking of having a contest. People can send in their ideas for the most dead-end job in Calgary. Rosa thought we could do a feature on Calgary's most un-cool night spots."

"Really?"

They look at each other and break into giggles like a trio of tipsy teenagers.

"What's so funny?"

"Is just a joke, Thelma," Rosa says, rather patronizingly Thelma thinks.

———

TWO GLASSES OF WINE later, Rosa, pursing her little rosebud mouth, asks: "So, Alvin, I do not know this, how long have you been writing your book?"

"Ten years. I keep changing it. I'll read a book that will knock my socks off and give me new ideas. I spent my youth with a book in front of my face most of the time. I even walked to school reading."

Rosa laughs. "I understand. I also loved to read novels. I read Guillén, Garcia Marquez. Oh, and Carpentier, I loved him."

"David Carpenter, yes, he is a fine writer, rather under-rated, as many Prairie scribes are, unfortunately. It's the nature of our country you see, the west gets ignored, not that I'm a Western Separatist or anything, and I sure wouldn't vote Conservative."

Rosa is looking at Alvin with a mixture of politeness and incomprehension. "You wouldn't vote..."

"...Conservative, no, they'd just get rid of the Canada Council and any other..."

"More risotto anyone?" Thelma interrupts.

Alvin helps himself to what is left on the platter and continues: "...grants, I mean I don't know a single writer who survives on his creative writing that is. Well, of course, with the exception of the biggies, Ondaatje, Atwood, Vassanji, maybe. I don't know about the plight of the writer in Cuba, but perhaps you have the same thing."

"Perdón, Alvin, what thing is this?"

"The marginalization of writers from outside the centre. I guess in Cuba it would be outside of Havana. So I am surprised and thrilled that you know David Carpenter..."

"No, Alvin, I mean the Cuban writer Alejo Carpentier."

"Oh."

"But I'm sure this David Carpentier is a fine writer."

"Carpenter."

"Carpenter?"

"Like the ant."

"His aunt?"

"The insect."

"Insect?"

Poor woman.

"Carpenter ant. I mean, I could see how you might think he's French, there is a sizeable French population on the prairies, Manitoba, where Gabrielle Roy hailed from originally, of course..."

Rosa looks at Alvin, brow furrowed, trying to follow.

Thelma wants to pinch him. Give him a little kick under the table. Give him a book on conversational skills.

"Have some risotto, Rosa, there's plenty more," Wally urges.

"Thank you."

"This is delectable, hombre. If you have any leftovers, I'd be happy to take them off your hands. Save me from opening cans next week."

"Yes," said Rosa, delicately wiping her glistening lips. "This is absolutely heavenly, Wally."

Thelma's husband turns the colour of the wine.

"Thank you, Rosa. That means a lot to me."

"Where did you learn to cook so well?"

"I liked to help my mom cook when I was little. Even though my dad didn't think it was manly, my mom indulged me."

"I'm glad she did! You are an artist. You give the food so much love."

"Gracias. In university, I lived with a couple of guys and neither of them wanted to cook so I decided to learn."

The timer buzzes. Wally ignores it.

"I started with basics from my mom's *Joy of Cooking*. The guys liked what I did so I branched out into Italian, French..."

"The cake, Wally."

"I under-timed... Spanish, then I got an Indian cookbook..." Rosa is leaning forward, expectant.

"Excuse me," Thelma mutters, going to the kitchen, turning the timer off and removing the cake from the oven. It falls a little.

"Then I started experimenting with Thai," she hears Wally saying, "the flavours are so wonderful, and from there I branched into Malaysian, and Japanese."

"So interesting," Rosa enthuses.

Alvin walks in the kitchen with plates.

"Where should I put these, Thelm?"

"By the sink."

"I'm blowing it, aren't I?"

"Well, Alvin, can I give you a hint. When you're talking to Rosa, try to ask her some questions, express interest in her ideas, and compliment her."

"I don't want her to think I'm sexist."

"I think she'd like it. I mean, do it discreetly. You wouldn't talk about her body parts or anything."

"Oh."

"You wouldn't, right?"

"No. Of course not. I'm not good with small talk. Especially with women. Attractive women."

"It comes with practice! The more you try, the better you get."

"I know, I..."

"You can do it. Get back out there, tiger." She pats him on the back, and follows him out to the dining room where Wally and Rosa are huddled together talking sotto voce.

"Writing secrets?"

"No, no, Thelm," Wally answers too quickly, gathering up some errant forks.

"You look very hot tonight, Rosa, "Alvin mutters.

"Oh, no, I'm not too hot, thank you, Alvin."

"I mean good."

"Oh."

"You, your dress, I mean skirt and uh, blouse, top. It's, they're, um, good." Good? He's a writer. Where are his adjectives?

"Thank you." Rosa colours a little.

"Great necklace, too." He eyes the spot where the sun disc hangs.

"Gracias."

Thelma sighs, knocks back the dregs of her wine, and refills her glass for the fourth time.

Or is it the fifth?

# CHAPTER 5

*Cuba*

THELMA HAS TO PHONE Gisela. She'll be at her night job, cleaning the offices in Thelma's building. Thelma imagines Gisela dipping her finger into her African violet's soil, adding a little water, then dusting around it; singing *Quimbara* with Celia Cruz, her mop Johnny Pacheco as they salsa around the kitchen. Gisela will know if her friend, Rosa, is in Cuba. She can also retrieve the lunch bag Thelma forgot in the fridge, see if Wally left a note in it.

When Thelma told her friend and office cleaner, Gisela, she was going to Havana, Gisela squealed with excitement. She was full of advice. "Stay in Vedado at the Inglaterra hotel, is very beautiful. You must walk on the Malecón, by the sea, but be careful after dark. Watch out for your husband with the young women."

Thelma laughed. "Wally doesn't chase young women."

"Maybe they will be chasing him."

"What? My rumpled old Wally?" Thelma laughed. "Is Cuba dangerous?"

"No, it is a safe country. For example, you want to hitchhike alone, no problem, no-one will hurt you."

"If you're a man, you mean."

"No, I mean for women. It is better if you are a woman alone, especially if you are beautiful. Easier to get a ride."

"I won't have much luck, then."

"But Thelma, you are pretty, with your complexion. Apples and cream, is that how you say it in English?"

"Peaches and cream. Though apples and cream is a better descriptor given my skin's propensity to resemble a red delicious after a few hours in the sun."

Gisela went on about the beaches, the museums, the ballet, and the salsa clubs.

"It sounds like a paradise."

"No, Thelma, not paradise." she said. "There are lots of problems, and not all of them are a result of the U.S. embargo. Por ejemplo, you cannot criticize the government publicly or..." Gisela drew a finger across her throat.

"You're killed?"

"No, but maybe you lose your job. Maybe you are sent away for re-education."

"What about freedom of speech?"

Gisela laughs. "That is one thing I have noticed about Canadians. You think that the world is full of justicia, that everything is as decent and proper como es en Canada."

"Are you saying we're naïve?"

"Not just you, Thelma. Your whole country. This is very sweet. But also a little dangerous, no?"

She has to phone Gisela, but all of a sudden, jet lag (combined with those mojitos) wallops her, and she has to lie down.

Thelma dreams the old dream. She's in a helicopter, flying over a frozen lake, a cirque surrounded by high mountains. She looks down into the ice. Sees, trapped there, grass, stones, small bushes. Sees her father under the ice, curled up like a fetus on a bed of yellow leaves. Then she is in a cave with her father and Professor Smythe. They are looking for a Mayan glyph of Ixchel, the moon goddess; but the men are way ahead, she has no flashlight, there is water all around her, she's only a little girl, she's all by herself, she can't see! Why have they left her?

Wakes up shaking, her eyes wet. Lies in the dark, thinking about the last time she had the dream. Wally woke her then.

"What's the matter, honey?"

"What?"

"You were shouting something in Spanish."

"I was?"

"You said 'papa, por favor, esparame.' What does that mean?"

"Papa, please wait for me."

Wally had gone back to sleep. But Thelma couldn't. She got out of bed, dressed quietly and slipped outside. A lone Canada goose trailed the disappearing moon, Ixchel, with her baby rabbit, across the sky. She walked up the 19th Street hill. Dead flower heads bent over dry stalks, orange leaf bags with carved pumpkin faces awaited Halloween. On the lawns, piles of leaves invited jumping. The sky that day was wide, a grey Chinook bowl with blue leaking from the edges.

At the top of the hill, she met the wind and entered the dog park, strolling along the footpath lined with swirling grasses, looking down over the neat grid of houses, the yellow-leafed poplars and red-berried mountain ash trees lining the streets, the Bow River bisecting the city. To her left, 14th Street fell to the river, then ran south like a prairie sacbe, the straight Mayan roads Professor Smythe introduced her to in the Yucatan.

In the field below, a man threw a stick for a golden lab. The dog streaked after it, his fur rippling like water.

———

THE BEDSIDE CLOCK reads 9:05. Her tongue is furry with rum, and the room is stifling.

She's slept too long. Gisela's probably finished cleaning and on her way home by now. Thelma picks up the phone by her bed, dials zero, and gives the operator Gisela's number.

Her neck is tight as a hospital sheet, and a headache is thrumming along nicely. As she waits for the call to go through, she counts the number of burnt-out bulbs in the chandelier. Five, six if you count the flickering one.

Gisela's cell phone rings, once, twice, three times, four. C'mon, Gisela, answer.

"Dime." Speak to me.

"Hello, Gisela?"

"Si."

"It's Thelma."

"Thelma, hello, how are you? Where are you? How you like Cuba? How is the hotel? I read on Cubaweb they have a frente frio, I hope you can still enjoy the beach. Here it is so cold, minus twenty. I wish I could be there, I could show you so many places. Where have you been? How is Wally's researches?"

"It's fine, it's beautiful, listen, Gisela, I'll cut right to the chase..." The line hisses and pops.

"Gisela?"

The hisses crescendo.

"Hello?" Decrescendo.

"I'm here, Thelma. I see the phone lines there are still muy malos. When

28

I try to call my friend, Patricia, in Holguin, ah, dios mio, is a big problem. First, I must call her sister and then, if I can get through, she have to go to Patricia's house down the street, it's a nightmare. I am waiting and the money is going out of the drain, is that correct?"

"Going down the drain."

"Not out of the drain."

"No. Listen, Gisela, are you still at work?"

"Yes."

"I need you to do something. Go to the fridge and find my purple lunch bag. Then look inside and see if there's a note from Wally."

"OK but why do you need the note? Wally is there with you."

"Yes, well, uh, can you just check? It's something, important, a poem, a poem he needs for his research."

"The poem is in your lunch bag?"

"Gisela, please..."

"Okay, wait a minute."

Another bulb begins to flicker. The ceiling fan makes a scratching noise, like a cat trying to get in. Thelma pictures Gisela walking through the dark office, past the looming forms of computers and filing cabinets, light from the street sliding between the slats in the blinds, striping the floor. Is she scared to be there, at night, alone? Thelma has never asked.

"I am walking to the fridge now. I have been leaving food for the little bunny outside, like you ask me."

"Thanks."

Thelma misses feeding the small, orphaned bunny that lives outside her office. Bringing carrot tops and lettuce, leaving it by the tree he often sits beside.

"Tell me, where did you visit? How do you like the beaches? Did you go swimming? Cubans are not swimming, I am sure. It is too cold."

"We haven't gone anywhere yet. I just got here, remember? Wally is, he's busy with his researching, so I'll be on my own in Havana for the next couple of days. Where should I go?"

"Ah, if I am there with you, I could show you so many places. I think tomorrow you can arrange at your hotel to go on a tour. You can visit Old Havana, José Martí monument, Museo de la Revolución, the Malecón, maybe see the cañonazo. It is a very interesting ceremony, where they fire the cannon every night at nine to close the harbour. Remember I told you once. The men dress like in the old times. You can watch and look out into the bahia, see the stars, it is very beautiful, very romantic."

The line begins to hiss again.

"Great idea. Did you find the lunch bag yet?"

"I am just there now. I am opening the fridge, let me look, here is a green one, orange..."

"Purple, Gisela. It's purple."

"I don't see purple."

"Then can you look at the schedule on the fridge and see who was on kitchen duty last week."

"Yes. It is Jennifer."

Jennifer in accounting, a junior position, though you wouldn't know it the way she supervises the fridge's contents. It's rumoured she takes home still edible lunches at the end of the week.

"Leave a note on her desk, please Gisela. Tell her I'm going to e-mail her. Tell her to check her e-mail first thing tomorrow."

"I will. I wanted to tell you, too, Thelma, when you got back. They are leaving me notes, again, the girls, to dusk their desks every night. You know I have ten floors to clean, only half hour for this floor. It is not possible to dusk their desks every night."

"No, it is not possible to dust every night. I'll speak with them when I'm back."

"Thank you, Thelma. You are a good friend. Enjoy yourself. Cubans are friendly and, how do you say, encantador?"

"Charming?"

"Charming, yes. Be careful of the men. Some think they are Casanova."

"I'll be careful."

"But have fun."

"I will."

"I wish I could be there. When I get my Canadian passport we will go together."

"Sure. And Gisela, one final question. Have you seen Rosa lately?"

"Rosa. No. We had a little fight. I..."

The line goes dead.

———

*To: jsloan@cityofcalgary.org*
*From: info@palco.cu*
*Importance: high*
*Jennifer*
*I see you were on kitchen duty last week. I left my purple lunch bag in the fridge and Gisela tells me it's no longer there. Can you e-mail me at this address and let me know where it is. There is an important paper in it.*
*T. Dangerfield*

*To: info@palco.cu*
*From: jsloan@cityofcalgary.org*
*For Thelma Dangerfield Confidential*
*I threw away the contents of your bag as per the policy on kitchen clean-up duty. I put the bag on your desk.*
*J.*

*To: jsloan@cityofcalgary.org*
*From: info@palco.cu*
*Was there a note in the bag? On yellow lined paper?*
*T. D.*

*From: jsloan@cityofcalgary.org*
*To: info@palco.cu*
*Yes. The note says:*
*"That's how I used to live and love that life and there was nobody or nothing that could change me because time passed so fast by my time that the days were only the waiting room of evening and evenings became as short as appointments and the years turned into a thin picture spread..."*
*G. Cabrera Infante, I Heard Her Sing.*

Thelma looks over at Carlos, the Palco manager whose computer she has been usurping for much of the morning.
"May I print something out?"
"Of course."
"Muchas gracias."

"De Nada. Everything is OK at home?"

She told him there was a family emergency. "I hope so."

He retrieves the email from the dot matrix printer, looks at it and hands it to her.

"Ella cantaba boleros."

"I'm sorry, who sang boleros?"

"It is the name of the story by the Cuban writer Guillermo Cabrera."

"Oh? You know the story Wally is referring to? What is it about?"

"A jazz singer before she was famous, and also about artists and our country before the revolution."

"I would like to read it."

"You will not find it in Cuba."

"Why?"

Carlos strokes an invisible beard. Castro. "Cabrera went into exile. He died in London."

She reads the passage again. Why would Wally put a quote like that in her lunch bag on the day he left? Why choose that particular passage? Was it meant as a clue? A warning? That the way they used to live, their thin picture spread of a life together was about to end? If she asked him, he'd probably say: no reason, Thelm. I just thought it was a lovely piece of writing.

"Where the hell are you, Wally? Could you be with Rosa? Though why would Rosa choose Wally?"

"Pardon me?"

"Sorry, just talking to myself."

Why not? Wally is sweet, erudite, a fountain of knowledge, a fabulous cook, a good lover. Though not a fabulous provider. He made just $5000 from his writing last year.

"Are you OK?"

Thelma nods.

It isn't until he hands her a tissue, that Thelma realizes she's crying.

"I'm sorry about your family problem."

"Thanks. It's nothing. I...I mean, I'm sure everything will be fine."

# CHAPTER 6

*Calgary, 2004*

OUTSIDE THELMA'S OFFICE window, a row of aspen protect the grass from dirt blowing in from the vacant lot. Though the lot won't be vacant for long—daily Thelma hears the low moans of the bulldozers, moving earth, preparing the ground for a new strip mall. She pulls her hands from the sleeves of her wool sweater and touches the radiator. It's as cold as Wally's feet in the middle of the night. Not surprising, given that the heating system usually rumbles to life about mid-Wednesday.

Around the corner, she hears her assistant, Ardeth's, squeaky top drawer opening, the jingle of her keys being dropped in.

Now she'll turn her radio on, Thelma thinks and sure enough:

*"Power 107 plays today's best music,* a caller declaims. *"Now show me my money."*

Thelma looks out the window, thinks where did the fall go, wonders what delectable gourmet lunch has Wally has prepared for her today. She fishes the purple insulated lunch bag from her briefcase (the only thing in it, but it wouldn't do for a manager to be seen going home without one). There's a sandwich in Tupperware. She lifts the lid. Salmon with avocado and havarti. But on white bread—strange. Yesterday, lunch was a spinach salad with raspberry vinaigrette, corn bread and slices of fresh mango.

She peers into the depths of the bag, spies a mandarin orange and two shortbread cookies.

A yellow note lies at the bottom of her bag. She picks it up, reads:

> *"Things have suddenly changed. My peaceful existence in Gentilly*
> *has been complicated. This morning, for the first time in years, there*
> *occurred to me the possibility of a search..."*
> Walker Percy, *The Moviegoer*

It's from the book Wally was reading last summer. About a moneyed guy in New Orleans, who philosophized, watched movies and fantasized about women.

"So what did you do this weekend?" Ardeth calls from around the corner.

"Indian food at the Taj on Friday. We had some friends over for Wally's famous chorizo lasagna on Saturday, went to the antiquarian bookshop on Sunday so Wally could look for a rare text on knight errantry. He went to his writer's group on Sunday night."

"How's that novel of his coming?"

"Pretty well, I think. Though his writer's group gets to see a lot more of it than I do."

"Writer's group?"

"Yeah, a bunch of guys that get together and critique each other's work. Well, not just guys now, there's a new woman in the group—Rosa. A poet. A Caribbean Dorothy Livesay, Wally calls her. Her work is apparently suffused with 'Communist Eroticism'."

"Communist what?"

"Just what I asked Wally."

Thelma nibbles the edge of the sandwich, thinks the salmon tastes a bit off.

"Rabbit, hard left," says Ardeth, coming around the corner.

Beside an aspen sits the office bunny, an orphan Thelma is sure, his coat almost white. How many hours has she spent watching the little guy furtively, out of the corner of her eye, while she smiles and pretends to pay attention to whoever is in her office? Waiting for Jennifer, for instance, to come to the point of her problem: too many people want to use the microwave at lunch, generating long line-ups and short tempers. Jennifer thought there should be a sign-up sheet.

"Like for exercise bikes at the gym?" Thelma asked.

"Exactly," Jennifer concurred. "But more long term, like for a squash court. You could sign up for, say, a ten-minute spot up to a week in advance."

"Do people plan their lunches a week in advance?"

"I know I do."

Thelma's e-mail beeps, an annoying feature of the new computers that all Parks and Rec managers have finally received after years of begging. There must be some way to turn the beep off. She'll have to ask Ardeth.

To: tdangerfield@cityofcalgaryrec.org
From: wtdanger@shaw.ca

*Thelm*

*Just noticed there's a sale on at Arnold Churgin's (40% off all pumps and loafers). You might want to check it out after work. The new Tomás Gutiérrez film,* Guantanamera, *is on at the film festival. The group is going. I'll see you after the show. Your "hombre sincero,"*
*W.*

Why didn't he tell her this last night or this morning? She thought they were going to rent a movie and relax.

Thelma scrolls through her inbox and wonders if it is possible to die of boredom. How many middle managers are found slumped over their desks in the middle of the day? Dead as the proverbial doornails. Or is it doorknobs? Surely boredom must shorten one's life, lead to early Alzheimer's. Senile plaques multiplying faster than you can say 'manager's meeting.'

It used to take her and Ardeth three weeks to prepare the budget, they'd work late, and then take a break to watch the sunset and eat take-out roast beef sandwiches from the cafe across the street. Sometimes Gisela took her break with them, sharing her rice and black beans, Moros and Cristianos she called them, Moors and Christians. Thelma used to enjoy the challenge of putting together the budget until centralization became the new buzzword, and preparing the budget involved correcting her boss' mistakes. Thelma stretches, prints an e- mail, and walks down the hall to see if there are any new job postings.

"Thinking of applying for something?" Ardeth asks, following behind her.

"Maybe."

"What?"

"Well, here's one for a manager in Waterworks."

"I think they want an engineering background."

"I've got an archeology background. I'm good at unearthing things."

"What kind of things?"

"Watery things."

Outside her window, clouds have moved in, throwing the bunny, huddled under the big pine tree now, into shadow. She wonders how he will survive the winter. Last winter it was -30 for ten days in a row. Do rabbits build burrows, like gophers? Will someone adopt it for the winter? Could she? She glimpses a yellow bulldozer between the trees; hears a faint roar. Where will the bunny go when his peaceful existence is disrupted? When they dig up his Elysian field and put in the strip mall?

# CHAPTER 7

*Cuba*

THELMA LIES IN HER king size bed, listening to strains of *I Feel Love* by Donna Summer float down the hall. When did she last hear Donna? 1977. That Halloween Party at UVIC:

Thelma slouches on a bench against the wood paneling of the residence's multi-purpose room, watching her friend, Diana, dressed as a playboy bunny, dancing with a cute math major. Across the room, another Playboy bunny sits on the lap of a giant phallic carrot. A third is draped around a frizzy-haired Gene Simmons who periodically yell-sings, I wanna rock and roll all night and part of every day. Shouldn't it be party every day?

At least her pirate costume is original: eye patch, bandanna around the head, hoop earrings, striped shirt, suspenders, cardboard and foil sword. She spent a lot of time on the shoes, removing the buckles from her two best belts and attaching them to a pair of Diana's black Mary Janes.

The damn things are killing her, squishing her toes together and mashing her instep. She eases her feet out of them and downs the rest of her over-proof rum and coke. She should just bite the bullet and ask someone to dance.

At the next table, two guys are having a drinking contest. The giant wins; the peanut is a close second. Not dancing material, she decides. Across the room, Einsteins shoot tequila.

Deciding she needs a drink, Thelma walks across the minefield that is the dance floor, maneuvering around a tipsy Fred Flintstone, swiveling to avoid a clown lurching toward her with an armful of beer. The mirror ball throws ovals across the floor. A guy dressed as a tree dancing with a gypsy stomps on Thelma's toe as she tries to slide by.

The tree stops, his construction paper branches brushing against her face. "I'm sorry. Did I hurt you?" he shouts over Donna's *Love to Love You, Baby.*

"Apparently toes are not absolutely necessary for survival," she shouts back into his branches.

He laughs. Nice white teeth. "But they still have nerve endings."

"True."

"Great costume!"

"Yours too."

The gypsy, who turns out to be from her res floor, Tracy or Trixie or something like that, puts an arm around the tree's waist, bumping her hips back and forth against his, humming 'that's the way, uh huh, uh huh, I like it.'

"Sure you're OK?"

Before she can answer, Tracy/Trixie pulls him close. "C'mon, Wally, this is our song!"

Thelma negotiates the remainder of the dance floor and joins the line-up at the bar, and then finds an unoccupied chair.

Ashtrays and beer bottles litter the floor, couples, including Diana and the math major, are lip-locked in corners. She quickly picks up a longish butt from the ashtray and lights it. Tries to look nonchalant. Exhale coughs. Very attractive, Thelm. Should send the guys running right over. Though it goes against her feminist principles, maybe next year she'll go as a Playboy bunny.

When did she see Wally next? Right, it was in the res dining hall. He was alone and she sat beside him, they started talking and found they were in the same Intro to Psych class. Thelma smiles, remembering how they chatted, lamenting their names: his, Wallace, an old family surname, hers belonging to her father's favourite aunt. Then Thelma brazenly invited him to her room, to study.

————

WALLY IS SITTING on her dorm room's only chair. Thelma perches at the edge of the bed across from him, her textbook in her lap.

"So do you want to review the Humanists or the Freudians first?" she asks.

"Freudians, they're so much more interesting."

"How so?"

"All the hidden sexual stuff. Is that a slip I see?"

She blushes. What? Damn it. She thought she put her underwear away.

"Gotcha."

"Oh, I get it. Freudian slip, ha ha."

Wally picks up one of the platform shoes she has shoved under the chair to make more room.

"You sure have small feet."

"Size five."

"A very attractive size in China."

"Really?"

"Yeah. The binding of feet began in the Sung dynasty. Court dancers had very tiny feet. Then two hundred years ago, the Empress Taki was born with deformed feet. So she wouldn't get embarrassed, her father announced that only women with very small feet could be desirable."

"Good for her. But not so good for the rest of Chinese womankind."

"True. But shoes were always a way for rulers to establish dominance over the ruled. Men over women. In nineteenth century India, Indians had to remove their shoes when entering British homes but the arrogant Brits just left theirs on when traipsing through mosques and Hindu temples."

"That's terrible."

He puts her shoe down. "Yes. And did you know that red was a royal shoe color, worn by Louis the 14th?"

"I didn't. I must be royalty then." She swings her naked foot back and forth. "So, um the Freudians, then?"

He is cute in a nerdy sort of way. Long curly hair, freckles, wide mouth. Ropy arms. Skinny but not too skinny. He knows so much. As much as her dad. More even.

Wally points at her blistered toe.

"What happened?"

"I wore my friend's shoes to the Halloween party. They were too small for me."

"It's your lucky day. I used to be a boy scout. I've got my first aid badge and I'm especially good at treating blisters."

He moves from the chair to the bed, puts his hand on her knee to stop her foot moving, then cups it in his hand. He touches the blister, carefully probing its watery centre. His hand is warm, soft. Thelma takes his other hand and pulls him over.

# CHAPTER 8

*Cuba*

THELMA STANDS AT the edge of her tour group in the sunny Plaza de la Catedral surveying the tourists. That man by the cathedral could be Wally. Same height, though she doesn't recognize the green baseball cap as one in his extensive collection. The man turns. Not Wally.

Their guide, Caridad, a no-nonsense woman around Thelma's age, with aubergine hair and not very sensible but very cute espadrilles, is saying something about the cathedral. Thelma can't hear exactly what because a trio in the café beside them has launched into a rousing version of Guantanamera: 'Yo soy un hombre sincero,' they sing. I am an honest man.

The Wally she knows is honest. Was honest. She thought. Reliable as— what?

Clockwork, the setting sun? She feels her shoulders tighten. Calming breaths, Thelma, he'll be back soon. Tomorrow. The day after at the latest. He said three days tops.

A young woman moves to stand beside her. Black curly hair like Rosa's. She glances at the her. Same lovely cafe con leche complexion, though she's never seen Rosa in a t-shirt, let alone a Nickelback one. Wally said Rosa was helping him with his research. Maybe he meant literally. Gisela warned her to watch her husband with the young girls. Did she mean Rosa?

Thelma fans herself with the tour itinerary and looks longingly at the shade cast by the baroque Catedral de la Habana. But Caridad walks them into full sun, to the Castillo de la Real Fuerza, the castle fort that guards the harbour.

They pause in a courtyard full of cannons, are instructed by Caridad to look up to the bronze weathervane of La Giraldilla: a woman, her robe fluttering in the breeze, looking out to sea.

"She is Isabel de Bobadilla," says the guide. "The wife of the conquistador Hernando De Soto."

Isabel! Wally's Isabel. The woman from his novel. The woman who climbed the tower ofthe fortress every afternoon for four years, to scan the horizon for her husband's returning ships. Pay attention, Thelma. This could be the clue you need.

"The family were conversos, originally Jewish before they converted to Catholicism. Isabel's father was Pedrárias, the governor of Panama and Hernando De Soto's patron. De Soto went out to Panama at the age of fourteen and proved himself loyal to his future father-in-law. Later De Soto and Juan Ponce de Leon bought ships to use in their Indian slave trade business. They lent some of the ships to Francisco Pizarro to go to Peru. De Soto went with the Pizarros and also participated in the conquest of the Incas and became rich from the gold."

"What about Isabel?" Thelma asks.

"I will tell you in a moment, Madam," says Caridad. "De Soto and Pizarro had a big fight about who'd be second in command in Peru after the Incas were defeated. De Soto lost, and so he went back to Spain. He married Isabel who was apparently beautiful, but no longer young. Her father's tendency to murder his daughters' fiancés hadn't helped her marriage prospects. Her dowry was impressive though—all of her father's cattle in Panama."

Interesting dowry. Thelma squints up at the buxom Isabel. Her crowned head is raised high and she holds what looks like a scepter.

Wally told her that after Isabel and Hernando married, he became bored with Spanish court life and decided he wanted to return to a life of adventure. The King of Spain helped him mount an expedition to Florida, to look for gold and new land there and threw in the governorship of Cuba to boot. So, he and Isabel, their servants and his army, set off for Cuba.

Thelma wiggles herself to the front of the group.

"When De Soto and Isabella arrived in Eastern Cuba, he sent Isabel with the ships to Havana and set off on horseback. Then he heard his ships were blown out to sea and drifted way off-course, so he rushed to Havana by boat."

"What happened to Isabel and the ships?"

"They were tossed around by hurricanes for forty days before they made it to Havana."

"And De Soto?"

"He arrived in Havana, got his ships and men together and left for Florida."

"He just abandoned Isabel and their children?" Thelma asks.

"They didn't have children together. He had some from previous liaisons."

"He was a philanderer, then?"

People are staring at her, frowning, looking at their watches. She is asking too many questions, delaying the lunch stop. She doesn't care.

"He had mistresses," Caridad concedes.

"Who?"

"A Spanish woman in Nicaragua and an Inca noblewoman in Peru."

"And he also abandoned these women and his children?"

"He didn't completely abandon them, Madam. He made provisions for some of them in his will."

"He abandoned Isabel, though."

The man beside her sighs loudly and points to his watch.

"He settled Isabel on a cattle ranch. He provided her with slaves and a house. He made her governor."

"May we go inside the fort now?" someone asks.

"Yeah, it's hot out here."

"I need a bathroom," says watch man.

"Of course," said Caridad. "Come this way."

"What happened to De Soto?"

"You are very interested in our history."

"Yes, well I am. My husband is." "De Soto's ships landed at Tampa Bay and headed north. He sent one of his commanders, Maldonado, back to Cuba the next year to report on his progress and get more supplies. When Maldonado returned to Florida there was no trace of De Soto and his men. Maldonado left messages in trees and returned twice more, but De Soto had disappeared. Isabel never saw him again."

"He didn't come back to her?"

"No. He died of fever on the banks of the Mississippi."

"Did he find gold?"

"No, there was no gold."

"My husband told me he was looking for the fountain of youth."

"That is just a legend," Caridad replies, stopping and turning to the group. "Please everyone, wait here by the entrance. I will get the tickets."

Thelma stares up at La Giraldilla. Poor Isabel, waiting every day for her husband's return. A husband, seduced by greed, by the promises of more wealth. An errant husband.

———

THELMA IS PERCHED on the malecón seawall across from the tour bus waiting for their 'free time' to finish. The rock is limestone with embedded shells that scratch her bare legs. A couple saunter by, two young women stand in the grass across the road, looking at a map. The rest of her group is nowhere to be seen. She watches the stream of bicycles and cycle rickshaws, their drivers straining against the weight of oversized tourists. On the sidewalk, couples stroll hand-in-hand; schoolboys in white shirts, red shorts and neckerchiefs sit on the seawall, their skinny legs hanging over the side.

Thelma turns to look at La Giraldilla. Imagines her walking the widow's walk, morning and evening, scanning the horizon for signs of her husband's returning ships. When did she give up and decide he was never coming home? And why is it that women are always waiting for men? Waiting for them to phone, to change, to act, to apologize, to take out the garbage, to publish their award-winning novel, to come back from some godforsaken wild goose chase across the country.

She walks toward the National hotel. Across the street is a man: Wally's build, same colour hair, same height.

"Wally!" she yells, darting into the road. "Wally Dangerfield!"

"Señora, cuidado!"

The startled face of a Cuban, his bicycle wheel twisted sharply to the right.

"I'm sorry."

"This is the bicycle lane, Señora."

She steps back onto the sidewalk and walks toward the man who is a good half a block away from her now.

"Hey," she calls, running. "Wally!"

The man keeps walking.

She waves her arms. "Over here! Across the street."

The man turns. Not Wally.

Accept it, Thelma. He's not in Havana. He'll phone. Maybe tonight. Tomorrow at the latest. If he wanted to go off with Rosa, he would have done that in Canada. He's not like that writer-philanderer in his book who drove across Cuba, seducing women as he went. Relax. You are in a tropical island paradise. Try to enjoy yourself.

BACK AT THE HOTEL, Veronika is working the front desk. She smiles at Thelma, a little sadly, as if to say there's the poor woman whose husband ran away.

Thelma approaches the desk. "Hi Veronika. I was just wondering, could you tell me about any places he might have visited before I came?"

"There is a small beach across Quinta Avenida I recommended to him to visit. Also, he wanted to see the authentic Cuba so I told him to go take a picnic to Lenin Park. For history and culture, I suggested Finca Vigia, the Hemingway House."

# CHAPTER 9

*Calgary*

SUNDAY, GLORIOUS SUNDAY. She's slept late, then finished reading a book she borrowed from Wally about a guy (the writer-philanderer) who drives a 57 De Soto across Cuba. She likes the author's description of the landscape but parts of the book she finds unsavoury. For example, the author's penchant for sleeping with the local women, the younger the better as far as Thelma can see. Too much information, buddy, she wants to tell him.

Wally has dropped his pajama bottoms on the bathroom floor and left a damp towel on the toilet seat. She folds the towel over the rack, sniffs the pajamas then throws them in the hamper. What is it with sloppiness and men? How much more effort does it take to hang up a towel than to leave it on the toilet seat?

She can hear the coffee grinder whirring downstairs. At least Wally cooks, drives a reasonable Japanese car rather than an old American gas-guzzler, and he doesn't sleep with women half his age.

She showers then pads downstairs, wondering what he has concocted for her breakfast. Homemade waffles with strawberry compote? Eggs Florentine? Fresh fruit salad with homemade yogurt? OK, he has never actually made yogurt. But he's researched it.

The tie to the striped robe from his university days is lying on the stairs. She picks it up.

"Morning," she calls, rounding the corner.

"Good morning."

"What delicious breakfast do I not smell but which you are undoubtedly going to prepare for me in just a few minutes?"

"Huh?" He's sitting on the couch, bent over a pad of paper, scribbling furiously.

"After your flash of brilliance, I mean."

He looks up at her, frowns, returns to scribbling. Touchy. She peers over his shoulder. "What are you composing?"

"Just writing down some ideas before I forget them."

"What kind of ideas?"

"Thoughts."

"About your novel?"

"Sort of."

She dangles the tie. "You lost this."

"Umhm."

"So, what's for breakfast?"

"Juice."

"And?"

"I dunno, cereal, toast."

"And?"

He looks up wearily. "What do you want, Thelma?"

"Well, for starters, a husband who will talk to me. A poached egg Florentine or some of your homemade pancakes would be nice as well."

He continues scribbling. "No eggs."

Thelma sighs, goes to the kitchen and opens the fridge. He obviously hasn't been shopping lately. There's a browning head of lettuce, two shriveled apples, some milk, a tetra pack of orange juice, a past due container of cream. She takes out the milk and puts it on the table then plugs in the kettle.

"I finished that book," she calls.

"What book?"

"The one about the American guy who drives across Cuba."

"Oh. I didn't know you were reading it?"

"Why? Wasn't I supposed to?"

"No, it's just for my research, that's all."

"You're researching philanderers?"

"He's not a philanderer."

"He is so!"

"He's experiencing the seductions of the island."

"Oh, please. Carrying them out more like. And what about his penchant for under-age women?"

"They weren't all under-age."

"Come on. One was fourteen."

"He didn't sleep with her."

"He didn't admit to it in the book anyway."

Wally doesn't answer. He's staring out the window at the bare poplars. The grass is covered with brown, soggy leaves he should have raked up weeks ago.

"And then there's his charming tendency to call the kettle black. Denigrating the pot-bellied middle aged men with their Cuban mistresses while he—a little younger, a little cooler and a little less rotund, perhaps—is doing the same thing."

Wally puts down his notebook. "What do you want, Thelma?"

"Besides breakfast?"

"Yes, besides breakfast. Listen, I'm reading the book to get some Cuban ambience for my novel. That's all. Besides, all of his relationships were consensual..."

"I wouldn't call them relationships. Anyway, is it consensual when he has the power and the money, and they're poor and have no money?"

He stands up and closes his notebook. "I'm not arguing with you, Thelma."

"Where are you going?"

"Back to bed."

"What about breakfast?"

"What about it?"

"I'm famished. And I thought we were going for a walk in Nose Hill Park today."

"You go," he says, disappearing around the bend in the stairs, his bathrobe tie trailing behind.

# CHAPTER 10

*Calgary*

THE DANGERFIELDS ARE dressing for Rosa's party. Wally has rejected her shirt suggestions: the light green dress shirt her mom and Peter gave him for his birthday, the dark blue turtleneck she got him last Christmas, saying they don't go with his Che beret.

"You mean the one the black one with the falling off red star?"

"I sewed it back on. I'm going to wear my new red shirt."

When did he start matching his clothes?

"What new red shirt?"

"The one I bought last week."

"You went shopping?"

"Yes."

"By yourself?"

"I'm not completely helpless you know, Thelm."

"Let me see the shirt."

He takes it out of the plastic wrap, shakes it out. Thelma has to admit it is a handsome shirt, looks like nice quality, a cotton/linen blend. Hell to keep wrinkle-free though.

"I thought you hated shopping," she says, searching in the closet for her good black dress pants and her turquoise blouse. She'll wear her new turquoise earrings, maybe the necklace and bracelet too, though that could be overkill on the turquoise. Gisela said the blouse made her look young. Well, maybe she didn't say young. Younger.

"I do, but I needed a shirt that would go with the beret."

"Interesting approach to accessorizing, it's usually done the other way around. You're going to iron the shirt, right?"

He shakes his head and starts to put the shirt on. Nice colour on him. She sighs. "You can't wear it like that. Give it to me. I'll iron it."

"Seriously?"

"Yes."

"Thanks, hon."

———

MERENGUE MUSIC SPILLS out the sliding doors of Rosa's apartment, elbows its way past the people crowding the balcony, eight steps down into the street, swinging its saucy hips. Greets Thelma and Wally as they walk hand in hand through the warm, Chinook-windy night. They follow the music up the stairs to the third floor apartment. Wally knocks and Rosa opens the door, wearing a gold lamé top and black leather skirt.

"Wally, Thelma, I'm so happy to see both of you. How wonderful of you to come," she yells over the wa-wa of trumpets.

Kissing each of them on the cheeks, she leads them into the living room. The furniture is against the wall, the area rug rolled up for dancing. People are grouped at the edge of the dance floor, in twos and threes. The crowd is about half Cuban and half Canadian. Mostly young, late 20s, early 30s, the women in dresses and sparkly party chic.

"Hey, Thelm, Wall!" Alvin puts an arm around each of them. He's wearing a button down candy cane shirt, black jeans and a skinny black tie, an outfit last seen in the 1980s. At least she's not the only person who dressed wrong, in work rather than party clothes. Poor guy, though. He's obviously made an effort.

"Great party," he shouts.

"Yeah, we just arrived."

"Do you want a drink?"

"Wally can get..., she turns but her husband has disappeared. "Where'd he go?"

"Kitchen I think? Have you seen Rosa?"

"Just at the door."

"What?"

"Door!" she shouts in the direction of his ear.

He turns.

"She's not there anymore, Alvin. Look for gold."

"What?"

"Gold lamé. Top she's wearing."

Alvin vanishes into the crowd and Thelma heads toward a table laden with bottles: whiskey, Havana Club rum, coke, sprite.

"Excuse me," she shouts, reaching an arm past a man for the rum bottle.

"Brat," he says.

Rude. She was just trying to get to the bottle.

"Sorry."

"Brad."

Oh. "Thelma."

He's young, tall, sporting a little goatee, a gold earring in each ear and a tight black t-shirt.

"How do you—?"

"Pardon"? The music has risen to floor shaking level.

"Rosa. How do you know her?"

"She's in my husband's writing group."

"Your husband's what?"

"Writing group. His name is Wally Dangerfield."

"Wally, yeah, heard a lot about the man. I'd like to meet him. He here?"

"Somewhere. What did you hear?"

"Rosa talks about him."

"Does she?"

"Yeah, he helps her a lot. With her writing."

A man pushes by Thelma, jostling her arm. Rum and coke spills onto her black dress pants. Damn.

Thelma heads for the bathroom, closes the door, takes some Kleenex and blots at the spill. It's quieter in here, at least. Rosa's blue seashell shower curtain is partly open. On the edge of the tub a razor, shampoo, soap, something rubbery and round. A diaphragm out in plain sight.

She opens the door to *Oye Como Va, Cubana*, makes her way back to the kitchen table and pours herself another rum and coke. Alvin is at the table, dunking pieces of bread into the spinach dip and, in rapid succession, popping them into his mouth. A young woman in a red off-the -shoulder dress is whispering into his right ear.

She taps his left shoulder. "Alvin, have you seen Wally?"

He barely glances at her. "With Rosa."

"Where?"

"They'll be back."

"They left?"

"Yup."

"Where the hell did they go?"

"Dunno."

The music changes, electronic with a thumping beat. She thinks it's called techno or house, something like that. Putting on an 'isn't this a great party' smile, she elbows her way through the kitchen to the living room. She is going to kill Wally. He was the one who insisted she come and then he deserts her, like a latter day Hernando De Soto.

"Did you find your husband?"

"Oh hi, Brat, Brad. No, no I didn't. You haven't seen him have you?"

"Nope. Wanna dance?"

This young pup is asking her to dance? What the hell. She nods and he takes her hand and leads her onto the dance floor. The electronic music stops abruptly. The next song is a rumba and Brad obviously doesn't know how to dance to it. He shuffles back and forth in front of her until Thelma takes his hand, places it behind her back, takes his left in her right.

"Alright if I lead, Brad?"

"Um, sure, OK. Hey you're good."

"Wally and I took some Latin dance classes a few years ago."

"Do you lead Wally?"

She laughs. "Well, sometimes I have to. My husband is not the most assertive of dancers."

Brad's picking up the beat, he's getting it, she can feel his back muscles flexing under his t-shirt, he probably works out.

"You're doing great!" she says.

"Thanks. You're a good leader."

"Too bad my work team doesn't think so. Ha-ha. But I have a question. In an apartment bursting with gorgeous young women, why are you dancing with me?"

"Well, to tell you the truth, you remind me of my 9th grade English teacher. I had a crush on her."

Thelma laughs. "I'll take it as a compliment."

———

She looks out the window just in time to see Wally opening their car door for Rosa.

Something he never does for Thelma. They head toward the building, Rosa holding a large metal pan. Damn him. She pushes through the crowd to the door, letting Rosa pass, and putting her hand on Wally's shoulder to stop him.

"Where the hell were you?"

"I had to leave for a bit."

"What? Why? You convinced me to go to this party. I don't know anyone. And you frigging disappear."

"Rosa's car wouldn't start and she needed to go pick up her friend Isel and the tamales she spent all day making, so I offered to take her. But when we got to Isel's, we had to wrap the tamales, then we ran out of tin foil so I had to go to the Co-op and..."

"You could have told me."

"I couldn't find you."

"Whatever, Wally, I drank too much rum, I'm starting to get a headache, let's just go home."

"Oh come on, Thelm, its only 10:30."

"We go to bed at 10:30."

"Not on a Saturday night."

"When we were twenty-five we didn't go to bed at 10:30 on a Saturday night. But now we do."

"I don't."

"You do so."

"Last Saturday I was up past midnight."

"Oh for God's Sakes, Wall!"

Rosa appears above them holding a plate of tamales. "Thelma, thank you for lending me your husband. Please, have a tamale."

"No thanks. We have to go."

"Oh no, please stay, the night is, how do you say?"

"The night is a storm-tossed temptress?"

"The night is young," says Wally.

"But we're not."

# CHAPTER 11

*Cuba*

THELMA CAN'T GET across Quinta Avenida. She wants to, knows the beach lies somewhere on the other side. But the streaming lines of traffic won't stop—Ladas like the one that Tomás drove, lumbering Fords and Dodges with tailfins and shiny metal grills; cyclists, businessmen with briefcases balanced on their handlebars or women riding side saddle behind, both the men and women looking fresh as daisies despite the heat rising from the asphalt. She looks up and down for a crosswalk. There isn't one.

She wants to get to the beach that is supposed to be on the other side of Quinta Avenida, the beach Wally visited, according to Veronika the hotel clerk, the day before he checked out. Finally, a break in traffic. Thelma runs across, a car screeches to a halt in front of her. Jesus. Where did he come from?

Pay attention, Thelma, she tells herself when she's safely on the far sidewalk. This is your second near-accident today.

A couple saunter in front of her, arms around each other's waists, the man whispering in the woman's ear. She speed walks past them. She sees the building Veronika described, a former amusement park, now abandoned, the windows barred with wood, yellow paint peeling from the baroque facade. Thelma walks down the gravel road toward it, pulls at the heavy, wooden door. It's locked. Damn. She walks back and forth in front of the building, trying to figure out how to get through the tall wire fence and then to the beach she can see behind the building.

Ah, there, beside a straggly hedge, someone has cut a hole in the fence. Thelma gathers her dress around her legs and crouches through the hole. On the other side is an expanse of dry, brown grass that looks like it hasn't seen water or a lawn mower since the Russians left in 1991.

She walks across the grass to the narrow beach. A group of little girls splash at each other, giggling and screaming. Two pale, aging men lie beside Cuban women a third their age. A trio of skinny boys hurl themselves off a dock. She scans the beach. There is no one else.

One of the young women is massaging lotion on a man's back. She imagines Rosa in a bikini, the sun disc going down as she massages lotion on Wally's white, freckled back.

She strides over to the men. As disgusting as she finds them, she needs to know if they've seen her husband.

———

THE ITALIAN MEN haven't seen Wally. He has left no more messages. She made Veronika check three times in case the messages were mis-filed. The chambermaid doesn't think anyone visited Wally in his room. The waiter at the poolside bar scrutinized the only photo she has of him in her wallet: an old one, admittedly, he had more hair and fewer wrinkles, and shook his head.

Thelma knows she is driving the staff crazy. It's been two days and he hasn't contacted her! Well, maybe he's tried. Maybe he can't get through.

"Well hello there."

Thelma looks up to see Cathy.

"Oh hi, Cathy."

"Writing home?"

"Um hm."

"Who to? If you don't mind me asking."

"My mom and her husband."

"Are your parents divorced?"

Nosy Parker. Her dad used to call her, when she'd come into his study where he'd be pouring over geological maps of Northern BC, the Yukon, NWT, planning out his next trip. She'd climb on his knee, pretend to read the maps with him.

"No. My mom re-married after my dad died."

"Did your dad die recently?"

"No."

"I, well, I know a little about how it feels. To lose someone. My husband."

"Oh. I'm sorry. When did he, uh, pass on?"

"John didn't pass on. He just passed on me. He's alive and well and living in the wilds of Riverbend in Southeast Calgary."

"I see."

"At least I have my little Sara." Cathy rummages through a sunflower covered cloth bag and withdraws a small framed picture of a blond, green-eyed girl with a gap tooth and a bright smile.

"She's very sweet."

"Smart, too. And still so curious about the world. I hope that curiosity never leaves her. Do you and your husband have children?"

Ah. The million-dollar question. Thelma doesn't feel like giving her the 'answer,' that they are content without children, and they didn't want to bring children into an over populated and uncertain world.

"No we don't."

"Oh, of course, lots of people don't. John wasn't so keen on kids, but he changed his mind when his little girl was born. He dotes on her. I always hoped to have more but I'm 39 and I don't think it's going to happen unless I meet someone soon. I, I don't want to pry but did you try to have children?"

Nosy, nosy parker.

"OK, sorry, sensitive subject. I'm going for a swim. Want to come?"

Thelma, not trusting her voice, just shakes her head.

# CHAPTER 12

*Calgary*

IN HER SECOND LAST semester at the University of Calgary, the penulti-
mate semester, Wally called it, Thelma stopped going to classes. She didn't
tell Wally or her mom. She ignored Professor Smythe's phone calls, asking
why she hadn't been in class; was she ill; did she need help with her term
paper; the final one a request to come and see him immediately. But Thelma
couldn't call him back. She couldn't study. She couldn't seem to do anything
except walk.

She got up (usually), threw up (sometimes) then left the apartment and
took the bus downtown. Got off at City Hall and walked over to the W.R.
Castell library where she spent a few hours reading whatever was lying on
the tables, sometimes copying passages and making notes in a small notebook.

Trout have an excellent growth rate, take well to crowding in ponds or
tanks, *(dad would be appalled!)* are fairly disease resistant *(good thing!)* and
are in great public demand. They are a popular sport fish because of their
fighting and jumping characteristics and because they readily take a shal-
low-water lure. Simenson, A. Trout Fishing in America. *Field and Stream*,
vol 4, #5, spring, 1975.

A young toddler needs limits. Don't give in to tantrums. Give him choices,
but only two: juice or milk. Soda pop is not an option. James, B. (1976) *How to
Raise a Happy, Healthy Child*. Parent Books, N.Y.

She started crying when she read that one and a man wearing a number
of sweaters offered her a handkerchief.

Sometimes she'd wander up and down 7th avenue, watching women in
platform shoes running for buses and men pushing shopping carts filled
with bottles along the sidewalk.

Sometimes she'd perch on an orange vinyl stool at Ye Olde Sandwiche Shoppe drinking watery coffee and eating day old crullers, watching the moms and tots entering and leaving the daycare across the street.

Other times, Thelma would wander further afield, up to 9th avenue where she'd walk east, past the Palliser Hotel and the Calgary Tower, through the dead stretch where trains shuttled back and forth, banging together, connecting and disconnecting. She walked the bridge across the Elbow River, past the Deane House, and the Alexandra Centre, turning down eventually to meet the bike path by the Bow River. She crossed the river and walked past the zoo, stopping at a secluded bench to listen to the haunting cries of the peacocks. Other times, she headed west on the path along Memorial Drive, stopping to rest on the grass of the education building under the sculpture of giant skinny people holding hands. Were they playing ring-around-the-rosie? Their pockets full of posies, hush-a hush-a, we all fall down. Dead. The posies were for the smell, Wally told her. It was a plague song.

On 6th avenue, she'd occasionally stop outside the Knox United Church, its stained glass windows catching the sun, the building the same golden sandstone as Jain temples she'd seen in pictures of India, elegant mirages rising out of the desert. When she heard organ music, Thelma would slip inside, and sit in a back pew, staring at the stained glass windows while the notes washed over her like waves. One day a young girl came in, her greasy hair pulled back into a ponytail, her baby in a stroller, the old-fashioned perambulator kind with a hood. The minister appeared from a side door and the girl went to talk to him, leaving the baby in the aisle. Thelma slipped to the edge of the pew, peered inside the stroller at the tiny dark-haired infant in pink pajamas. She dangled a finger. The baby grasped it.

"Her name's Annette."

The mother was young: 16, 17, 18 at the most.

"She's beautiful," Thelma said, her eyes filling with tears.

"I know," the girl said. "My girl. My precious girl."

Some mornings Thelma walked north, turning east on the path at the Louise bridge where walkers, bikers and aggressive Canada geese with their newly hatched chicks were fewer. At Edworthy Park, she'd sit on a bench overlooking the Bow River. Thought about how the river started high up on the Wapta icefield, descending mountain passes, meandering its way through Banff and the wide Bow Valley to Calgary. In spring, it was a torrent, rushing through the city on its way to the Oldman where it slowed eventually into summer torpor, becoming, finally, an unassuming little prairie river.

Some days she thought about the river and some days she thought about the girl who'd jumped from the bridge at Edworthy Park last year. The Herald said she was a straight A student, a quiet girl from a good family. She worked on the yearbook, played in the band, had lots of friends, a devoted boyfriend. No one knew why she jumped.

Thelma knew.

And so the term ended.

Most nights, Thelma went over to Wally's, thinking she'd tell him she was pregnant, but he always seemed be in the middle of something important, making outlines of Russian novels, constructing charts of the characters' names and nicknames and diminutives. Or working on his grad school applications. Occasionally, he'd ask her why she never had any homework. You're amazing, he said when she told him she'd got it all done during the day, kissing her absentmindedly on the cheek and returning to his novels and applications.

Thelma wrote to do lists: tell mom, tell Wally by w/end, get pregnancy test. But she didn't need a test. She hadn't had a period for two months and 23 days. She wanted children. She did. Just not now.

One night, her grades were waiting for her. She got an undeserved C in Professor Smythe's class, Ds and Fs in her others. Wally called that night. He received four A's and one B+.

Wally's family came up for his convocation. Thelma didn't go, said she didn't believe in all that pomp and ceremony. Her mom wasn't able to get off work anyway, thank God, and Peter was recovering from hernia surgery. They gave her a suitcase for a grad present. Like I'll be going anywhere anytime soon, Thelma thought.

One day on a walk, she passed the Canada employment office and went inside. Filled out an application for a typist in the City Parks and Rec department. Wrote that she could type 90 words per minute. They didn't check. They didn't ask for a medical either. She got the job. She lost the baby.

# CHAPTER 13

*Cuba*

THELMA PUSHES HER stomach out, runs her hand over it, imagines her belly skin stretched.

Imagines her lost baby shifting, his movements rippling her skin.

Why did she get married? After the miscarriage, there was no reason. She could have made up the missed semester, written the GRE. Dr. Smythe would have written her a letter of recommendation for Grad school.

Why? Because Wally asked her? Because it was his baby? Because she didn't think anyone else would want to marry her? Because she loved him?

Her friend Marianne got pregnant and quit school in grade twelve. When Thelma visited her, there were always baby clothes strewn across her couch, dishes in the sink. Marianne's hair hung in ropes because she had no time or energy to wash it; because a baby stole away her days.

She watches Eugenio, today's poolside waiter, expertly balancing drinks while negotiating loungers. His curly hair reminds her of her high school boyfriend, Ron. He distributes the drinks to a group of Italians. At least she thinks they're Italians. They could be Spanish. Colombians, Argentineans, French. She could use a drink. It's early but what the hell. When in Rome....

Thelma raises herself up in the chaise, raises her hand. Eugenio saunters over.

"Buenas dias, Señora. Quisiera tomar algo?"

He remembered she speaks Spanish! "Si, un mojito, por favor."

"Si, Señora, ahora mismo." He stops. "Y tu esposo?"

She doesn't know how to say my husband is still missing so resorts to "no esta aqui."

A family walks by, a mom and dad, two teenage boys. The dad barks at the boys in French. The boys scrape chairs across the cement. Across from her, two women about Thelma's age, wearing white sunhats and designer sunglasses, have removed their bikini tops. Where do they think they are? Cannes? The Cote d'Azur? Have they no modesty?

Her mojito arrives. She scrawls her name and room number on the bill, and reaches for her suntan lotion. On the stereo system, Tito Rodriguez sings *Cuándo, Cuándo, Cuándo*. Tell me quando, tell me when. The sun is warm but not too hot, just the right temperature for tanning for an hour or so before she returns to interrogating the staff about the possibility of lost messages and missed calls. She reclines the chaise, turns over. Oh my darling, Tito sings, tell me when.

———

THELMA WAKES TO find her chaise in shade, the paper umbrella submerged in her half-finished mojito. The French family and the topless women have left. Thelma touches her back, winces. Burned. Damn it. How long has she been asleep?

The sun has almost gone. Thelma pulls her t-shirt over her bathing suit. She drags the chaise into the last corner of sun. A few metres away, a man stands and walks toward the pool. She is unused to seeing men in tiny speedos, aside from Olympians, and she's never seen a Canadian man wearing one. But she likes the way the material caresses his bum. Wally favours knee-length Bermudas. His current pair, she recalls, feature orange dolphins frolicking in an indigo sea.

The man turns to her and smiles. She blushes. Did he see her looking? He looks just as good from the front, a nice broad chest and what do they call it, a six pack? Wally used to have one, but it's been replaced by a little paunch and love handles. You're one to talk, she thinks, sucking in her stomach.

———

"HELLO, VERONIKA. I was wondering...."

"We haven't heard from your husband, Ms. Dangerfield."

"OK, can I rent a bike from the hotel, please?"

"Certainly."

"A ten speed or higher."

Veronika laughs. "Sorry, our bicycles have one speed only."

When was the last time she rode a bicycle? High school? When she and Ron and Marianne rode out to Paul Lake but had to call her mom from the

McDonald's in Valleyview because they were exhausted and couldn't make it up the overpass home? Now here she is, grinding up the hills on Calle 146, past gated mansions in all their crumbing glory, trying to get the bike she rented to change gears. Thelma passes a man, a woman perched side-saddle behind. They pass her on the next downhill. A man calls out "hola linda" as she passes. Yes, she must look absolutely stunning, with her hair plastered to her head and sweat streaming down her face. On the next uphill, she passes a teenager on a *Forever* bike, and an old man walking his bike, a car tire strapped to the carrier rack. He lifts a hand and flashes a smile as she stands and pedals past. A truck roars by. She rides through a cloud of black exhaust. The kid on the *Forever* flies past on the next downhill. On the flats, she tries to catch him but he speeds up, turning around to look at her for so long that she calls out, cuidado! Be careful.

"De donde es?" the kid asks when she catches him at the lights.

"Canada."

"Canada. Very good. Where you going?"

"Lenin Park."

"Why?"

She shrugs. Because Veronika said she thought Wally had gone there. He looks down at her shiny bike.

"Cambio?"

Thelma looks at the rust on his handlebars, the tread-less tires, smiles and shakes her head. No, she doesn't want to change bikes. The light turns green; the boy sprints ahead then turns right at the next corner. She pedals on, wiping the sweat from her brow; watching loose clusters of people at the bus stop re-form as a smoke-spewing bus lumbers toward them.

She passes a gaggle of schoolchildren. They wave and for the first time since she's arrived in Cuba, she's happy. Happy to be riding through this mass of humanity on a week day, to be hot and sweaty in early March instead of in her office, her camel hair coat over her shoulders, shivering and calling out to her secretary, Ardeth, to please call the building maintenance guy again and tell him if he doesn't fix the heat by noon she's calling his boss. Wind would be blowing the snow over the brown grass and frozen bulldozer tracks, flinging it against her window, a warning that more cold was coming, that her car might not start, that the motherless rabbit who lived in the field outside her office window had better stay in his burrow.

Here the sun streams through high clouds. What are they? Cirrus? Stratus? Her dad taught her cloud names. She used to know them all.

At the corner of Avenida 51 and Calle 100, Thelma spies an open-air snack bar and turns into the empty parking lot beside the road and rests her bike against a lamppost. Los Van Van proclaim *Havana Si* from scratchy stereo speakers. She orders a Tropicola at the window and asks what they have to eat. "Nada," says the young boy behind the counter. He's eight or nine, with hooded dark eyes and a shy smile.

She smiles at him. A woman in a white apron comes up behind him, says something in rapid Spanish.

"Si, Señora," says the woman. "A sandwich is possible. "Conejo? I will make."

"Rabbit?"

"Yes. We raise for the meat."

"Well, uh, no thanks I think I'll just have the cola. Do you have bread, cheese?"

"Yes."

"A cheese sandwich."

"Okay, sit, I bring for you."

While she waits for her sandwich, Thelma wanders over to the guarapo stand. An old man with watery eyes sits beside the press in an ancient armchair; its brown fabric bleached almost grey, white stuffing coming through the threadbare cloth of the arms. "Un vaso, por favour," says Thelma.

He pushes himself out of the armchair. She watches him press the sugarcane, watches the juice trickling into a glass below.

"Hielo?" he asks. Thelma is about to say no then thinks, what the hell, it's hot, live dangerously. She nods. The man opens an enormous turquoise coloured GE refrigerator, a 50s relic with rounded corners, and removes some ice cubes. The fridge is like the one at the cabin her family rented at Shuswap Lake, a round blue fridge where her dad kept the fish they caught. He sliced them down the middle, took out their bones and guts. Their dead eyes stared at her, accusingly, every time she opened the door.

"Señora? Tu guarapo."

"Gracias."

The boy brings her the order, lingers beside her table. "A donde vas?"

"Parque Lenin."

"Very good place," the boy says.

She thinks to ask him to sit down, buy him a cola, but his mother beckons from the snack bar.

It shouldn't be too far away now. She'll visit the lake, Lenin's statue, the monument to Celia Sánchez. When she gets back, she'll call the airport taxi driver, Tomás, see if he can take her to Finca Vigia tomorrow, Hemingway's farm in San Francisco de Paula, outside of Havana; she thought it looked interesting in the movie *Memories of Underdevelopment*.

———

LENIN HUNKERS AT the top of the hill. His head only, jutting out from a huge piece of white marble. Thelma gets off her bike and stares at the chiseled profile. If Wally were here, he'd be taking pictures, telling her interesting historical facts about the Russian revolution. She plops down under a nearby tree and looks up to the fronds of the coconut palm above her, then back over to Lenin, trying to remember who came first, Marx or Lenin, and how Trotsky fit in.

After a short rest, she cycles on through the park. The Celia Sánchez museum is located in a small house at the end of a shaded drive. Leaning her bike against the house, Thelma tries the door. It's locked. She knocks. An old man dressed in a starched blue guayabera and trousers ushers her in.

"Bienvenido," he says. "Pase, por favor. De donde es?"

"I'm from Canada."

"Ah, Canada. Your prime minister, Jean Chretien, he visited Cuba. And Pierre Elliot Trudeau, of course, was a good friend of us."

"Yes, of course."

"Please come and look. Here are pictures of Celia, with the heroes of our revolution." The walls of the house are lined with pictures of young Celia, Celia and Fidel, Celia and Haydee Santamaria, Celia and Camilo Cienfuegos. Celia and Wally's hero, Ernesto Che Guevara.

"I understood there was a statue of her."

"Yes, is waiting outside."

The man indicates the doors on the other side of the room. Thelma steps outside, walks down a path to a fern-lined amphitheatre where a bronze sculpture of the woman is set in stone. She sits on the grass, then takes out the guidebook from her pack. During the revolution, Celia ran the intelligence and supply networks to the guerillas. She was Fidel's secretary, friend and his lover. Did she want to marry him? Or was her first love the revolution? Like Fidel, like their university friend, Pedro? His first love was the revolution he and his group were going to start in Ecuador. His second love was his country. Third his family and fourth his girlfriend, her friend, Anna.

Pedro took them to a movie once, *Between a Marxist and a Naked Woman*. To show them, perhaps, that revolution was a calling and trumped everything, including love.

Thelma thought she had a calling, once. Archeology. Excavating and studying the things people left behind, the things they threw away, things hidden deep in the earth.

———

"HELLO, THELMA. Hope you had a nice ride and a lovely day. No messages," Veronika calls cheerily as Thelma drags her sweat drenched body by the front desk. Yes, she had a nice day with Celia and Vladimir. And she wasn't even going to ask about Wally.

# CHAPTER 14

*Cuba*

IT'S RAINING AND the chandelier lights are flickering, threatening to die. She lies on the bed, staring at the drops sliding down the window. She tried to call Tomás. The first time, the phone emitted a series of squawks. The second time, she couldn't understand the person who answered and then they were cut off. The third time, the phone rang five times and then stopped ringing.

Goddamn Wally! Damn him to hell. It's been three days. Why hasn't he called? If she stays by herself, in her room, she'll get angrier. She should see if Cathy wants to get a taxi and go out somewhere. Where could they go? Thelma doesn't know the names of any bars, any clubs. Except the Tropicana. And the idea of watching young, beautiful, scantily clad women dance does not appeal.

———

THELMA'S IN THE SHOWER when the lights go out. They say blackouts are responsible for many babies here. What else do you do in the dark? She imagines an apartment building filled with amorous couples, calling to each other ah, Miguel, Lazaro, Doris, my amor, mi vida, their words echoing out the doors, down stairs and around corners, out windows where they are carried in the breeze down to the malecón and the narrow, cobbled streets of old Havana where couples press together in darkened doorways.

She fumbles for the knob, turns the water off, steps cautiously out of the tub. Shouldn't have closed the door. The bathroom is pitch black. She feels dizzy, suddenly, slides down the wall to the floor. Thelma smells smoke.

"Hello," she calls. "Is anyone there?"

White Owl cigars. The kind her dad smoked.

No answer.

Her dad died in a room at the Royal Inland Hospital in the middle of the night, his breath tightening in his chest then stopping. No one could tell her why he left her.

His red plaid fishing jacket, the one she kept, smelled of his cigars. When the smell faded, she went to the little store on Greenstone Drive, bought some more cigars, telling the proprietor they were for her uncle. She hid behind the hawthorn trees in the side yard, lit a cigar, blew the smoke back into the jacket. Her mother caught her and grounded her for a week but Thelma didn't care. She wanted his smell back.

———

THELMA, HAVING DISCOVERED Cathy is out, is drinking cuba libres in the Palco's patio bar and listening to the evening pianist playing *Toma Chocolate*, *Guantanamera*, *Yolanda* and *Hasta Siempre*, songs she has come to recognize as the tourist standards, when a couple wander in, hand in hand. They pull their barstools close together, whisper and giggle, nuzzle each other's necks, kiss.

The women wears her black hair up, her neck and back are tanned to a coppery sheen, her halter dress is a soft pink.

They unlock their lips briefly to order drinks.

When the waiter returns with them, the man tosses him an American twenty and tells him to keep the change.

"We're on our honeymoon," the woman says. The waiter offers congratulations.

"How do you say honeymoon in Cuban?"

"In Spanish, it is the same. Luna, moon, de miel, of honey."

Thelma heard her friend's uncle once say he was going on a honeymoon. She asked her dad if it was a type of moon. He laughed and said a honeymoon was a place where people went after they were married but Thelma didn't need to think about that for a long, long time.

Her parents discouraged talk of brides and weddings. 'You need to be able to support yourself,' they said. Her mom worked as a nurse before she was married, before she got pregnant with Thelma. After her dad died and her mom went back to work, her mom went on about how lucky she was to have finished nursing school, even though she was a single mother, she was a single mother with a profession.

When she was a teenager, Thelma thought if she married at all, it would be when she was very old, in her thirties, at least. She didn't expect Wallace Alexander Dangerfield to propose. He was the third most interesting person she'd met so far in her life, after her father and Dr. Smythe. How many twenty-two-year-olds can talk passionately about history? Not just Canadian or world history or the history of the Blue Jays, but of ideas, shoes and dogs and the Napoleonic wars and the Anglo-Indian novel. His knowledge was encyclopedic. Not surprising, since he read the entire Britannica as a kid.

He proposed, and she said yes. Why? Even at the age of twenty-two, he looked like a future rumpled professor, wearing t-shirts, baggy cords, and old tweed jackets he bought from Good Will. She had to admit he wasn't bad in bed. Earnest, eager and happy to try anything she suggested. Maybe she married him because he cried sometimes at the end of sad movies. Because he knew about chaos theory and how to conjugate French irregular verbs and what the active ingredient of peyote was.

Very smart, her Wally. There were two brains in her high school in Kamloops, Tony Chu and Sandy Martíno. But neither of them could hold a candle to Wally's genius.

But, truly, why did I marry him? Thelma wonders. Because he said I looked good when I didn't. Because he told me all the things he loved about me: 'this,' he'd say, running his fingers over my toes, 'these eyes,' he'd say, humming the Guess Who song. What else? Besides the physical?' she asked. 'I love that you act so tough.' 'I am tough.' 'Ha! You couldn't fight your way out of a wet paper bag.' She loved it when he said that. Because her dad used to say the exact same thing.

She loved that he was sensitive. She liked the wounded look he'd get when she said something a bit mean. The way his nostrils quivered, rabbit like, when he was listening very intently, listening not just with his ears but with his eyes, nose and mouth. His whole body leaning forward in anticipation of what she was going to say. That was how she used to live and loved that life. Before the possibility of a search; before the years turned into a thin picture spread. To quote Wally's quotes.

————

THIS TIME THE DREAM is longer, more detailed. She's flying over a high plateau toward a line of mountains. A steep, dark mountain, dotted with small lakes left by retreating glaciers. The plane flies over three smaller, then a larger one, with ponds dotted around it like moons around a planet.

Ribbons of frozen water, white lace, knife down the surrounding slopes. The lakes are frozen at the edges. She reaches beneath her seat, touches the canister with her father's ashes.

She sees a patch of meadow, the helicopter descends, but the earth is rushing up, fast, too fast, her heart is pounding, Jesus...

Thelma opens her eyes. Where the hell is she? Oh. Yes. In bed. Home? No, too hot.

Cuba. Havana.

She'll go downstairs. Maybe Wally called while she was in the bar and there's a message.

Thelma runs a comb through her hair, slips on her sandals and slides into the silent hall.

The glass elevator is waiting, glides smoothly downwards, no calls interrupting its descent.

The lobby is quiet, the front desk empty. "Hola," she calls, her voice echoing across the marble floor: "hola, hola." Finally, a young man she hasn't seen before emerges from the back office.

"No hay mensajes, Señora Dangerfield," he says. Her message requesting reputation apparently precedes her.

Thelma nods and attempts to walk casually to a cluster of yellow flowered couches at the far side of the lobby, sits, looks out the window but all she can see is her blurred self. He's gone. This man she has lived with for half her life. She can't imagine life without Wally. His side of the closet empty, his drawers devoid of socks, underwear and t-shirts, dust and dryer lint in their empty corners. Her books falling onto each other in the spaces his left on the bookshelves. Can't imagine coming home from work to a dark house, rummaging through the fridge for leftovers, spending every second night eating by herself somewhere in Kensington or at the North Hill Mall food fair, hiding behind a book. Can't imagine weekends that go on forever.

The cold side of the bed. Watching movies by herself, no Wally to cuddle up against, to discuss them with afterwards. Can't imagine....

Of course, you can imagine it, Thelma, she tells herself. You just did. Alright, enough brooding. What are you going to do? Stay here and brood? Go to Cienfuegos to look for him? If she finds him, she will tell him the story Professor Smythe told her. How, for the Ancient Maya, adultery was a serious crime. The cuckolded party had the right to crush the lover with a rock.

Looking out the window, Thelma can see her second self, unhinged and floating in the dark.

IN A CORNER OF the basement bar, the only one still open, a man is smoking, his cigarette pulsing red as he inhales. Sweet smoke drifts her way. Not White Owl but sweet, close. Thelma orders a Taino beer. When it comes, she takes a long drink, plunks the glass down heavily.

Somewhere a floor is being vacuumed. She hears a car pulling into the driveway, doors slam, voices slip through the glass door: a breathless woman, a laughing man.

Though she hasn't smoked in twenty years, she asks the waitress for a package of what the man is smoking. Hollywood Verde. Orders another beer. By closing time she has smoked all the cigarettes.

As a little girl, she loved to spend time in the dirt-floored basement, watching him build things. Her dad's workbench sat in the corner across from the boarded up coal chute, the tools neatly lined up on the wall in the slots he built for them. Her mom didn't think it was healthy for her to spend so much time below ground. It's damp, Ev, she'd say to Thelma's father. She'll catch a cold. Thelmie's tough, her dad replied. She'll be fine.

When the men lowered her father's coffin into the ground in the cemetery across from the high school, Thelma didn't cry. She touched the warm, wet earth at the edge of the hole, smelled its leaf smell. She didn't cry when people told her she was a brave little girl. Because she knew something they didn't. Thelma knew he wasn't gone.

———

LAST YEAR, SHE went down to the basement, sat beside the hot water heater, and dug through files in a box marked T–univ. She found a term paper she wrote for Professor Smythe:

*The Tales Knots Tell: an examination of the Inca Quipu system.* 'Good title,' Professor Smythe had written below in black fountain pen. Quipus were knots, a record keeping and storytelling system. The Incas tied them in specific positions on the strings to represent numbers. Different string colors represented different concepts. Runners carried these knot messages along the roads of their empire. How exactly the Inca used the quipus to tell stories, Thelma couldn't remember. She liked the idea of a secret code the Spanish didn't know and couldn't break. Liked the fact that quipus might have delayed the conquest.

On the essay, Professor Smythe had written: 'an excellent, well-researched, meticulously documented paper. A+. P.S. Have you put in your grad school application?'

In the box were a well-thumbed copy of *Maya Archeologist*, and a tattered brown envelope containing five photos from her Ruta Maya trip from third year. In the first picture, she was standing below El Castillo at Chichén Itzá. In another, she had her arm on the shoulder of a blond boy in a safari hat, hipsters and a Grateful Dead t-shirt, as they posed beside a Chac-Mool.

"Last call," says the waitress.

"I'm good."

"Are you sure?"

"Sort of."

"Did you find your husband?"

She's never even seen this waitress before. Veronika is such a gossip!

"No. But he has to be on the island. He's researching De Soto, you know. Hernando. He's smart. Got a grant."

"De Soto?"

"My husband."

"Your husband is a professor?"

"No. He's a writer. I'm the one who should have been a professor."

"What subject?"

"Archeology."

"Ancient History?"

"Kind of, yeah."

CHAPTER 15

*Mexico, 1978*

THE GREY STONE benches in the Cancun long distance phone office are shiny, polished by the bums of the waiting. An old couple shuffles in and sits across from Thelma. A fan moves like a heat-drugged fly, barely stirring the thick air.

She ponders her lazy field trip classmates, who prefer to hang around the palapas, swim and tan, than explore hidden Cancun with Thelma, two other students, Cindy and Jeanine, and Dr. Smythe. After she calls Wally, they're going for lunch at a hole in the wall place Dr. Smythe knows that serves a spectacular pollo pibil. She's looking forward to trying the chicken. Then they're going to shop in the market. Maybe she'll get Wally one of those colourful serapes for his bed. Or a hammock, a big one they could hang on his balcony and cuddle up in together.

Something resembling her name is called. A woman motions her into a glass booth. She picks up the phone. It rings. And rings. And rings. It's 8:00. Why isn't he answering? His phone is right by his bed and they planned that she would call him today. God damn it, she mutters, hanging up after the thirtieth something ring. She'll have to figure out how to get to town later to call him again and who knows if he will be even home.

———

PROFESSOR SMYTHE has arranged for them to stay at some huts down the beach from Tulum. The male and female students are segregated; each group has a thatch-roofed palapa with no sides, a concrete floor, and hooks for hanging hammocks. Some of the girls sleep on foamies, but Thelma imagines the snakes and cockroaches and scorpions that could crawl on her in the night and decides to sleep in a hammock. You get the breeze higher up and once you find a good position, it's almost comfy.

She can't sleep. It's too hot, and she misses having Wally sleeping beside her, his hand slung casually across her stomach. Although she shouldn't miss him too much, since he seems to have forgotten their phone date. She pitches herself out of her hammock to pee. Outside is black velvet, the new moon invisible. The moon is visiting the land of the rain gods, dipping her white self in a cool cenote, perhaps, Thelma thinks, wishing she could dip herself in one, too.

The next night there's a party on the beach. A fire. Logs to sit on. Beer and tequila. Thelma sits by the fire for a while, drinking Dos Equis, but then she gets too hot and goes to sit on a little sandy ridge. She watches the waves advancing, receding. Stares at drunken couples weaving down the beach together, looking for a quiet make-out spot. Wishes Wally was with her, beside her, his long fingers resting on her bare shoulders. She walks back to the fire, stepping over a couple of people passed out on the sand beside it.

A drunk girl stumbles by. From somewhere in the dark, someone giggles. From down the beach, the sound of retching.

Jerome from her trip ambles by, drops his lanky body beside her.

"Are you looking forward to Chichén Itzá" he asks.

"Yeah." Don't want company, thanks. Have a boyfriend. One who doesn't answer the phone.

"Me too."

A little breeze flickers the fire, rushes down her bare arms.

"You're cold," he says, sliding down the log toward her.

"Nope." She fake-yawns. "Well, time to hit the hay."

"It's early. Why don't we go for a walk on the beach?"

"I'm tired. You know, all the digging in the hot sun."

"I like your hair," he blurts.

Thelma fingers her braids. "Thanks. Gotta go. See you."

His droopy brown eyes glint up at her. Nice. But not as nice as Wally's blue ones.

————

THELMA, JEROME, AND CINDY are waiting under the ceiba tree for Professor Smythe. The morning light is a soft orange and she can smell the smoke from nearby cooking fires. Thelma wonders if they'll have huevos con frijoles or huevos rancheros for breakfast. Or maybe just hot tortillas with butter and jam. Jeanine saunters over to them, her make-up perfect, her white cut-offs spotless. She spends every night with a flashlight and bar of yellow laundry soap at the cement tub.

"Here he comes," Cindy announces.

She turns. Professor Smythe is bending his long body under the clothesline strung with Jeanine's bikini day-of-the-week underwear.

This is the part of the day Thelma likes best. Before the heat becomes oppressive, the ruins too crowded, before her fellow students couple up or wander off in search of shade, water, beer, or a make-out place.

Professor Smythe is wearing a pair of creased khaki pants and what looks to be a woman's gardening sun hat. Balancing a pile of papers in his arms, he surveys the four of them.

"Where is everyone?"

Jeanine giggles. "There was a party..."

"Well it was good of you four to rouse yourselves."

He lowers himself to the ground, organizes his notes in piles, anchoring them with rocks. "I'll begin then. Today I'd like to talk about the Mayan calendar and recording of time. As you know from your readings there are a number of calendar systems, used to record the past and predict the future. Whenever a period of time ended, a katun, twenty Mayan years, or especially a baktun, which is...?"

"144,000 days, sir," Cindy pipes up.

"That's right, just less than 400 years. Whenever a baktun ended, the Maya redoubled their efforts in temple building because it was at the end of each period that the possibility of calamity, even the end of the world, could happen. The current baktun began in 1618 and will end—anyone?"

She knows that, she just read about it, damn, it's 2000 something.

"December 21, 2012," offers Jeanine.

"Exactly. Thirty-four years from now."

Just before Christmas. Thelma imagines people scurrying through malls, picking up a last minute bottle of perfume for a sister-in-law, some more candy for the kids' stockings. Would there be an announcement: 'the world will end in fifteen minutes, fifteen minutes ladies and gentlemen. Please complete your purchases and head to the nearest exit.' Would people file slowly and obediently to the exits or, would there be panic, broken perfume bottles, chocolates strewn across the floors, cars smashing into each other in the parking lots?

In 2012, she'll be old. Older than her lost father ever was. What will her life be like? For sure, she'll have her PhD in archeology, specializing in something Mayan. Wally will be a professor in English or History, though most likely English. They'll probably be married with a couple of kids, maybe three, two boys and a girl.

"Thelma?"

"I'm sorry, sir?"

"Why did the Itzá built Chichén Itzá?"

"The, uh, well the Itzá were dreading the new baktun and the coming of the death lord because the death lord would preside for the next four hundred years. And they wanted to stop that from happening."

"Exactly." He beams at them, even at Jeanine who has only answered one question and Jerome who hasn't answered any. "And not long afterwards, the great Mayan city states declined, fell into disarray, and the people retreated into the jungle. Though, of course, the Maya, the day keepers, the stories and rituals, their view of the world, are still with us."

"Are they, sir?" asks Jerome.

"Of course they are. The past is always with us."

———

AN HOUR LATER, the hung-over having been woken and fed tortillas and coffee, they are on their Bluebird bus en-route to Chichén Itzá. Thelma has snagged the seat behind Professor Smythe. She wants to talk to him about the coming end of the baktun but Dr. Smythe is hunched over the wheel, taking the potholed road at a bone jarring speed.

Thelma pulls a map of Chichén Itzá from her pack, unfolds it and begins to plan her day. She'll start at the Nunnery where there are some Rain Gods/ Chacs she wants to see and sketch. She's thinking about doing her final assignment about the Chacs. Judging from the discussion around the campfire last night, most of the guys are heading straight for the more gruesome parts of the site—the temple of skulls where eagles are depicted tearing open men's chests and eating their hearts; the ball court where players from the losing team were decapitated. She should have the Nunnery and the Rain Gods all to herself.

Dr. Smythe floors the shuddering Bluebird past men on bicycles, machetes swinging from their belts, blue uniformed children waiting for a school bus, women in beautifully embroidered huipiles carrying water jugs on their heads.

They arrive at Chichén Itzá ten minutes before opening. Professor Smythe hands out maps, a sheet of questions, a meeting time and place (the sacred cenote).

Jerome falls into step with her.

"So, Thelma, where are you going?"

"Right now?"

"Yeah."

"To the bathroom, actually."

She doesn't want him following her around, looking at her with those droopy, expectant eyes. She has serious work to do.

"After that?"

"I'm not sure. I need to go. Pee I mean. See you at the cenote later."

———

SHE IS THE ONLY person at the Nunnery complex. The church, La Iglesia as the Spanish called it, is rectangular, constructed of grey-brown stone. There's a door in the centre of the complex, the hooked question mark noses of the Chacs hanging above it. Thelma stares up at the crumbling roof comb. The air is warm but not too hot yet. She stares at the Chacs, thinking about how this city was abandoned, how it lay covered in jungle until Edward Thompson "discovered" it in 1904. She takes out her notebook and begins sketching.

She hears voices, noisy, nattering voices. A group of women burst into the clearing. They swarm past Thelma, crowd the doorway, perching their elegantly dressed butts on the ancient stones, patting down their hair, freshening their lipstick, posing for pictures.

"Don't," she yells to a woman who has taken out a cloth to rub dust from a Chac's nose.

"No English," the woman replies, extending her camera. "Photo me?"

Thelma politely takes her camera, and waves her hand for the subject to back off.

"A little to the left so I can frame you," she calls.

"Like this?"

"Perfect." Thelma cuts off her head and hands the camera back.

She is just returning to her sketch when a man, dressed in white and holding a bright red flag, leads another group towards the Nunnery.

"Goddamn it!"

Angrily, she picks up her pack. She'll go to look at the Chac-Mool and come back later.

The famous Chac-Mool: his head turned to one side, his belly a bowl for blood from sacrifices, his arrogant almond-shaped eyes facing west, death, darkness. Professor Smythe told them an archeologist climbed the Chac-Mool pyramid during a storm. He was struck by lightning and died instantly.

———

AT THE SACRED cenote, the sun blasts down from the centre of the sky. All moisture has been sucked out of the air. This could be Kamloops in August. The waterhole is surrounded by spindly trees. Vines and bushes cling to its banks. Thelma imagines swallows building their nests in the mud banks, flying back and forth above the pea green waters like they do on the Thompson River.

"Any questions, people?"

A hand shoots up. "What are Chacs again?" asks a guy they call Hoser. She doesn't know his real name. Did he even look at the assigned reading?

"You've undoubtedly seen them today with their hooked noses, snakes emerging from their mouths. The rain they brought was both needed and feared. And they are not just ancient gods. They are still worshipped today in some parts of the Yucatan. Shrines are prepared, young boys are tied to altars. They croak like frogs, encouraging the Chacs to bring on the rains. Remember, the cities were abandoned but the Maya are still here."

"The past is always with us," Thelma adds. "The past predicts the future, according to the Maya."

"Exactly. Yes. Very good, Miss Roberts. Excellent."

Thelma beams.

"So, a cenote is, like, a well or something, right?" asks a guy whose name Thelma has forgotten.

"Like a well? It is a well. Cenotes, generally, are doors to caves, under-ground rivers and the watery underworld where the Chacs and jaguar spir-its reside. Any other questions? No, well let's meet at the bus in half an hour. Miss Roberts, would you mind staying here to let the stragglers know?"

"OK," she says, though she'd prefer to get herself back to the Nunnery.

Her classmates scatter in four directions. A tour guide and his group march to the edge of the water, blocking her view.

"This is the sacred cenote," the guide begins. "Where young virgins were thrown, sacrificed to the bloodthirsty Gods."

Not true!

"There are nine levels of watery hell," he declaims, "populated by diseased death lords spewing excrement. Picture it in your mind, ladies and gentlemen. Can you see it? Yes?"

She is so lucky to be with Professor Smythe.

———

THELMA IS SITTING on hot stone at the edge of the Mayan ruins of Tulum looking out to sea. Dr. Smythe and the other students are still at the top of El Castillo. She imagines them, in their baseball caps and straw hats they bought at the tourist stalls outside Chichen Itzá, their cameras clicking in unison. She has already climbed the stairs, noted the serpent columns, and examined the Diving Gods, with their wings and birds' tails: Gods of the bee and honey. She's examined the famous mural of Ixchel, seated on her throne, receiving offerings.

Thelma takes off her Tilly hat, lets the sun enter her body. Dangles her hand through a large opening in the rock. Cool hand, hot everything else. Her hand in midair, surrounded by limestone that was formerly the ocean floor, which now leads to ocean.

Thelma peers down the opening. It is just wide enough for a body to pass through.

She wants to slip inside it, slide down smooth rock and into a cave where stalactites hang from the ceiling, where light pencils through tiny holes to freckle the dark water. Wants to slide down the tunnel to the underworld, to the home of the Rain Gods. Her own small cenote. Her own private cave. She imagines walking through it, the water ankle, thigh, waist deep. Swimming, finally, toward the light where she imagines her father is, emerging into the turquoise sea.

The sun dances off the breakers. From cliffs, children hurtle through the air like so many diving Gods. She imagines Professor Smythe finding her bottle, her backpack, her book, *The Ancient Maya*, that she has left on its stomach, spine cracked, glue dissolving in the heat. She and her father will float on the waves, swim with children and dolphins, and come ashore eventually. Like the 16th century Spanish Conquistadors who, from their ships, saw the brilliantly painted red, blue and white buildings of the Maya, and came to land.

———

SHE MANAGED TO convince Dr. Smythe to drop her at the phone office, explaining she'll take a taxi back, which she will get Wally to pay for.

In the long distance booth, the phone rings, once, twice, three...

"Hello." A woman's voice.

"Hi. Is this Etta?" She didn't know Wally's sister was coming to visit.

"No."

"Is Wally there?"

"No.

Who is this?"

"Deirdre."

"Deirdre who?"

"A friend."

"Really?"

"Yes. How can I help you? Can I take a message for Wally?"

"No. Yes. Tell him Thelma, his girlfriend, called."

"Yeah, sure." Click.

Rude girl. She's never heard of a friend of his called Deirdre. Unless she's an old friend from Nanaimo. Or a friend of Etta's who is in town and crashing on his floor. If that's the case, why didn't she say so? Why did she hang up on Thelma? What the hell is she doing at Wally's place? And why isn't Wally there?

There had better be a good reason for this Deirdre person being at his place. Like they were studying late and she fell asleep. He fell asleep. They both fell asleep. In separate rooms.

———

HER BELLY FULL of huevos rancheros, Thelma's back in the booth, the last time she's going to try. She pulls at her t-shirt, which is sticking to her sweating body like elephant skin, counting the rings. Pick up, pick up, she mutters.

He answers on the tenth.

"Hello."

"It's me."

"Thelma, hi, how are you? How's the trip? I was just reading about the ruins, the temple of skulls at Chichén Itzá sounds pretty impressive. Where are you?"

"Cancun. Listen I don't have much time. I just wanted to ask you something."

"Sure, shoot."

"Why didn't you answer the first time I called?"

Silence. "Sorry, I, I pulled an all-nighter. Studying. Must have crashed in the living room."

"Well, it's not exactly easy to phone from here you know."

"Sorry."

"And who answered the phone when I called earlier?"

"When?"

She didn't tell him.

"This morning." Or he's lying.

"What?"

"I called at 7:00 this morning. A woman answered."

"Really?"

"Yes, really. A woman answered and it wasn't Etta or your mom. So unless you've acquired a housekeeper..."

"Well, uh, maybe..."

"Maybe what, Wallace?"

"Maybe it was Deirdre."

"Who is?"

"Pardon?"

"Who is?"

"A friend."

"What kind of friend?"

"You're coming back a week Tuesday, right? I've got your flight info, I'll pick you up. We can talk about it then."

"Are you sleeping with her?"

"Thelm!"

"Are you?"

"Why are you even asking me that?"

"I think it's rather obvious why I'm asking you."

"Thelma, please! I'll see you on Tuesday. OK, listen, I have to get ready for class. Have fun and I'll see you soon. Bye."

The phone emits a strange sort of shrieking sound. Her hand is shaking. If he is sleeping with Deirdre, that's it. It's over.

She walks outside into the mid-day furnace. On the sidewalk, a woman and a little boy hold out their hands: un peso, Señorita, por favor, Señorita, por favor.

She finds herself on a bench in a litter-strewn park. Two boys kick a piece of rubber that was once a ball. Another follows a snake into the long grass. A shit filled diaper lies beside a thorny bush. The sun is fierce, the park absolutely without shade.

If he is sleeping with Deirdre... If he is sleeping with her...

She blinks back tears. He better not be.

———

THE NEXT AFTERNOON at the palapas, she washes her hair in cold water, lies in the grass with it spread around her to dry. Later, she puts on a blue halter top, the lacy white skirt she bought in the market, mascaras her lashes in the cloudy mirror hanging above the outdoor sink.

At the fire on the beach that night, she sits beside Jerome.

"How's it going?"

"Thelma! Hi. Wow, you look great. Good, it's going good. I was looking for you this afternoon. We played volleyball. I wanted you on my team."

"You did?" Thelma smiles brightly. "That's sweet. Sorry I missed it. Hey, I bought some tequila at the market yesterday. Want some?"

She pulls the bottle out of her bag, takes a swig and hands it to him.

"Wow. Sure, thanks Thelma. Thanks a lot."

———

A FEW STARS HAVE come out, pin pricks in a moonless sky. There's no more wood and the fire is dying. She and Jerome have polished off most of the tequila and run through their repertoire of jokes. She stands up, waits for her head to clear.

"Hey Thelma, wher'ya going? Come back here."

"Gotta, you know, pee."

She staggers off down the beach. When she thinks she's far enough away, she squats, pulls her panties to one side, like she used to do as a kid when she couldn't be bothered to take off her wet bathing suit, and pees in the sand.

Back at the fire, she somehow misses the log and lands, unceremoniously, in the sand.

"Whoa, there, Thelma. You OK?"

"Yeah, log jumped. As did some sand, into my mouth." She spits. "Omigod, that tequila is strong."

He slides down beside her on the sand. It is.

79

Then, all of a sudden, he is kissing her. He's not a bad kisser, a bit sloppy but maybe he's a little drunk, too. He slides his tongue into her mouth and she lets him. He groans, and pushes her back onto the cool sand, then slides on top of her, his hand reaching under her top.

She pushes him off, sits up.

"What's the matter?

"I have a boyfriend."

"I don't mind," he says, nuzzling his face into her hair and kissing her neck.

"Jerome, no listen, I think, oh no, I'm going to be sick."

She turns and throws up the rice and beans she had for dinner, the chicken from lunch, the tequila.

"Are you alright?"

She throws up again.

"No," she says, wiping her hand across her mouth. "Damn two-timing Wally."

"Pardon?"

"Nothing."

"Come on." He helps her up and steers her toward the girls' palapa. "Let's get you to bed."

———

WHEN SHE WAKES up, it's still dark. She's wearing her nightgown, lying on a blanket on the concrete floor. Jerome has put his jacket on top of her. In the hammocks, girls rustle and cough. Her back is stiff and her mouth tastes like puke.

She stands, waits for her head to stop spinning, and then stumbles out of the palapa and down to the beach. A few embers from the fire still smolder. A guy and girl sleep beside it covered in a blanket, their clothes strewn on the sand around them. She looks more closely.

Jeanine. And the Hoser!

Thelma walks away from them, down the beach. She wanders over to a cove and wades into the water. It's warm, soothing. She lets the waves carry her out, away from the beach, the smoldering fire, the palapas. Turns on her back and floats. The stars slide away, light edges up the horizon. It is a pale lavender, the colour of the blanket she made for Marianne's baby, the colour of the earrings Wally gave her for their six-month anniversary, the colour of lilacs in her backyard in Kamloops. She floats, remembering the sweet smell of lilacs, how her mom used to cut them, bring them into the house, how the living room became full of their scent.

"Miss Roberts!"

Dr. Smythe stands at the edge of the sea, waving his arms.

"Wait. I'm coming!" He's taking off his shoes.

"Stay there. I'm fine," she calls back.

"There's an undertow!" He's walking fully clothed into the sea. She starts swimming back to shore.

"Hold on, Miss Roberts!"

A wave picks her up, rolls her and spits her out. She gasps for breath just as another breaker pulls her down, scrubs her body against the ocean floor, she needs to get to the surface, needs air. Then suddenly she feels arms circling her chest, pulling her up. Dr. Smythe. She lies against his back as he kicks toward shore. Then they're pulled under, she can feel him kicking them up, they surface but another wave pulls them down, Dr, Smythe tightens his grip. Finally, the wave spits them up a few yards from the beach.

"I, I'm OK now," she gasps. But he won't let go of her, picks her up and deposits her on the dry sand.

"I'm sorry, Dr. Smythe," she says, when she can speak.

"What in heaven's name were you doing way out there?"

"Just, um, just swimming."

"Swimming to Cuba?"

"No."

"Well," he gasps. "That's where you were heading. And I very much doubt you would have made it, young lady."

# CHAPTER 16

*Calgary*

WALLY'S HAIR-SHIRT SOFA prickles the back of Thelma's legs. Which is appropriate, given her prickly state since she returned from Mexico. Wally sits across from her on a plastic Ikea chair.

"Wow, Thelm, did I tell you how good you look with a tan?"

"Yup."

"So tell me about the Mayan ruins, about Mexico."

"First you tell me about Deirdre."

"What do you want to know about her?"

"The usual: who is she, how did you meet, is she pretty, did you sleep with her?"

"Thelma! She's in my Canadian history class. She asked me to help her with an essay on Louis Riel and..."

"And?"

"You look good, Thelma. Your hair got longer. And blonder." He reaches across the coffee table, tries to take her hand. She removes it from her lap. "I missed you, you know."

"So you didn't sleep with her, then?"

He looks down. "No."

"No you didn't sleep with her or no my assertion is incorrect?"

"Well, I kind of..."

"You kind of slept with her? Either you did or you didn't, Wally."

"OK, listen, we uh, we, we just fooled around one night. She brought over some beer and I was helping her with her essay and then all of a sudden..."

"All of a sudden...?"

"She just came on to me and..."

"And you were powerless to do anything? Reverted to some kind of infantile state? Your brain went missing in action?"

"I didn't sleep with her, Thelm, honest, we just fooled around, you know, I mean she wanted to but..."

Thelma stands up. "Spare me the fucking details!"

"Please, Thelma." He blocks her way. "I'm sorry, it doesn't mean anything. I'll make it up to you."

She tries to slam the door on her way out but the damn thing sticks in the frame.

———

SCHOOL STARTS, SHE stays in the library until it closes most days, taking the last bus down Crowchild Trail to her apartment. She works on extra credit projects for Dr. Smythe, on her honour's paper. Dr. Smythe is sure she'll qualify for grad school and a scholarship. She's acing all her tests, her GPA is sure to be the highest ever.

One Saturday evening in mid-November, Thelma opens the door to her building to find a shivering Wally waiting for her in the vestibule. He has dark circles under his eyes. His hair looks like it hasn't been brushed in weeks. He's wearing a thin jean jacket despite the fact it's minus five outside, the vestibule only slightly warmer.

"Thelma! Hi. Thank God. I've been waiting for over an hour. Is it ever cold in here. I can't feel my fingers and toes anymore."

She declines to respond.

"How are you?"

"OK," she says frostily, opening her mailbox.

"Well, I'm not so fine. Listen, Thelm, I've been trying to phone you, where have you been?"

"Around."

"You never answer your phone."

She picks up her mail and starts up the stairs. He follows. She searches her pockets for the house key. Finds it but can't get the damn thing to fit in the lock.

"I haven't seen you at school."

"I've been there."

"Can I come in?"

She jiggles the key and, finally, the bloody deadbolt slides open.

"What for?"

"I just want to talk. If you don't want me to come in, we could go out for a coffee or..."

"I'm busy."

"You look great, Thelm. I missed you, you can't imagine. I haven't seen Deirdre at all, she phones me but I tell her I can't see her. We didn't do anything. Nothing really. I can understand if you don't want to go out with me anymore, but can we at least be friends?"

She turns to him. "I don't think so."

"Don't you miss me, even a little?" he asks, his sleepy dog eyes searching her face. She does miss him reading his Russian novels to her in bed at night. Shrugs.

"Deirdre was nothing."

"I'm sure she'd be thrilled to hear that."

"You know what I mean."

She did let Jerome kiss her. Would have probably done more if she hadn't been sick.

Though that was after she found out about Wally. And she was drunk.

"Can I at least come inside to warm up for a sec?" He's shivering like a wet dog.

She walks in, leaving the door open behind her.

———

THELMA SLEEPS WITH Wally on a cold day at the end of February, three and a half months after she found him in her building's vestibule, two months after she agreed to try being friends. They went skating at Bowness Park. She invited him in for hot chocolate. While she was stirring the cocoa into the milk, he came up behind her, lifted her hair and kissed the back of her neck.

She didn't realize how lonely her body was. How greedy. That her body could betray her like that.

# CHAPTER 17

*Cuba*

IN THIS DREAM, she and the Tomás, the taxi driver, are walking along Quinta Avenida. A car glides up beside them, a man leans out into warm night, asks *taxi*? Tomás dismisses him with a wave of his hand. They pass colonial houses, pillared and porticoed, chunks of plaster missing, some with their doors ajar, revealing families watching flickering black and white televisions. In front of them a man, his smoke from his cigar beckoning them down the street. A scooter glides by. She sees red letters on a wall: Venceremos. We will overcome. From a second story window, snatches of music drift down, a song of lost love, Yolanda, Yolanda, Eternamente Yolanda. A cyclist appears out of the dark, passing so close Thelma can feel his rough cotton pants against her leg. He has a cage on the back, with a rabbit inside.

Tomás presses her elbow, guides her down a dark side street that smells like the sea. The yellow amusement park shimmers out of the dark. Tomás slips through the hole in the fence. She stops, thinking 'I should be afraid, it's dark, I don't know him, who he is, what he wants.' His hand brushes against her thigh, searching for her hand, she bends and he guides her to the other side. At the edge of the beach, her silent partner slips off his sandals. She does the same. The sand is gritty and cool against her soles. She looks up to the moon, thinks she sees rabbit tracks there. A little breeze shimmies down her arm and up her dress as if to say, what are you waiting for?

They walk across the warm sand, out to where the moon meets the water. She dives under the moon. Water cradles her body like a pair of loving hands.

Then Thelma is alone and walking behind Wally and Rosa who are strolling down the malecón, arm in arm. She walks quickly but they are faster, their outlines become smaller, their laughter receding. Shapes appear out of the blackness, men offering cigars, rum, themselves. She ignores them, jogging now after Rosa and Wally, but they keep receding, she speeds up, sprints, and suddenly she's falling down a long, earth tunnel. She lands on damp earth. The air smells like hibiscus. She wanders through the humid darkness. Then a man is beside her. Eugenio, the Palco waiter/bellman. He leads Thelma to a grassy meadow beside a cave. She holds out her arms and the man removes her blouse, unbuttons her skirt so easily it seems he must have watched her put it on.

Then the waiter turns into her high school boyfriend, Ron, and they're running on a grassy bench above the Thompson River under a blue summer sky, falling into grass and burrs and stickweed. He kisses her, hard, grinds his pelvis into hers. She tries to push him off. Crows squawk and wheel above them.

She wakes to the click of the fan, all twisted up in the sheet, pinned to the bed. The only light, the green phosphorescent numbers of the clock: 4:52:10. Thelma flips on the bedside lamp.

Her father wouldn't like this hotel. The too dark wood, the heavy velvet draperies. He would like the marble floors, though, might remind her that marble is crystallized limestone, that there are marble quarries in Cuba. If he was here, he'd want to camp. He'd pitch his tent in a grove of trees off the side of the road. Their grey canvas, mushroom smelling tent.

Every summer when she was a girl, before they went camping, he took the tent out of the basement, set it up in the back yard to air. The mushroom smell faded with the airing but never went away. They'd pack the car with coolers, lawn chairs, the propane stove, sleeping bags, food and set off. They drove north, to Williams Lake, Blue River, Barkerville, Hundred Mile, Smithers. Once all the way up to Prince Rupert. Her dad always picked the quietest, most remote campsite he could find. One year, when she was nine or ten, they pushed wheelbarrows full of food and camping gear through mud to reach that isolated place on the Skeena. It rained and rained. They sat in the malodorous tent playing endless rounds of rummy, crazy eights, king in the corner. They slogged through mud on 'nature walks,' searching for chocolate lilies.

5:05:14.

The first fingers of dawn slide under the curtains.

She never wanted to go on another nature walk in her life after that trip. But she'd go on one every day if her father was still here.

———

ON HER WAY to breakfast, Veronika calls her over to the desk, hands her a sealed white envelope.

"When did this arrive?"

"I don't know, I just arrived. Is it from him?" Veronika asks sotto voce, Thelma's not sure why since every person on staff seems to know about her missing husband.

She rips it open, reads.

> *Thelma*
> *I knocked on what I thought was your room this morning and woke up an amorous Italian and his Cuban girlfriend. The front desk wouldn't give me your room number. I am going to the cannon ceremony tonight. Would you like to come?*
> *Cathy room 352*

"Damn!"

"Bad news?"

"No. Yes. It's not from my husband." Thelma jams the note in her purse. Veronika shakes her head sympathetically. "Hombres!"

Cathy wants to go to the cannon ceremony Gisela told her about. She'll call Cathy, but first she's going to write a note to Wally telling him she's leaving.

———

> *Wally.*
> *What the hell do you think you're doing? I've been waiting for you for four bloody days now. You haven't called. Are you actually with this so-called Professor Sánchez I met a woman, I met someone who is willing to travel with me. I'm not going to let you ruin this vacation for me.*
> *Thelma*

She crumples it. Needs more anger.

> *Wally*
> *You truly are a selfish jerk, you know. How many days do you expect me to sit around the pool waiting for you? Luckily, I have met a handsome Cuban man who has agreed to escort me around this lovely*

*island. I'll see you back in Calgary. Maybe.*
*Thelma*

Not bad. Maybe she should allude to his other shortcomings, too.

*Wallace*
*I'm tired of spending my life waiting for you. To write your novel, to*
*get it published. At least before you cooked good meals. Now you can't*
*even seem to manage cooking – except when Rosa is coming over.*
*TD*

She takes up another sheet of hotel stationary. Perhaps short and simple is best.

*Wally*
*Tired of waiting around.*
*See you back home.*
*T.*

Her fury exhausted, Thelma puts down her pen and lies on the bed. Why has he gone? It makes no sense. Or does it? Were there clues she missed? Hints she overlooked? She can't remember any, but her short term memory is no longer the well-oiled machine it was in her twenties. The recent past: today and yesterday and tomorrow all seem to blend together, though the distant past is as clear as the Havana sky this morning. Her first date with her high school boyfriend, Ron, she can recall in Technicolor: a Bruce Lee double feature at the North Shore drive-in. She wore a striped blue and red halter, light blue cotton sweater and her best cut-offs.

She remembers grey metal speakers attached to their car windows like Martian ears, the purple sky and the row of cypresses lining the fence like sentinels. In the car beside them, a bare foot dangled from an open window. Ron offered her a piece of juicy fruit gum. She remembers being glad to have something to do with her mouth. While Bruce Lee was dispatching horse thieves, he slid across the plastic seat of his mom's Dodge, put her hand on his shoulders and kissed her. His lips were chapped but soft, like toasted marshmallows. They tasted like apricots. Why apricots she's not sure, but that's what they tasted like.

She's experienced hundreds of kisses since then, of course, but the feel of that first kiss, she's never forgotten.

And yet, Wally's first kiss, strangely, she has forgotten. Not the circumstance of the kiss, no, she remembers the night in her dorm room quite clearly. It is the actual taste, the actual feel of it, the smell of it she can't remember. She recalls kissing Wally at other times: the night they arrived in Frejus on the train from Paris. The air was steamy, backpacks clung to their sweating backs, they'd tramped all over town trying to find a hostel or a one star hotel only to discover it was Bastille day and there was not a room to be had. Dejected, they got back on the train (thank god for their Eurail passes), which was full of drunken soldiers who kept bursting into their carriage and song before lunging out and into the next carriage as if they were performers hired for the amusement of the passengers.

The train pulled into a station and they stumbled off and onto a dark, deserted platform. Wally found a flashlight in his pack and they walked silently up the steep road, following the narrow beam of his light. The road intersected a bigger one, on the corner of which was an auberge with a restaurant and a fixed price menu featuring bean soup, ratatouille, lamb stew and lemon tart, which they ordered and devoured, washing it down with red wine followed by glasses of yellow pastis. They laughed at their luck, having stumbled onto this cafe filled with French families and a big orange dog that lay in the middle of the aisle.

Later, in their tiny room above a lavender filled courtyard, she and Wally fell into the sagging single bed and each another.

———

SUN SLANTS IN THROUGH the half open blinds, covering the sky blue bedspread in stripes of light and dark. She doesn't want to move; just wants to savour the taste of the dream-memory of she and Wally in the narrow French bed. They lingered in that Southern French town, whose name she can't remember, for five days; eating baguettes and drinking café au lait for breakfast, hiking in the nearby hills. They took the train to the Picasso museum at Antibes where, holding hands, they sauntered through Grimaldi Castle, lingering over Picasso's flute playing satyrs and dancing goats; his *Death of a Toreador*, the sideways head of the bull, looking, they thought, like a moose with two displaced horns. In Nice, they hiked up a small path from town to the Chagall museum, a building surrounded by trees and full of paintings of the resurrection, angels falling to earth, winged brides and bridegrooms on flying horses.

How old were they? Wally had just finished graduate school, and was being pressured by Dr. Maria Scarletti to do his PhD in English. She said he had a future in academia ahead of him, especially if he continued to specialize in Renaissance literature. There were promises of TA-ships and scholarships. An editing job with the university press was a possibility and U.B.C. was interested in him. All very confusing. So they left their tiny apartment in Calgary and escaped to France to ponder their future.

Thelma drags her body out of the bed and into the bathroom. The woman who stares back has black circles under her eyes, grey hairs sprouting like some invasive species.

———

SITTING ON THE BALCONY, watching the sun sliding down the sky, sipping a mojito that Eugenio, doubling as room service waiter, has brought up, Thelma feels almost content. Sunset is her favourite time at work. When everyone has left and the setting sun fills her office with light. At this time of day, she could work on a project without interruption, without someone knocking on her deliberately closed door to complain that so and so parked in her parking space, or demanding the budget numbers for tomorrow. She could watch a flock of Canada geese flying low, on their way to the river. Or recite the Robert Graves poem her father loved. One that Wally also knew, he put it in her lunch every year on the anniversary of her father's death.

*The untamable, the live, the gentle.*

*Have you not known them? Whom? They carry*

*Time looped so river-wise around their house*

*There's no way in by history's road*

*To name and number them.*

One evening, Gisela slipped through the half-open office door and they watched the light slide from rose to saffron, to indigo.

"Such a beautiful sunfall."

"Yes."

"In La Habana, I used to watch the sun fall over the bahia, the bay. At night, sometimes, when I went to the cañonazo."

"What's that?"

"It is a cannon ceremony, a re-creation of how the English fired the cannon at night to close the city gates and entrada to the harbour."

"The English were in Havana?"

"Yes, in 1762. They ruled for one year, then traded my country for Florida. People call this the 'time of the English,' 'la hora de los mameyes.' The hour of the mamey. You know mamey?"

"No."

"It is a fruit, large and red like the Englishman's uniforms."

"Like a watermelon?"

"A little, but thicker and much, much sweeter. So delicious."

"I'd love to taste one."

"You don't have mamey in Calgary. I have looked everywhere."

What did Thelma know about Cuba then? A few details about a Spanish colonial past, revolutionary battles. Had time looped like a river around Gisela and Rosa's country, Hernando and Isabel's country, leaving oxbows and silting up history's roads?

———

BEFORE HER FATHER died, she spent her summers by a river. Two rivers really, green and brown, the North and South Thompson, two rivers that met and became one, and looped through her town, cleaving it in two. Her father held out his arms: swim to poppa, come on, he'd cry, while her mom lay on a towel, covered in baby oil, her skin reddening under the relentless sun. When they were finished swimming, they'd walk on the banks above the river, searching for arrowheads or remnants of old kekulis, the underground pit houses the Shuswap people used to winter in. She sees her lost father, his back bent, his battered grey field hat at a tilt, digging in the dirt, pulling out an arrowhead, polishing it on his t-shirt and giving it to her. Watches the two of them sitting on the ground pulling cacti and burrs out of their pants. Sees her dad pointing out evening grosbeaks, pine siskins, purple finches, and red-winged blackbirds that flit by this river of memory. His mouth is open and he is speaking, but she can't hear the words or the sound of his voice.

———

CATHY'S KNOCKING could wake the dead. By the time Thelma gets up from the balcony, she's opened the door, which Thelma has apparently not locked, and is in the room.

"Ready?" Cathy asks. She's wearing an off-the-shoulder white peasant blouse and a flouncy cowgirl skirt embroidered with flowers.

"Yeah. Just let me just grab my purse."

"I've been so looking forward to this," Cathy enthuses as they board the Vaiven tourist bus to town. The vehicle lurches down Quinta Avenida, passing a double-humped bus pulled by a transport truck with the people inside packed tight as matchsticks. A little buck-toothed boy smiles at her. Sweet little guy. She waves and he waves back.

"We should try the camellos," Cathy proposes.

"Camellos?"

"Camels. That's what they call those buses like the one that just passed us. 'Cause they look like camels."

Thelma wrinkles her nose. "Look how crowded they are!"

"But it would be fun, don't you think? To travel the way the people do. Sara would love it."

"I suppose she would." Thelma pictures the little green-eyed girl, wide eyed, watching everything.

They plunge into darkness as the bus enters the tunnel under the Almendares River. On the other side, the ocean and the malecón are to their left, to their right the pastel blues, pinks and yellows of crumbling multi-storied houses. Pretty, until you notice the peeling paint, the missing plaster. She remembers a story Gisela told her about her friend's car. How it was parked in the street and a balcony from one of these houses fell on top of it and crushed it.

Cathy is reading her guidebook. Thelma notes the unrestrained use of pink highlighter.

"What shall we do first?" Cathy asks.

"What do you suggest?"

"Why don't we start with the Castillo de Los Tres Reyes del Morro. It means castle of the three kings of, well—according to my Spanish-English dictionary, morro means nose or snout, but I can't imagine it is called Castle of the Three Kings of the Snout. Anyway why don't we start with the Morro Castle, then we can have dinner at one of the restaurants at the Castillo de San Carlos de la Cabaña, then wander in the museums there until the cannon firing at nine."

"Sure. How old are those castles?"

Cathy begins enthusiastically flipping pink pages.

"Let's see, construction at the Morro Castle began in 1589, it was built by slaves and took forty years to complete. It kept lots of pirates out until the British landed outside Havana in 1762. They held Cuba for a year until trading it for Florida. La Cabaña, next door, was built from 1764–1774 following the English invasion and..."

"Thanks," says Thelma, making a mental note to keep historical questions to a minimum. "I get the idea."

———

"THE MUSEO DE FORTIFICACIONES y Armas is supposed to have a wonderful collection of armour."

"Indeed," says Thelma. She peers at the model of La Cabaña.

"Look over here," Cathy exclaims. "It's the execution wall where Spanish sympathizers were shot during the 19th century wars of independence. It was a military prison under Machado and Batista, and then a prison for counter-revolutionaries after the revolution. And, oh look, here's the curtain wall where...."

"Great, listen, I think I'll just wander around on my own now." Having Cathy explain every single thing here will drive her crazy.

"Oh. Are you sure?" Cathy's face falls. "I mean, I have the guidebook and, and everything."

"Why don't we meet for dinner in, say, an hour. Where would you recommend?"

Cathy rallies. "There are the Bodegón de los Vinos and La Divina Pastora, well that one's a little farther away."

"Why don't we meet at the Bodegón one"?

"Do you want my map?"

"No thanks. I'll find it. I'll see you there at 7:30."

Thelma leaves Cathy and walks down the long cobbled path, stopping to listen to the drums and chanting of two men dressed in white, surrounded by tourists. Santeria devotees. Elegguá, the men sing to the God of Destiny, Elegguá. One side of the cobbled street is in light, the other is in shadow. Children in school uniforms run past her. Thelma follows them onto the shadowy side of the street. They enter the Che Guevara museum. She keeps walking, toward a chapel with blood-red walls. The door to the chapel is slightly ajar. Thelma pulls open the heavy door and sits in a back pew.

In the semi-dark she can just make out the swirl of baroque carvings in the ceiling above. A man kneels at the altar of Santa Barbara/Changó, the God of War. The back of the man's head, the close-cropped hair, the wide, straight back, look so familiar. Behind her, the door opens then closes completely. She sits in the dark, the smell of dust and candle wax held in the warm air.

Then the door squeaks open again, flooding the church with light. The man is gone.

At the Bodegón, Thelma sips her wine, letting Cathy chatter about her plans to visit Hemingway's finca or farm the next day. Cathy seems to have done very well post-divorce, with all her plans. Maybe that's where she and Wally were heading. A divorce. She could go back to school, finish her archeology degree. Take early retirement. Travel. She's doing fine here on her own without him.

After dinner, they climb a staircase to the curtain wall and find a place to sit among the crowd. She watches a man in a kilt walking on the parapet beneath them.

Sees her dad in his red tartan sweater kneeling before their fireplace, carefully arranging twists of newspaper and kindling. This is how you build a fire, he says. Newspaper first, then kindling, then when it's going, a couple of small pieces of wood. Leave spaces for the air so the fire can breathe. Can I light the match, dad, she asks, and he hands her the long box. She scrapes the match down its side, once, twice. There's a smell of sulphur, then a blue-orange flame appears. She guides the match to paper, the ends darkening, the fire licking in front. She moves toward the flames...

"Thelma! It's starting."

Men in scarlet uniforms appear, led by a drummer and a fife-playing man.

"Soldier, soldier will you marry me, with your musket, fife and drum. Oh how can I marry such a pretty girl as thee, if I've got no shoes to put on."

"That's a nice song."

"One of my dad's favourites."

A trio of men carrying torches march toward the cannon. Thelma leans over, looks down. On a ledge below is a wide-shouldered man, his arm around a little girl. A torch bearing soldier approaches a cannon, the fire disappears inside.

The little girl buries her face in her daddy's shoulder as the explosion echoes across the courtyard.

# CHAPTER 18

*Cuba*

THELMA OPENS THE closet. Inside she's hung her two new dresses, and the pashmina wrap she brought for evening. She hauls out her suitcase, removing her new sexy camisole and panties set, two pairs of shorts, three skirts, five blouses, eight pairs of underwear. Her evening shoes are wrapped in plastic bags in the corners. As she takes them out, she feels something square in the top zipper compartment. What did she put there? An extra book for beach reading? She unzips the compartment, pulls out a red leather-covered notebook. Not hers. Wally's. How the hell did it get in here?

They did argue about the suitcases. Wally wanted this, their biggest one, said he needed space for papers and books. She convinced him to swap for two smaller suitcases, one for his clothes, one for his books and papers. She needed the big one for her shoes. How many pairs of shoes do you need? Wally asked. Thelma told him. She needed sandals for the beach, walking shoes for, obviously, walking, two pair of dress shoes (open and closed toe, the latter in case it rained), hiking boots for, yes, hiking, and running shoes.

She runs her fingers over the book's soft leather. Expensive. Wally didn't usually buy such pricy diaries. She slowly opens then closes it. None of her business. No. It is her business. He left it in her suitcase. He's bloody well missing! It could contain some kind of clue to his disappearance.

*October 12*

*The bike path in October is a singularly un-crowded place. The odd woman pushing a baby jogger, old men walking small dogs. I ride toward the city, past the lopped off poplar trees, haul the bike up the stairs and ride across the bridge over Memorial to the curling club hill. I stop half way up the hill to get my breath. A guy on a racing bike shoots by on my right, another on my left. At the top of the hill, on Crescent Road, I look at the city spread out below me: the silver towers of Bankers Hall shimmering; the Petrocan buildings like Lego in the sky; high rise behind high-rise, a pop-up book of buildings. I turn onto Twelfth and wind around Crescent Heights past porched bungalows with weeping willows sweeping the ground like golden brooms; stately mountain ash trees, their bright orange berries and olive-gold leaves waving in the wind; a Siamese cat in a tree. The sun warms my back. My new getting-in-shape regime won't be so bad if I can cycle on days like this. I cross Edmonton Trail, pedal down 8th, swoop down the hill into Bridgeland, then speed along Centre Avenue, past the old General Hospital site, now an empty expanse of pavement, turn left on to Edmonton Trail and cross Memorial where I meet the bike path again. I cycle past amputated trees, mirroring the fate of some of the WW1 soldiers they were planted for. Why were they pruned?*

*Were they diseased? Or did their roots push through the tarmac, were they taking up too much space? I'm wondering this when a guy comes speeding toward me on a fancy racing bike.*

*"Get on your own side, asshole!" he yells.*

*"What did you call me?" I scream at his disappearing back.*

*I stop, get off my bike and throw it into the grass at the side of the path, inhale huge gasps of air. My hands shake as I lift the water bottle, cold water dribbles down my chin and onto my jacket.*

*I imagine myself riding up behind him, pushing him off his bike then jumping off mine and hitting him. Over and over. My fist in his gut.*

She didn't know he had a getting-in-shape regime. And he didn't tell her about that incident.

Poor guy.

———

COMPROMISE CAN BE a slippery slope. You start gradually, giving in to, say, your partner's need for tidiness. She nags you to put your shoes in the shoe cupboard so, after a while, that's the first thing you think about when you come into the house. Before you take off your jacket or fold your umbrella, or remove your hat. Or say, with cooking. You use different bowls for grating the cheese, mixing the salad dressing, for putting the cut vegetables in while you brown the meat. But, as your partner points out, she's had a tough day at work and it's she who has to wash all those things you dirtied. So you learn to use just one, small bowl.

She does not make him use just one small bowl. He's being unfair. She'll tell him, if and when she sees him: I don't care if you don't put your shoes away immediately but when the front entrance is so crowded I can't even push open the door, what am I supposed to do? And you do use an inordinate number of bowls.

No, of course, she won't tell him. Then he'd know she'd read his diary.

Maybe Wally was having a bad day when he wrote it. Maybe it was a melancholy, grey November afternoon, a dreary Sunday and they'd just had a fight about the dishes. Maybe the sky was low and he looked out a dirty window at the bare poplars lining their street and felt full of despair.

The next page is blank.

On the following page this:

> ...the waiting room of evening and evenings became as short as
> appointments and the years turned into a thin picture spread...
> Guillermo Cabrera Infante, I Heard Her Sing

The quote from her lunch bag!

*Rosa lent me the novella. It is exquisitely written, about a lost photographer, a big jazz singer, La Estrella, musicians, women, and Havana night life. An elegiac piece, full of long, beautiful sentences that wind back on themselves, like the streets of Vedado our protagonist wanders in the early morning hours: the madrugada. It is about the end of an era, and the beginning of another, where it is raining: "the rain erases the city but it cannot erase memory." Cabrera's parents were Communists, and so was he. Until he lost his job for criticizing the revolution, and left the country.*

The end of an era and the beginning of another. Does he mean them?

———

*IN THE ALEXANDER ROMANCE, Alexander the Great and his servant, Al-Khidr, were lost in the Land of Darkness, the Forest of Abkhazia, where the descendants of a Persian emperor were trapped because they'd persecuted Christians. Alexander was searching for the water of life, the spring that restores youth. He found it. His servant drank the waters and became immortal.*

*This myth, known to the Spanish Conquistadors, was reinforced by Arawak tales of the land of "Bimini," a land north of Cuba, an earthly paradise where a magic fountain restored men's youth and virility. It spawned the legend that Ponce de Léon, and De Soto after him, heard. They went to Florida, the story goes, to search for the Fountain of Youth.*

*What happened to poor Alexander in the Land of Darkness?*

*Did he wander there for years, aging as his servant got younger? Lost, with no bread crumbs to show him the way home?*

———

HOW TO MAKE YOU *behave? I've got you, Isabel, right where I want you, on a widow's walk at the top of the castle, the moment a sail appears on the horizon. Maldonado's ship. Maldonado who will inform you Hernando is dead. Dead of fever and lying at the bottom of the Mississippi river. And you desert me and the widow's walk, return to your room where a totally minor character, Juan the man-servant, is waiting. For naught, all that research, hours in the university library (where I really got to see the sorry state of page ripping and article defacing).*

*Useless all those index cards mapping out scenes. "Who's controlling who, er, whom?" I yell at you.*

*I knock and you come to the bedchamber door, wrapped in a gown of blue silk, stomp your feet at me in a most un-governor like way, order me out and return to the smooth talking Juan. Ignoring your administrative responsibilities even though they say you were an exceptional governor, Isabel, practical, pragmatic and detail-oriented, better, in fact, than the impetuous, romantic Hernando ("you want to look for the fountain of youth, oh please, husband, hadn't we better solve the corsair problem first?").*

*No, Isabel, you will stay exactly where I've placed you, on a grey, rain-soaked Sunday afternoon, looking out to sea. The wind whips your black cloak and heavy gold cross; rain slaps your face and pulls your sodden hem to the ground. Behind the heavy wooden door, maids fuss, the minor character makes occasional sallies to beg you to come inside, says: "you will catch your death. Nothing good can come of all this watching and waiting." And me your creator, well, revisioner, wants you to be so in love with your husband that you can't do anything but stand at the edge of your roof-top walk, above the stench of the town, the mud, mosquitoes and pestilence, staring out to sea like the brave, worried woman you are (and, incidentally, looking a bit like Meryl Streep as Sarah in "The French Lieutenant's Woman").*

*Though perhaps, as the esteemed Mr. John Gardner says, I must be the story's servant. Alright, Milady, I will be the servant. Your servant. I will serve you on bended knee, offer you bits of wild goat cheese with fennel, red Malaga grapes, an herbed biscuit or two. I will bring you to my table, proffer cucumber soup, rack of lamb with mint and yam fritters, kirsch soaked strawberries dipped in chocolate. Or maybe you'd prefer a juicy mutton leg or a roast pig haunch instead? I do not expect any thanks. My pleasure at serving you will be enough.*

*You reject my offerings?*

*Alright, Isabel, you headstrong lass. Go ahead and do what you want. Run off with your manservant. Why did I give you a manservant anyway? According to history, you should have a lady servant, a white slave also named Isabel, a converted Moor.*

*Shouldn't, in fact, the manservant be with Hernando?*

*Ah my Isabel, you plot spoiling darling.*

He had shown her that scene from his novel. They even had a conversation about it.

"What do you think, Thelm?"

"It's kind of cute."

"Cute?"

"OK not cute. Funny."

"And?"

"Is revisioner a word?"

"Just give me your general impressions," he said testily.

"I like that you, the author, the narrator, the 'I' is serving her, Isabel."

"Thanks."

"But is the 'I' supposed to be chauvinistic?"

"What do you mean?"

"Well, why can't she take a lover, run off with the manservant if she wants? Her husband abandoned her, after all, to the mosquitoes, pirates, mud and pestilence."

"He had his reasons."

"Which are?"

"He was an adventurer, an explorer, a discoverer…"

"…a gold plunderer, an opportunist…"

"…had been since he was 14 years old, Thelm. Hernando would have been bored to death being governor. Cuba was nothing but a way station for ships on their way from Mexico and the new world to Spain. There was little silver and gold there. De Soto was like Che Guevara after the Cuban revolution. Che couldn't sit still, didn't want to just be a minister in the government. That's why he went to the Congo and Bolivia to start revolutions."

"But Che was trying to help the poor; De Soto was just trying to get rich."

"Let's just stick to the writing."

"Well, I like the lover. And I don't think she should behave. I think she and the manservant should have mad, passionate sex on the bedchamber floor."

"I am not writing a bodice ripper, Thelma."

She didn't feel bad at the time. But maybe she was too tough on him. He was always so sensitive about his writing.

———

*LAST NIGHT ROSA read us a poem from her "Imagines de Havana" series. About a boy, Jaime. His father, Basilio, left for Miami in the Mariel boatlift. Lydia, his mother, couldn't bear to leave her family so she and Jaime stayed behind. There's a lovely line about Jaime in Havana bay on his big inner tube, fishing, wondering if he can catch a marlin, like Hemingway's Old Man did, a marlin that will pull him all the way to Florida. To a paradise where the oranges don't rot on the trees for want of pickers and people eat meat every day. Rosa conveys, in a few, well-chosen phrases, the isolation, the homesickness he will face if he ever gets to "paradise."*

*We all agreed it was a breakthrough poem for her. She's going to enter it in a poetry competition. We're keeping our fingers crossed.*

*Thelma is mad at me again. Something to do with Rosa, I know, though she said it was the noise we were making atwriting group meeting last night.*

*With Gary taking a break from the group (I suspect he's packed in the novel) and Charlene moving to Ottawa, it was getting dull with just Alvin and Tim and I. I'll admit it's nice to have a woman in the group. To be told one is "intelligente" and "gentil." But Rosa's like that with everyone. Thelma might say she's using her feminine wiles, but I think this is how she is. She still loves her country passionately. And she's so animated. When Rosa gets excited about something like she did last week about Ondaatje's writing in Anil's Ghost—her brown eyes fill with fire and she slips into Spanglish, losing her word endings and s's and speaking so quickly that all we can do is sit and marvel at all that passion.*

*Could such a creature possibly be interested in joining a trio of balding men, with expanding stomachs and contracting possibilities?*

Thelma slams the diary shut. He is obsessed with Rosa! So—she knew that. Rosa's beautiful; she likes him. Rosa wouldn't tell him to put his shoes in the shoe cupboard, and would likely be non-judgmental about bowl use. She'd take him to experience the Havana night life Cabrera described. But would he run off with her? And would she want him? Wouldn't there have been some signs? What would they do together? Wally, in a threadbare old t-shirt and faded bathing trunks with Rosa, turning heads in a tiny bikini. What would they talk about besides poetry? How much poetry is there to talk about?

The phone.

"Wally!"

"Thelma?" Shit. It's a woman. Rosa?

"Yes. Who is this?"

"It's Cathy, silly. I was wondering if you'd like to have dinner with me tonight. There's a great little place not far from here just off Quinta Avenida."

"I can't."

"Oh. Maybe tomorrow? That is, if your husband doesn't..."

"Maybe," Thelma says quickly. "I'm sorry; I'm in the middle of something. I'll talk to you later."

She re-opens the diary, turns to the next page. But it's blank. There's nothing else. Just those six entries. Six entries she was not meant to read. Or maybe she was. Is her errant husband sending her on some sort of a quest? What exactly is she meant to be searching for?

———

"THELMA, MY GOD, its four AM, what's the matter?"

"Wally's gone, Cathy. He not coming back, I just know it."

"Hold on, Thelma. Come in, sit down and start at the beginning. I thought he was in Cienfuegos."

She lets Cathy lead her into the room and sit her on the bed. Blows her nose into the tissue Cathy hands her.

"He could be, I don't know. He's disappeared. He was supposed to be back from Cienfuegos already. I found his diary, I, he, he might, he almost beat up a guy on the bike, maybe he's depressed. Oh God, I think. I think maybe he's with, with..."

"With who?"

"With...." If she doesn't say it out loud, it might not be true.

"Oh, I don't know," Thelma says finally, sniffing and wiping her eyes.

Cathy puts an arm around her shoulder. "Don't worry, Thelma, I'm sure there's a reasonable explanation. Listen, why don't we go and try to find him."

"What if he comes back and I miss him?"

"We'll leave a note. We'll leave lots of notes so he can't miss them. We'll pin them up behind the front desk, in the restaurant, at the bars."

"On trees.

De Soto's searchers nailed notes to trees. The searchers who Isabel sent to Florida to look for her husband. Did she send them back year after year, unwilling to give up hope that he might still be alive, that he might come back to her?

Cathy laughs. "Sure, on trees, too, wherever you like."

Thelma blows her nose. "I do know a couple of taxi drivers we could hire."

"Great. Listen, it will be OK. We'll call the taxi drivers first thing in the morning." Thelma manages a small smile. "Yeah, alright."

"Now go back to your room and try to get some sleep."

"I know I can be sharp with him sometimes, I forgot how sensitive he is, he's like a little child, I..."

Cathy puts her hand on Thelma's. "We'll find him. Don't worry. He's got to be here somewhere. It's a small island. He can't have completely disappeared."

"Hernando De Soto disappeared."

"Well, he's not Hernando."

"Maybe he thinks he is."

# CHAPTER 19

*Cuba*

SHE WAS TWELVE when her papa first returned. The first time she was scared, thought he was an intruder, called out for her mom. Sometimes she thought she could see him, a faint outline in the dark. After that, whenever he appeared, she felt happy and full of peace.

Sometimes she woke to a draft, as if her window was open, though she knew she'd closed it. Sometimes there was the smell of White Owl cigars.

She started rituals to summon him: wearing the same blue flannel pajamas as the last time he visited, even in the summer when they were too hot; making sure the glass of water on her bedside table was in the same place; that her sheets were the same ones. She wouldn't let her mom put different ones on, insisting the flowers on them helped her get to sleep.

At first Thelma didn't say anything when he appeared, was quiet like when they read their books after dinner, sitting together but spaced apart on the living room couch. Then she began talking to him in her head. She told him that the girls in her science class were cliquey and the student teacher for Social Studies was cute but strict and she didn't know what options to take next year. He didn't answer in words, but after he visited, she knew just what to do.

But her poor mother didn't.

"How come you never make a fire?" Thelma would grill her.

"Thelma, for goodness sakes, when do I have time to make a fire? With work, I barely have time to buy groceries and cook, let alone run all over town looking for wood to make a fire."

"I'm just asking. You probably don't remember how to make one, anyway."

"You're right."

"You forgot what dad taught us on our camping trips."

"I guess I did."

"How can you have forgotten already?"

"I honestly don't think your father taught me how to build a fire."

"Well he did. I was there. I bet you don't remember his favourite movie."

"*The African Queen.*"

"Wrong. It was *The Rainmaker.*"

"No, Thelma, I'm sure it was *The Af...*"

"Favorite food?"

"Chicken cacciatore."

"Right. Favorite..."

"I'm not playing this game, Thelma Marie."

"Favorite legend?"

"I'm not playing."

"Favorite legend: the rabbit in the moon. Favorite gemstone: ruby, favorite cigar, White Owls, favourite..."

Her mom started crying then, tears flooding her eyes, streaming down her cheeks. But Thelma was full of meanness and she couldn't stop.

———

THELMA CAN'T REMEMBER exactly when she started seeing Doc K. It was her mom's idea. Because Thelma was in denial. Because Thelma wasn't grieving properly. She had to go to the health unit once a week, wait in a lobby with orange plastic chairs with big cold, silver screws in the seats that shivered her bum, and a play centre for little kids. She hoped no one she knew would see her there. Decided, if she saw anyone, she'd say she missed getting her shots at school.

To make her mom think Thelma was making progress, she let her take the boxes of her dad's clothes from Thelma's closet and give them to the Sally Ann. All except for the scratchy Cowichan sweater with the broken zipper, the red plaid fishing jacket and the lumberjack shirt, which Thelma hid in her bottom drawer in a black garbage bag under her old Brownie uniform. For herself, she kept the rock collection with the arrowheads they found together up at Paul Lake and the dinosaur toe he discovered in Horse Thief Canyon in Drumheller. She kept his rock hammer, which she wrapped in an old t-shirt and put in the back of her closet where her mother never went.

He showed up less often as she got older. At fifteen, her dad only visited when she was extremely upset, like after she and her mom had a fight about the white halter dress she wanted to wear to the end of the year dance, and her mom threatened to ground her, which was laughable because Thelma could lock her door from the inside and sneak out the bedroom window, and her mom wouldn't even know.

On the sixth anniversary of his death, she woke up at 4 AM and couldn't get back to sleep, kept thinking about the time they went canoeing on Shuswap Lake, how he taught her to steer the canoe, her proud ten-year-old self J stroking it across the lake to Copper Island.

By the time she was eighteen, he only appeared a couple of times a year: on her birthday, on his death day. She'd wake in the dark to a warm presence at the end of the bed, a cool breeze from an open window, his voice in her head.

Then she went to university. She met Wally. Since then, he's only emerged in her dreams.

# CHAPTER 20

*Calgary*

"THELMA, CAN YOU hold the puffs while I fill them."

"I'm tired, Wall."

"I thought you just had a retreat today."

"Just? We spent three hours wordsmithing the mission statement, followed by two hours visioning the entire Parks and Rec organizational structure, followed by a 'frank discussion' about the crisis in arenas."

"What crisis?"

"Too many teams wanting ice time, not enough ice, no money to build more arenas."

"Please Thelm, the group will be here in half an hour."

Serve the group store bought cookies or defrost one of the cranberry-orange loaves in the freezer, why don't you, she thinks.

"I just need you for a sec."

She pulls herself up from the couch. Cream puff shells line the green granite countertop like soldiers. Frothy cream filling sits in a glass bowl by the fridge. She dips a finger into the bowl.

"Hey!"

"Sorry."

"I had to throw away the first batch of pastry. Damn things didn't puff at all. OK, I'm ready."

She steadies each fragile half-shell while he fills it from the pastry bag. "How long did they take you to make these – two or three hours?"

"About that. Why?"

"Guess you didn't get much writing done today."

"I find participating in the writing group as valuable as writing."

"OK, OK."

He was making cream puffs for his writing group while she sat in a meeting, exhausting as only a six-hour meeting with twenty people who love the sound of their own voices can be.

He puts the pastry bag down. "You're upset because I made cream puffs?"

"I'm not upset. It just seems like a waste of time."

"Was the hand rolled spinach ravioli I made for dinner last night a waste of time?"

"No. OK, forget I said that."

She picks up the *Joy of Cooking*, which Wally has covered with plastic wrap, reads: 'for a marvelous tea-teaser, put in the base of a puff shell a layer of: whipped cream. Lightly insert with the pointed end up: a flawless ripe strawberry.'

"Are you adding the strawberries now?"

"No. I don't want to stain the cream."

"Strawberries cost the earth this time of year."

———

FROM HER BASEMENT EXILE, Thelma can hear the writing group carrying on upstairs in the living room. Even with the T.V. on and the gas fireplace humming. She thought writers were supposed to be quiet types but the four of them, Alvin, Rosa, Tim and Wally, are as noisy as teenagers on New Year's Eve. Picking up the remote, Thelma starts flicking, through hockey, curling, Friends, nothing she wants to watch, then turns off the TV. Wally has left *The Collected Works of José Martí*, bilingual edition, beside the fireplace. Martí. The guy who wrote *Guantanamera*. Her mom and Peter have the song on an old Pete Seeger album.

She skims the introduction. Martí is Cuba's national hero and poet. He was born in Havana to poor parents in 1853. Arrested at sixteen for criticizing the Spanish, sentenced to hard labour in a quarry then deported to Spain. He lived, taught and wrote in Mexico, Guatemala, and New York City, where he organized the second Cuban war of independence. He returned to Cuba in 1895 to fight and died on the battlefield.

She flips through the poems. Reads one called I Dream Awake.

> *Day and night*
> *I always dream with open eyes*
> *And on top of the foaming waves*

*Of the wide, turbulent sea*
*And in the rolling*
*Desert sands,*
*And merrily riding on the gentle neck*
*Of a mighty lion,*
*Monarch of my heart,*
*I always see a floating child*
*Who is calling me.*

Lovely, she thinks, reading on to find out it was written for his son, José Francisco. Is this boy the floating child Martí sees? Is it his son who calls to him? This child who was once curled up in his mother's womb, thumb in mouth, sleeping in her briny waters.

There's a burst of laughter from upstairs. Thelma picks up the remote again, turns up the volume. But even the cries of 'hurry hard' on the Tournament of Hearts can't drown out the laughter. Surely discussing writing should involve a lot less noise. She's going up there to get a drink.

They're lounging on the floor around the glass coffee table which is strewn with sheets of paper. Rosa close, too close, to Wally.

"Hi Thelma," says Rosa, not moving away from her husband.

"Hello."

"How are you doing, Thelma?"

"Fine, Tim, you? How are Gina and that sweet little Esme?"

"Great."

"You have to read Alvin's new story." Wally tells her. "It's hilarious."

"He had us in stitches. Stitches, is that correct?"

"Si, es correcto," says Alvin.

"You are doing exceptionally well with your idioms, Rosa," Wally adds.

"Well the hilarity explains the floor pounding," Thelma notes drily.

"Sorry about that. In the story, this farmer from Watrous Saskatchewan starts to find messages from Wallace Stegner written on his barn walls," Wally says, before collapsing in a fit of giggles.

"Sounds like a real barn burner. Don't let me interrupt. I'll just get myself a drink and head back to the dungeon."

Rosa smiles. "You are not interrupting. It is your house."

"Yes it is. I pay the damn mortgage."

Downstairs, the Tournament of Hearts is heating. The score is 4/4. The skip is yelling hurry hard. Rocks smash. The crowd roars.

# 2

# CHAPTER 21

*Cuba*

THE HOLE IN THE fence where she and Cathy are supposed to meet the taxi was not hard to find. Pulling their suitcases behind them, they trudged down the hotel driveway, turned left at the main road, and again onto a cul-de-sac, its grey concrete looking like a pile driver broke it up and forgot to take the pieces away.

"Can't you meet us on the road outside the hotel?" Thelma had asked when she finally got through to Tomás on his aunt's phone, and explained the need to go to Cienfuegos to find Wally and Professor Sánchez.

"It is the daytime," he said, by way of explanation. Meaning, she thinks, he is afraid someone from the hotel will see him. "Don't worry. The hole in the fence leads to ISA, the art institute. It is easy to find and close to the hotel. Just follow the students."

It was easy to find. The taxi, however, is not.

Cathy is guarding the suitcases beside the hole in the fence and showing photos of her daughter to a couple of teenagers. Thelma stands at the corner. She has already waved down two Ladas, neither of which contained Tomás and Jorge, though one was driven by a man who was willing to chauffeur them to Cienfuegos for free, in return for guaranteed immigration to Canada.

It's 10:00. Tomás should have been here an hour ago. The sun is burning the top of her head. The smell of rotten meat and composting vegetables rises from the pile of garbage at the edge of the road. Sour and oniony. She wishes she had a hat and some water.

She could be back at the hotel, eating a leisurely breakfast by the pool, or sipping her second cup of café con leche in air-conditioned comfort. Where the hell is Tomás? Is he coming? She should have hired a woman taxista—at least a woman would be reliable.

"Thelma," Cathy calls from her perch on the suitcase. "Do you have any pictures of Canada I can show these kids?"

Thelma shakes her head.

A taxi drives by. A proper taxi, a shiny red Nissan. Thelma waves, the driver stops, rolls down his window. She feels a whoosh of cold air, notices the comfortable looking leather seats.

"Cuánto cuesto para ir a Cienfuegos?"

"Dos cientos dólares," he says. Two hundred dollars is too much. Thelma waves him on. At least Tomás is cheap.

Her feet hurt, she wants to sit down but there is no place to sit, except the ground or her suitcase.

A car turns off Quinta Avenida, a boxy car, it could be a Lada, yes, it is Tomás' orange Lada belching black smoke, its engine chugging ominously. It pulls into the cul-de-sac and stops beside her.

She turns toward Cathy, who is now distributing Canada pins to her new-found friends.

"They're here!"

Tomás leans out the window. His hair has recently been cut. He smells lemony, like the aftershave she gave Wally for Christmas last year.

"Hello Thelma," says Tomás.

"Hello, Thelma," echoes Jorge from the back seat. "We are late. Sorry. There was a problem, but don't worry, everything is resolved."

"What kind of problem?" She doesn't like the look of the black smoke and the way the Lada's engine is misfiring. There wasn't any black smoke at the airport. Or maybe there was. It was dark, after all.

"Small problem with the car, don't worry. All is OK now. How are you?"

"I'm hot, dehydrated, I have a headache, my husband is missing. Other than that, I'm great, Jorge."

Tomás says something to Jorge in Spanish, too fast for Thelma to understand.

"Yes," Jorge says finally. "We are very, very sorry. About the lateness. About your husband."

Cathy appears, having left the suitcases she is supposed to be guarding.

"Hola, Buenos Dias, I'm a friend of Thelma's, well not a friend, more of an acquaintance, but I'm sure we will be friends soon, anyway I'm Cathy." She offers her hand through the open window. "I'm coming to help find Wally."

"Tomás," says Tomás.

"Jorge," says Jorge.

"Suitcases," says Thelma.

"Tomás, can you get the ladies' luggage?"

Tomás gets out of the car, saunters over to the suitcases and carries them back. He unties the rope that is keeping the trunk closed, and heaves them aboard.

———

TOMÁS INSISTS THELMA take the front seat because of her headache. Cathy and Jorge are squeezed together in the back, Jorge behind the driver's seat. Thelma yanks the passenger door open, showering her shoes with filigrees of rust. Nice. And here's the cracked black vinyl seat with the jutting spring. She sits to the left of it, jamming her knees into the gearbox.

"I thought we could stay at the Rancho Luna hotel in Cienfuegos, Thelma," Cathy suggests.

"Great."

"It is supposed to have a fantastic folkloric group that performs traditional Cuban dances every evening at 7 and 9. Also, we can visit the Castillo de Jagua, a seventeenth century Spanish fort that is supposed to be haunted by the wife of the governor."

If only she could haunt Wally.

"Remember, Cathy, we are looking for Thelma's husband," Jorge reminds her.

"Errant husband," adds Thelma.

"What is errant, Thelma?" Jorge asks.

"Not doing what he's supposed to be doing. Screwing off."

"I thought it had something to do with knights off looking for adventure," Cathy says.

"That, too."

"I can't wait to get to Cienfuegos!" Cathy says.

"Today would be good," Thelma mutters under her breath.

Tomás finishes smoking his cigarette, throws it out the window. He turns the key. The engine gives little whir-like moans but doesn't catch.

"Oh-oh," says Cathy.

"Not to worry. Like a woman, she needs a little time to warm up," Tomás pronounces.

"Charming analogy, Tomás," Thelma remarks. Now he's flooded it.

Cathy giggles. "She's not warming, Tomás."

"Not to worry. In Cuba we can solve any problem."

"I hope so. Because I don't know the first thing about cars, boys."

"Try adjusting the choke."

Both men look at Thelma.

"Yes, I know about cars."

"Did you take a course in Calgary? One of those car mechanics for women courses? I've heard they're great!"

"My dad taught me."

———

THE GARAGE SMELLED of oil, dust, and mold. Piles of magazines: her dad's *National Geographics*, her mom's *Nursing in Canadas* loomed from dark corners. But I don't want to, dad, she whined when he called her to help him change the oil or replace the spark plugs. You need to learn about cars, most mechanics see dollar signs when a lady walks in. I'm not a lady. OK, when a little girl walks in. I ain't little.

Oil changing was his specialty. He was the surgeon and she was his capable assistant, like Dr. Rex Morgan MD's nurse, except she passed him tools instead of scalpels. Her dad's legs stuck out from the car, black sweat pants and red runners with holes in the toes.

Screwdriver, he'd call. Wrench. Hammer. Pliers. She'd search the green toolbox for the right tool, say got it, and he'd slide part way out on his little wheeled pallet, extend a tool, and she'd take it and press the new one into his disembodied hand.

"Maybe you should try the choke, buddy," Jorge says in Spanish. Tomás tries it. The engine turns over.

———

THELMA THOUGHT THERE would be more hills in Cuba, more mountains like the Sierra Maestras in the east. But the Autopista Nacional, the main highway, is mostly flat. When he wants to pass another car, Tomás leans on the horn then veers into the middle of the road, where they chug past other, even more ancient and decrepit cars, people on bicycles, horse-drawn carts.

In the distance, a group of people mill at the side of the road.

"What are they doing in the middle of nowhere?" Cathy asks.

Jorge laughs. "There's no middle of nowhere in Cuba."

"They're waiting for a ride," adds Tomás.

"We have room," Cathy ventures.

"I don't think so," says Thelma.

"Maybe they think we're one of those—what are they called—collective taxis."

"Boteros," Jorge offers.

"But we're not," says Thelma.

"The people wait for hours for a ride. Sometimes they wait all day."

"That's terrible, Jorge. Thelma, I think someone could sit back here with us. A smallish person."

"You and Jorge barely fit."

"So we are not stopping?"

"No, Cathy. We're on a mission, remember. My errant husband."

Sweat pools at the back of Thelma's neck. The spring pokes the side of her bum. She shifts to the left. She'll have to lift her knees when Tomás wants to change gears, but at least the spring is not gouging her. The acrid smell of smoke and exhaust fill the car, despite the open windows. Or maybe because of them.

An American car from the fifties, all fins and low-slung grace, passes them.

"Look at that," enthuses Cathy, snapping a photo.

"A conquistador," says Tomás, taking his hands completely off the wheel to light a cigarette.

"Yes, a De Soto," says Thelma.

"What was De Soto doing in Cuba anyway, Thelm?"

"He was a governor. Well, mostly his wife, Isabel de Bobadilla was. After he took off to Florida."

"That must have been a first. For a woman to be governor."

"It was."

"You are very knowledgeable, Thelma. Have you studied our history?" Tomás asks.

"A little. My husband has. For the book he's researching here."

Supposed to be researching. If he is actually with Professor Sánchez and not with Rosa.

Tomás blows a thin stream of smoke. "Many tourists come to study us: the Germans, they study our beaches and rum. The Italians, they study our beautiful women. The Americans study our cars. What do Canadians come to study?"

"Your joie de vivre," offers Cathy brightly.

"Ah, yes, our famous joie de vivre."

"Well, you seem to have it," she adds, uncertainly.

"We are merely clowns, Cathy, smiling on the outside, crying on the inside."

"Why is that?"

"Life is hard here since the Russians left. There is no electricity, sometimes, no water. Meat once a month, if we're lucky. People used to raise meat rabbits, but then they started getting hemorrhagic fever and dying."

"I can see it must be hard to live without electricity. Why, my washing machine goes on the blink for a day and I almost can't function."

"No transportation..."

Jorge clears his throat. "My friend Tomás is in a dark mood today, Cathy. Many Canadians come to escape the cold, I believe."

"Yes. You have a song. *Mon pays ce n'est pas un pay, c'est l'hiver,*" says Tomás.

"You know Gilles Vigneault"? asks Thelma.

"Bien sur. Il est trés Canadien, n'est pas?"

"You speak French?"

"Un petit peu."

"I can see that life is hard. But tourism helps your economy, doesn't it, Tomás?" asks Cathy.

"It helps the government."

"And what good things your government does," Cathy enthuses. "I was reading about Tarara, the camp where Fidel Castro brought the Chernobyl children for treatment. If only other countries could be so generous. And your education system is excellent. Children learn to recite poetry, learn the poems of José Martí by heart. Imagine, Thelma, a country where people go about quoting poetry!"

"¿Que importa que tu puñal/ Se me clave en el riñón?/¡Tengo mis versos que son/ Más fuertes que tu puñal!"

Cathy claps her hands. "See, Thelma! What does it mean?"

"Of what significance your dagger that thrusts into my kidneys? I have my verses that are stronger than your dagger."

"Wow!"

"¿Que importa que este dolor/Seque el mar, y nuble el cielo?/El verso, dulce consuelo/Nace alado del dolor. Of what significance that this sadness follows the sea and darkens the sky? The verse, sweet consolation, is born beside the sadness."

Cathy claps her hands. "How beautiful!"

"Do you like poetry, Thelma?"

"Yes, Tomas. My husband reads it to me, sometimes. Puts poems in my lunch bag. You?"

"Claro que si."

"Of course," Jorge translates, before muttering, "Inglés, amigo. Speak English."

Tomás moves over to pass a man driving a horse and cart with one hand, lighting a cigarette from the butt of the one dangling from his lips with the other.

"Can you slow down so I can get a picture?"

"Certainly", Tomas stays beside the man while Cathy fumbles with her camera. They're approaching a blind corner.

"Please, get on your side," shouts Thelma.

"Did you get your picture, Cathy?" asks Tomas.

"Yes, I think so."

"Christ," Thelma mutters, when he's pulled back over in their lane. Maybe she'll just keep her eyes closed the whole way.

"That old gentleman's face was so expressive. I'd love to paint it!"

"In the manner and palette of Cezanne, with oils I think."

"Yes! You're an artist, Tomás?"

"I am. Maybe you would like to see my pictures when we return to Havana, Cathy. I have one, in fact, of the children at Tarara. Also many watercolors: beach scenes; mountain scenes, historical scenes—a dying José Martí falling from his horse at Dos Rios. Some very close likenesses of the revolutionary heroes: Che Guevara, Fidel Castro, Camilo Cienfuegos. I do landscapes, cityscapes: the magotes of Pinar del Rio, the Malecón, the Plaza de Armas, La Catedral in Havana."

"Did you hear that, Thelm?"

"A."

"A what?"

"Thelm-a." She's being mean, but she's miffed that Cathy put their lives in danger for a picture.

"Right, sorry, I don't like it when people call me Cath, anyway did you hear, we're being chauffeured by an artist."

"Do you paint professionally?" Thelma asks.

"In a manner of speaking."

"Which manner is that?"

"The manner in which one paints when one isn't driving beautiful turistas such as you."

Thelma raises an eyebrow. "I see."

The car bangs into a pothole.

"Cuida la naranja," says Jorge. Be careful of the oranges?

"You have oranges in the car?' Thelma enquires.

"No, why?" asks Jorge, confused.

"La naranja."

"The car, I have named it la cacharra naranja," adds Tomás. "The bruised orange."

"A fitting description."

"Orange is a favorite colour of mine. Cathy, I would paint you in shades of orange. Because of your complexion."

"You would?"

"Yes. I would paint you in an apricot dress against a yagruma tree."

"Lovely." She giggles. "What does a yagruma tree look like?"

"It is soft and feathery. Like you."

"How sweet you are! Flattery will get you everywhere. How would you paint Thelma?"

"Please, Cathy."

"Hmm. Let me see." He turns and looks at Thelma so intently, her face reddens.

"Watch the road, please!"

"Si, miralo, amigo."

At least Jorge's backing her up.

"I would paint her with monos."

"Is that a kind of tree?" asks Cathy.

Tomás laughs. "No. Monos are monkeys. I would paint Thelma in an orange grove, surrounded by monkeys. Or perhaps in the jungle, with a little monkey around her neck. Like Frida Kahlo painted herself."

"Why monkeys?"

"Well, they are playful. Some say also a symbol of love. But no, I am joking about the monkeys. Besides, I like to paint what is in my country and we have no monkeys, except in the zoo. Let me see."

He looks at Thelma again. The car bumps through a series of potholes.

"Pay attention to the road!"

"I am, Thelma. With your complexion, I would put you in a blue sky dress."

"And would you paint her with yagrumas, also?"

"Perhaps."

The front tires dive into a pothole; water splashes up onto her arms. She shakes them out and closes the window.

"Jesus!" Thelma mutters.

"Sorry."

"Where would you paint her?"

"I would paint Thelma beside the sea. Like our goddess, Yemaya."

"He'd paint you as a goddess, Thelm!"

"Perhaps I could be wearing a crown and riding a dolphin, also."

"Buen idea."

Thelma's knees are cramping up from being jammed into the gearbox. She moves them slightly, sighs loudly.

"You are alright?" enquires Jorge.

"Fine except for this broken spring." And the exhaust and her temples pounding an insistent bass line.

"Here," Jorge hands her his jacket, "Sit on this."

"Thank you."

"And would you paint flowers in my hair, Tomás?"

"Claro. For you, Cathy, I would put bougainvillea."

"And for Thelma?"

"Please, Cathy, enough of the painting."

"Sorry, I thought we were having an interesting conversation."

"We are. I have a bit of a headache, is all."

"Do you need a pill?"

"No. I need you to stop hitting potholes."

Tomás laughs. "Is hard," he says, grazing the edge of one.

"Apparently."

They pass a grove of trees, heavy with oranges, then a truck, the box packed with teenagers. Cathy waves at them and the kids wave back.

"Where are they going?"

"To do voluntary work in the country, I think."

"Yes, I've heard of this part of Cuba's wonderful education system," enthuses Cathy, who appears to be once again on her mission to convince Tomás of his country's benefits.

Thelma closes her eyes. Tries to focus on something other than her head. How does your body feel, a voice asks. Wally's voice. Neck and shoulders wood-block tight. Lower back stiff as a board. Oh Wally, I could use a massage the way you do it, the way you find those tight balls of muscle and press into them until they release. And I would do the same for you, husband, if I knew where you the hell you were. Are you with Professor Sánchez? Are you massaging the lovely Rosa? Or have you disappeared into the wilderness?

Her head is pounding like Taino drums. Can you get high from leaded gas fumes? Can you get carbon monoxide poisoning? She'd look in her purse for a Tylenol if she thought it would touch the pain. She closes her eyes. Wally's voice whispers: relax your shoulders, arms, back...

She jerks forward.

"Tomás!"

"Sorry."

"You didn't see that one coming?"

"The steering she's not as responsive as a woman."

"Um hm. Maybe you could slow down so you can see the potholes coming. That and perhaps steer around them."

She closes her eyes, images herself in a roomy car with functioning shock absorbers, air conditioning, buttery leather seats. Imagining this, her neck and shoulders shed their tension and she sleeps.

———

When Thelma wakes up, they're on a dirt road. The landscape has changed from orange groves and sugarcane fields to grass and scrubby bush.

Jorge is snoring softly. Cathy is reading her guidebook. Tomás is smoking. They pass a man on horseback with a machete in his hand, looking like someone from another century.

"I thought we were on the autopista," says Thelma, stretching her arms and yawning.

"I made a detour, down to Playa Giron. We will drive to Ciudad Juragua, the nuclear city, and cross over to Cienfuegos."

"I thought the autopista went right to Cienfuegos."

"This is the scenic route. I thought you might prefer it."

"Because of the reactor, you mean?"

Tomás laughs. "Well, the nuclear reactor isn't on the travel brochures. But this whole area is very interesting; it is made of limestone and filled with dolinas and cenotes."

"Dolinas and cenotes?" asks Cathy.

"Pools that form where the limestone disintegrated."

"Limestone? Is that like karst?"

"Karst is an area of limestone where there are ravines and caves," Thelma replies.

"Si, and underground rivers to the sea. Much of our country is made of karst. It is why we don't have many lakes."

"But if you have limestone, you should have oil, shouldn't you, Tomás? Like in Alberta."

"No, Cathy. Your limestone is very old. Millions of years old. Ours is young, recent, only 30,000 years old. We were once connected to Haiti and the Dominican Republic, to the Yucatan."

"So Cuba isn't a volcanic island?"

"No, it was made when the Caribbean plate went under the Bahama reef," Thelma answers.

Tomás raises his eyebrows. "You are right. How do you know this?"

"I collect obscure geological facts. My father was a field geologist. He worked for exploration companies in B.C., the Yukon and North West Territories. He told me how they used electromagnetics to find the fractured zones in the dolomite, metamorphosed limestone where fluids have carried metals up to the surface."

"And you also studied geology?"

"No. Archeology."

"Archeology. A very interesting field. Does your father work in karst, in cenotes and dolinas?" asks Tomás.

"No. He would have liked to." They could have explored them together, lowering themselves on ropes down to the watery depths.

"Donde estamas?" asks Jorge in a sleep fogged voice. "No estamos en el autopista, hombre." Where are we? This isn't the highway.

"Yo se." I know.

"Eso no esta el autopista!"

"Si. Claro."

"Are we lost, Tomás?"

"Oh, I don't think they're lost, Thelma. I'm sure this road goes up to the highway eventually, right Tomás?"

Silence.

"Right?"

"I think so Cathy," he replies.

————

THE ROAD IS LITTERED with potholes. Tomas jerks the wheel, trying to avoid a water-filled crater but drives right into it. Now they are stuck. Tomás tries to turn the car around. He roars it back and forth, back and forth, grinding between first and reverse. The engine sputters, then stalls.

"Mierda!"

He turns the key. Nothing but the smell of gas. Tries again. No groans. No whines. No whispers. Nada.

Tomás lights a cigarette. Nice combination, fire and petrol.

"Don't worry," says Jorge softly. "We can resolver the problem."

"I have exactly two weeks in this country before we have to leave. Two weeks to find Wally. One and a half, actually. And we're stuck in the middle of nowhere."

"There is no middle of nowhere in Cuba."

She groans. "Well, maybe not, but if there was, this would be it."

Evening descends, riding down the sky and resting on the tops of the mangrove trees like a flock of birds leaving their red flight path behind.

"Don't worry, Thelm. They'll fix it," Cathy says.

Thelma decides not to reply. Cathy's the kind of woman who thinks that everything will work out for the best. But it doesn't always, sweetie. Not by a long shot.

Jorge and Tomás get out of the car. The hood squeals open. They're arguing, talking loudly and too quickly for Thelma to make out what they're saying.

Wally appears again, quoting from Robert Graves' "Through Nightmare":

*The untamable, the live, the gentle.*

*Have you not known them? Whom? They carry*

*Time looped so river-wise around their house*

*There's no way in by history's road*

*To name and number them.*

Why does she like the poem so much? Because Wally does and her father did? Because of the language, the emotion? She loves the references to those who don't fit into the time in which they live, who can't find a place in the modern world. It is a lament for those people and places beyond time, stuck in a tragic or a heroic history. This country.

We've come to an island that lives in the past, Wall. Every day, in the newspaper *Granma*, revolutionary battles are re-lived. The patron saint of the island is José Martí, a nineteenth-century poet. The blowing up of the Maine, Spanish-Cuban-American war, the taking of Guantanamo, why they just happened yesterday. Didn't they?

You told me De Soto left his love-struck Isabel in Santiago. Or maybe she wasn't so love-struck anymore, having been dragged across the Atlantic to Santiago, only to be sent on another ship to Havana sans hubbie, who'd decided to take the scenic route on horseback (looking for gold, Hernando. You and the Pizarros had the Inca gold, how much gold could one man possibly need?). Isabel's Spanish ship was tossed by hurricanes; she had only her slaves and a disgraced niece, Leonor (having found herself in the family way by Hernando's second in command) for company. Forty days later, she arrived in a Havana recently wrecked by pirates. When Hernando finally arrived, he prepared his ships and left for Florida. Leaving Isabel to do what? Govern, yes, a little of that. And wait, a lot of that. A hell of a lot of waiting.

Isabel bore no children. Was she past childbearing age? Did they die in utero? What was her life like? She had a brutal father and was married late, to a man who'd had several mistresses and children. Perhaps she didn't expect to marry at all. She was prepared to accept the hardship of the new world, long absences from family and friends, and from her husband. Did she also accept the cruelty, fornication, torture and murder of the native peoples as the right of the conquerors? And if she didn't accept these things, what could she do? What other choices did she have?'

Thelma had choices. Many choices. One of which was to marry Wally. To love and honour him. Though she did not agree to obey. She is not an obedient woman. Is Rosa obedient? Was Isabel? Or do they just dress in duty's trappings and pretend to be, as women often do, to survive.

Outside the window, a half-moon settles on the treetops.

Tomás lopes down the road. Going for help or disappearing, too?

# CHAPTER 22

*Cuba*

EVENING. SHADOWS brindle the path. Thelma walks quickly on a track through the trees, pulling her sweater closer. Mosquitos buzz around her face, darting in for bites. The breeze is cool, fishy. Away from the gas and cigarette fumes, the pounding in her head is almost gone.

Behind the trees, something snorts. She stops. Listens. Nothing.

She should have woken her dozing companions, Jorge and Cathy. But she couldn't stand to be crammed in that metal rust-box a moment longer. She needs to stretch her legs.

The sound again. Closer, to her right. Thelma turns. There's nothing.

One minute she's on the autopista, passing a pink De Soto, the next she's on a dirt track in the middle of nowhere.

Gisela said Cuba is a safe country. Nothing to worry about.

Except for the fact that you're with a Pollyanna and two strangers who say they are taking you to Cienfuegos. To find your husband. Except for the fact that your husband's disappeared, leaving a cryptic note. Except for the fact that your husband is not the disappearing kind.

She stops, look up to see a faint crescent moon rising. Ixchel, protector, holding her baby rabbit. She hopes the office bunny has found a warm place to bed down for the winter. That Gisela and Ardeth are remembering to feed him.

The path veers to the right, opens into a large meadow. Floppy eared, long horned cattle wander in the semi-dark, egrets riding whitely on their backs. In the near distance, she sees a structure. Barn? House? Whatever it is, there might be help there. She walks toward it.

———

THERE IS SOMETHING on the porch of the house. Someone or something moving in the gloaming.

"Hello," Thelma calls.

The moving stops. Thelma pauses.

"Hola," she tries.

No response.

"Por favor, estoy, uh, lost. Mi caro esta rompio." She thinks she is saying her car is broken. Or does caro mean heart?

On the porch there's a swishing, the sound a long skirt makes sweeping across a wooden floor.

A soft brush against her calf. Thelma stifles a scream.

A cow, Thelma. Only a cow, its horns white in the diminishing light.

"Señora, por favor," she calls to what is surely a woman on the porch, moving slowly toward her. "My car, mi caro is...I need help."

But as Thelma moves closer across the hummocky ground, the figure seems to be moving backwards into shadow.

"Señora?"

Then she's falling. Falling backwards. Down and down.

———

FOG HOVERS a few feet above the ground. The branches of the aspens are etched with frost.

Thelma walks to the side of the office where the office bunny lives, over the uneven, frozen ground. Her heel cracks a frozen puddle. Frost stings her lungs. From Memorial Drive comes the faint roar of cars. The bunny sits on his haunches a few yards away. She moves closer, and he breaks into a lop-sided run.

"Come here, little bunny," she coos. "I won't hurt you. I just want to see what you've done to your leg."

He stops, lifts a paw as if to look at an invisible watch and hurries on. Thelma follows him across the frozen mud, catches a heel, stumbles, and finds herself falling down a long, narrow root cellar with jars on shelves. She plucks one as she goes by, opens it and pulls a salmon sandwich with a note stuck on it that reads EAT ME. Lands with a thud on a pile of moss, her mule sling-backs dropping beside her. The bunny hurries down a narrow street bound on both sides by houses with wrought iron balconies, and a sign that reads "Gentilly."

Curiouser and curiouser.

Thelma is on an azalea-lined street, presently coming to a tiny, partly opened door. She can see a garden inside, with bright pink rhododendrons, white camellias and kudzu smothered trees. In the distance she can see Wally sitting and reading a book under an oak tree. He stands, then disappears into the ravine behind him. On a shelf beside the door, Thelma spies a bottle marked DRINK ME. Opens the lid and takes a sip: watery office coffee with too much coffee mate. She feels a curious sensation, as if her head is rushing away from her toes. She steps forward and bangs her chin on the top of a door. Damn, I've grown too big, Thelma thinks. She knocks back the rest of the disgusting office brew. On the other side of the door, her secretary Ardeth walks by with an armful of copy paper. Then Ardeth becomes Rosa. "Hey," she yells, managing to squeeze an arm and shoulder through the opening just as Ardeth/Rosa disappears down the ravine.

————

IT IS THE MADRUGADA. The early morning. Thelma wakes to discover she is lying on the ground in a meadow. A layer of fog lies across the grass. Ahead is an old house, vines climbing up the porch, the roof partially caved in. She focuses on the porch, but there is no one there. The back of her head and her foot throb. Has she broken her ankle? She stands, takes a couple of steps. The ankle holds. She has to get back to the car and the others. What if they've left? She's miles from the autopista. If they've gone, she'll have to walk to the next town. Which is where? And which way, exactly, is the car? Try to find the woman from last night. The woman will help you.

"Hola!"

A long-eared cow turns his head, looking at her with his angry eyes. Poor cow. So skinny. The cow snorts and Thelma sees that the cow is a bull: a bull with a ring in its nose, a rope attached to the ring and wrapped around his head. The bull snorts again then lowers his head. Huge horns jut forward. Breathing rapidly, Thelma backs toward the house, keeping her eyes on the bull. Back up and don't look him in the eye, that's what her father said to do if they encountered a grizzly bear. But does that apply to bulls? She feels dizzy, a combination of carbon monoxide poisoning from the Lada and fear. The bull waves his head from side to side. She turns around and, dodgy be damned, runs to the house.

SITTING ON THE WOODEN floor just inside the house, Thelma periodically peers through the door to see if the bull if still there (he is) and wondering if De Soto and Isabel might have passed this way. Lived here even? Ran a cattle ranch like many of the conquistadors did?

Wally told her that De Soto was born in Extramadura in Castile. Where was Isabel born? Spain or Panama? Was she a daughter of the old or the new world? Which did she prefer? For the men, the conquistadors, poor sheepherders and farmers who became landowners, the new world offered freedom and wealth. But for the women, were the stultifying customs of the day merely transferred across the ocean, combined with brutality (storms, pirate raids, uprisings, backbreaking labour), and hardship? Or did the new world offer them freedom, a chance to transform themselves and become something new?

———

THE SEÑORA WALKS across the field, leading the bull by his nose ring. Thelma walks towards them. She is not afraid. The woman takes her hand and places it on his nose. Together they stroke his velvet coat. "There," the woman says. "You see. He is just like a man. Seeming ferocious, but touch him the right way..." she laughs, a sound like spoons on china teacups.

"And if you don't touch him the right way? Perhaps he will take a lover," says Thelma.

"I don't know about that. My husband, he came to me older, tamed already."

"By other women?"

"So they say," replies the señora.

"He had children with those women?"

The señora smiles. "All I know is that I am the governor. And I am the one he calls wife."

———

THIS IS NO TIME to daydream, Thelma tells herself, looking outside. The bull is eating grass, his back to her. She slips outside, tiptoes across the porch and down the stairs, then starts walking as fast as her ankle will take her across the meadow. Glancing quickly behind her, she sees the bull look up, meet her eyes and return to grazing, as if he's been tamed. Ahead is the path through the trees. Thelma turns once more, but the bull hasn't followed. She stops and to Isabel, the Catholic with Jewish ancestors, she whispers "muchas gracias, señora. Muchisimas gracias, Doña Isabel."

———

THE BRUISED ORANGE, welcoming beast, hunkers down on the track ahead, its four doors open. Cathy and Jorge standing beside it.

"Thelma! Thank God," Cathy cries. "Where did you go? We've been so worried, Jorge went to look for you and then it got dark and he didn't want to get lost, but he went out again this morning. Oh my god, what happened? Where were you? Are you OK?"

"I'm fine."

"Gracias a Dios you are safe!"

"Yup. Safe and sound but really, really thirsty. Does anyone have water?" She collapses under a palm tree, massages her ankle. Cathy hands her a water bottle. She drinks while the two of them peer down at her like anxious parents.

"Despacio," says Jorge. Slowly.

"Go ahead, have the whole bottle. There, good. Now, tell us where you were. Jorge looked everywhere."

"While you guys were sleeping, I went for a walk, over there. I ended up in a meadow, where I guess I fell. I must have hit my head. Anyway, I was out cold for a while. Sorry to have made you worry. Where's Tomás?"

"He's not back yet, Thelm."

"He went to find help. He was going to walk or try to get a ride to a place with a mechanic. Not to worry. He probably stayed in a little caserio."

"Caserio?"

"A collection of houses."

"How was your night?" Thelma asks them, eyeing Cathy's smeared lipstick.

"It was a little uncomfortable, all squished up in the back seat." Cathy runs her fingers through her hair. "I must look a mess."

"Well neither of us are ready for our close-ups."

"I slept, of course, in the front seat," adds the chivalrous Jorge.

She imagines Isabel in her house on the cattle ranch. Alone. Well, not alone, she probably had servants. But alone in her thoughts. She was a woman who kept her sorrows to herself, Thelma thinks. A woman who got on with things. A tamer of men and bulls. A woman who did what had to be done. She may have to return without Wally. What would she do? Quit her job? Buy a little place in the country, near the hoodoos around Drumheller. Rosedale or Wayne. Hike coulees, bring home dinosaur bones and arrowheads, like her father used to do. Plant a garden, buy some chickens, join a book club, come to Cuba once in a while.

———

THEY ARE SITTING on the shady side of the car. Cathy fans herself with a tourist pamphlet while Jorge amasses a pile of small stones.

"So hot. Do you have another brochure?" Thelma asks.

"No, but you can have this one. Did you know Cienfuegos means one hundred fires?"

"All of which seem to be burning today. No, I didn't."

"Do you have any idea where Wally and the professor might be in Cienfuegos, Thelm?"

Thelma shakes her head and fans herself vigorously. "Jorge, do you know the professor's first name?"

"Professor?"

"The professor my husband went off with."

"Only I know she is Professor Sánchez."

Thelma stops fanning. "She?"

"Sí."

"A woman?"

"Yes."

"Is her first name Rosa?"

"Rosa, no, I don't think so."

"Why didn't you tell me she was a woman, Jorge?"

He reddens. "I did not think you would be interested."

"You didn't think I would be interested to know that my husband ran off with a woman?"

"Thelm, don't get upset, he didn't run off. He's just doing his research."

"Do you know the profesora, Jorge?"

"I don't know her."

"You know of her."

"Yes, everybody knows of her."

"Why?"

"Because of, because everyone know everyone who is famous in Cuba," says Jorge, suddenly keenly interested in rearranging a pile of stones.

"Why is she famous?"

"She went to Spain and found in some old documents there is a ship with gold, the King's royal fifth of gold that sank near Havana. The government located the ship."

"So my husband is with this woman? Not with Rosa?"

"Who is Rosa?

"Maybe that's why he didn't contact me. He's in some kind of trouble, he didn't have the proper permission to be with the profesora, the police stopped them and arrested him, they think he's after some of the gold, they..."

"Please, Thelma, calm yourself. He's a tourist. If there is trouble, it will be for her not for him. Besides, the ship has been found. They government already has all the gold."

He is not with Rosa. She smiles, the cool water of relief flooding down to her toes.

# CHAPTER 23

*Cuba*

THE AIR SIZZLES. Waves of heat bounce off the white track down which Jorge and Cathy recede, going for a walk. Thelma climbs into the front seat of the car, thinking it might be cooler inside but the black vinyl sucks the backs of her thighs like an ardent lover. Sweat streams down her chest. She pulls her skirt from her stomach and looks at the red puckers left by the elastic. I must be a sight, Thelma thinks. She pulls down the rearview mirror to check her face and the mirror comes off in her hand. She tries to press the thing back. It falls on the gearshift and cracks down the middle.

Shit!

If Wally were here, she thinks, I'd be somewhere cool. Swimming in a pool. Drinking mojitos in air-conditioned comfort. But he isn't here. Wally's with a woman. Possibly the profesora, or if that is a ruse, Rosa. And if he is with Profesora Sanchez, why didn't he mention that she was a woman? Did he just forget to mention it? Like he forgot to tell her about Deirdre.

Her neck is so tight she can hardly turn her head. It hasn't felt like this since her typing pool days. Once a week, at an ungodly hour, she stumbled from the house to the bus stop, pale and devoid of the make-up that she usually applied so carefully each morning. She'd get crunched at the chiropractor's, go to work, sleep better for a night or two, and then the neck pain would start all over again. She tried massage but the masseuse she went to seemed overly familiar with her body, rubbing her hands up and down Thelma's back in big, sloppy passes. She tried another woman who hardly touched her at all, holding her hands over different body parts to see where Thelma's energy was blocked. She wanted to put suction cups on Thelma's back. Thelma declined. Could leeches be far behind? A chirpy physiotherapist watched her walk, showed her how her gait threw her knees, hips and back out of alignment, how one shoulder was higher than the other, pushed them down two inches after Thelma had relaxed them. She showed Thelma diagrams of skeletons and muscles and sheets of stick people doing exercises that would cure the problem, if only Thelma would practice faithfully every day.

The only thing that seemed to help her neck was yoga with Julia, a lovely redheaded woman who came and put a block under her head, pushed on her back while she lay in child's resting pose, gently opened up her shoulders. Thelma asked Julia, once, why she had so much neck and shoulder pain. We hold feelings in our bodies she said. Anger and fear. She didn't mention the happy emotions. Were they, too, being held in abeyance, in Thelma's body, just waiting for the right yoga posture to release them?

She didn't have neck and shoulder problems when she was a girl. When she hiked and backpacked with her dad. She remembers hiking in to Egypt Lake campsite. Sliding their packs off, she and her dad sat down, removed their boots and socks, dabbled their feet in the cold water, feeling the breeze drying their t-shirts. She was so happy then, love filling and energizing her body. Like it did when she first met Wally.

Where are the famous Cuban breezes? Where the heck are Cathy and Jorge? Shouldn't Tomás be back by now? Thelma can smell her own musky armpits. The front of her new turquoise blouse is smeared with dirt. The underwire from her bra is gouging and her face is slick with oil and sweat. She needs something to cool her off. But what? She has no water but she does have baby wipes, she remembers, in her suitcase. Thelma unsticks herself from the seat, undoes the rope holding the trunk closed and hauls her suitcase out. Unzips it. Wally's diary is on top. She picks it up. A scrap of paper falls out from the back. She didn't notice it when she read the diary the first time, perhaps because of the blank pages between it and his entries.

*'Hubb' is love, 'ishq' is love that entwines two people together, 'shaghaf' is love that nests in the chambers of the heart, 'hayam' is love that wanders the earth, 'teeh' is love in which you lose yourself, 'walah' is love that carries sorrow within it, 'sababah' is love that exudes from your pores, 'hawa' is love that shares its name with air and with falling, 'gharam' is love that is willing to pay the price.*

*Lady Anna Winterbourne (British, married to an Egyptian, Sharif Basha). The Map of Love, Ahdaf Soueif. Bloomsbury, 1999.*

This beautiful, evocative passage, written with such care, is in her handwriting, Thelma's best handwriting. She remembers copying the passage down a couple of years ago when she was reading the book, and showed it to Wally. They both found it interesting that in Arabic there were so many words for love. While English has only one.

Though there are love's pale kin—infatuation, desire, passion, yearning, devotion, adoration. All to do with having and wanting. She reads the quote again. Teeh: her love for Wally that first spring they spent together in Victoria, walking in Beacon Hill Park, running down the stairs to the beach where they sat behind rocks oblivious to passersby, kissing and fumbling zips and buttons with wind-reddened hands. Spring leafed into summer. She didn't go home, told her mom and Peter that she'd found a great job in Victoria. The great job being a waitressing gig at the House of Pancakes, serving strawberry cheese blintzes, pigs in a blanket, and Dutch apple pankoeken to carloads of tourists, who pulled into the parking lot in dusty station wagons bearing yellow Alberta license plates, kids spilling out and into the restaurant to spill more: milk and juice and syrup, leaving the lids of the sugars unscrewed so when Thelma picked them up to refill, they crashed to the table.

She was known as the 'college girl' by the full-time waitresses who taught her how to fill the ketchups without spilling, to carry three plates on one arm, a pot of coffee in the other.

Though her feet burned, the white polyester of her uniform was covered with stains, and her fingers were always syrup sticky, Thelma didn't mind because she knew that the shift would end, that Wally would arrive in his orange Datsun B210 with the stickers on the back: *Save the Whales* and *Give Peace a Chance*, to whisk her away. They'd drive out to Sooke, find a stretch of deserted beach. She'd step out of her uniform, strip off her bra and panties and run into the ocean, letting the waves wash her clean. She and Wally camped there, sometimes. On clear nights, they took their foamies outside the tent and slept ishq-entwined under the stars.

Sababah: love literally flooding from her pores. Gloria kidded her, 'Thelma, your beau just walked in and he looks pretty hungry. For you.' Thelma blushed, her body prickled, she fumbled the creams and lost her order book when Wally slid onto a stool at the counter. She felt she would disintegrate in a brown sugar puddle at his feet, like the witch in the *Wizard of Oz*.

Hawa, love like air and falling: jumping from the cliff into Thetis Lake, plunging through air, into water, back up into air.

Is there is a progress of love? Does teeh lead to sababah, lead to hawa, lead to ishq lead to shaghaf? Is shagaf followed by sorrow—walah—and wandering the earth—hayam? And when does one fall into gharam and decide to pay the price?

What things did she love? Playing tennis with her father. Before he left her. Early in the morning, she and her dad drove to the ochre clay tennis courts down by the river, by the railway tracks and the Red bridge. The air smelled like leaf, like fish, like river, like manure from the stockyard across the road. Her dad would roll the clay, check the net's height, and then stand with a metal basket of balls on the opposite side, hitting to her forehand, backhand, a lob, a volley.

She tries to remember more details. What did her dad wear? Tennis whites? Did he wear the glasses he used to play squash, with the big black nosepiece? What did he say, exactly?

Take your racket back, she remembers that one. Step into the ball, that's a girl, follow through.

He taught her well. Which is how she came to beat Wally that summer when they were twenty-two, exactly half her life ago, the summer of love, the summer they played on the old city courts across from Craigdarroch castle in Victoria, courts that sloped, weeds growing through cracked black-top, and a metal net that was two inches too low, but impossible to raise.

When she was hitting well, when she and Wally were both hitting well, she loved tennis in the same fierce way as her ten-year-old self did, loved it because it was the only sport she could play worth a damn. She loved the rhythmic thwacks, the satisfaction of a cross-court forehand that whistled over the net, landing just inside the baseline. Way to get your racket back, Thelmie, brilliant follow-through, said her dad.

She was better than Wally when they first started to play. But he was determined and spent hours practicing against the backboard. Where once she would take her time getting back to the baseline after a wicked cross-court forehand, later she couldn't be sure he wouldn't make a desperate lunge and jab the ball, that it wouldn't come sailing back over the net. He'd grin. I've still got a trick or two up my sleeve, he'd say. Don't you be taking me for granite. You're more like limestone, she'd joke back. Porous and permeable.

After a hard battle, they'd sit in the park, kissing, so in love they wanted all the world to see.

And, of course, love in tennis is zero. Fifteen love, thirty love, forty love. Game. Set. Match.

Why did Wally keep the quote? Why did he bring it here? Did he find it, one day, on the floor, on the dining room table, in a pile of old bills and absentmindedly stuff it in the back of his diary? Did he forget to transfer the diary to his suitcase? Or did he put the note in the diary, in her suitcase, for a reason? For her to find and read? Did he imagine it as a love note? Though it was actually a love note from herself to herself, she read the book after all, she copied the passage and showed it to Wally.

She slides the paper carefully into the back of the diary, slips the diary into her suitcase. Searches below it for baby wipes that aren't there. Exhausted by the heat, she goes to the car, lies down in the back seat. However, the black vinyl sticks to her shirt, which sticks to her back. Her stomach grumbles. When was the last time she ate? Yesterday. A whole day ago. She has no food. Thelma looks around, notices that Cathy has left her bag on the floor. Cathy seems like the kind of woman who would carry extra food, for emergencies: crackers, a package of peanuts, a granola bar, fruit leather. She sits up, looks around, and reaches into Cathy's bag, pulling out a pink wallet with a picture of a mini Cathy in plastic. Sara with her missing front tooth and velvet hairband. Thelma sighs. She'd always thought she would have had a boy, but a little girl she could dress up, that would have been alright, too.

A comb, several tubes of lipstick, hand sanitizer, two packages of Kleenex, a digital camera, a set of keys on a Mickey Mouse keychain, a purple pen, a lilac coloured notebook, a zip lock bag containing Canadian flag pins, a pink silk teddy—interesting—and something squishy in a brown paper bag. A papaya! Food, glorious, food. She takes it out and bites into it, sucking the meat from the skin with her teeth. Juice drips down her chin onto the notebook. Damn. She wipes it quickly with the corner of her blouse, then opens the notebook.

No, she tells herself. Close it now. Put it away.

She will. After she takes a peek to make sure she didn't get juice on any of the pages.

*March 4, Havana, 2 AM*
*I needn't have worried about being on my own here. There are loads*
*of other tourists. I slept most of the morning (jet lag, washing and*
*packing every night last week, making sure that Sara's homework was*
*done, that she was ready to go to Hawaii). Hated to leave her, poor*
*thing, she started crying on the car ride over to John's and then*
*I started and was a red faced, sodden mess when we arrived. Does*

*it get easier, leaving your child? I know she'll have a wonderful time
in Hawaii.*

*John's a good dad, whatever else he is not.*

*Ate lunch at the Palco's poolside bar. A clubhouse sandwich
should always be eaten in the sun, on a chaise lounge under a fragrant
frangipani bush. Ah, the smell of sweet flowers. The only floral scent
at home this time of year is my plug-in air freshener.*

*Met another Canadian. Thelma. I don't think she meant to be rude
to me. I think she was just a little drunk. A lot drunk.*

Thelma remembers the other picture Cathy showed her. Little Sara's hair
done up in ringlets, a pink dress with matching tights and shiny black shoes.
If she'd had a little girl, she would have dressed her up that way too.

*March 8, Havana*

*Today was International Women's Day. El dia de las mujeres. How
wonderful that in Cuba they celebrate a day just for women (we have
Mother's Day but it's not the same). The men bring flowers to their
compañeras at work. John used to bring me flowers, bright orange
gerberas, pink carnations, yellow roses.*

*Thelma seemed nicer today but more worried. Her husband seems
to have run away. Well, he says he's gone to do "research," but from my
experience of husbands, he has run off! Stop. Replace those thoughts:
I am woman hear me roar. A woman without a man is like a fish
without a bicycle. What are the other ones I am supposed to say when
a bad thought comes up?*

Cathy's kind of funny. Less ditzy than she appears. But you're not going to
read any more, she tells herself. This is absolutely wrong. You are not going
to find any clues to Wally's disappearance here.

Thelma puts everything back in the bag except the teddy. It is beautiful, real silk, with an inset of lace above the V and around the bottom. She
thinks how cool it would feel against her skin. Wally used to buy her silk
lingerie like this. It would sure feel nice to slip off her underwire instru-
ment of torture for a moment, slip this on. Quickly, she undoes the buttons
of her blouse shucking it and her bra, and pulls the teddy over her head. It's
cut lower than anything she usually wears, is a little tight in the bust but

otherwise it fits alright. The silk is indeed glorious against her skin. She'll just wear it for a minute or two.

"Hello, Thelma."

Damn. Tomás is resting his arms against the window frame, looking in. Did he see anything? Blushing, Thelma crosses her arms over her chest.

"You're back. Finally! Did you find someone to fix the car?"

"Yes."

"Where is he?"

"He had to butcher some rabbits first."

"Of course he did. So how did you get back?"

"I walked."

"Was it far?"

"Ten kilometres."

"Each way?"

"Yes."

Tomás face is glazed with sweat. He has a faint five o'clock shadow on his chin, a few crow's feet around his eyes, but other than that his face is smooth as a baby's bum.

"So when's the mechanic coming? I need to get to Cienfuegos."

"Soon. But don't worry. We will find your husband and the professor."

"Did you know the professor was a woman?"

"Of course."

She uncrosses her arms, leans toward him.

"Why didn't you tell me she was a, a she?"

"I thought you knew. And we didn't want to mention it, to make you more angry. What is the saying – hell hath no fury like a woman scorned."

"Well, it's not been confirmed that I've been scorned."

"May I join you inside the car?"

"It's hot in here. I just came to get something."

"I like hot."

"Suit yourself."

She moves over and he slides in beside her. She can feel the heat coming off his skin, the faint smell of his underarms, musky, not unpleasant.

"I like your blouse."

Thelma reddens, re-crosses her arms. "It's not my, it's not a blouse. But, uh, thanks." How the hell is she going to get the thing off and back into Cathy's bag with him right beside her?

His thigh brushes hers. She tries to move her leg away but it appears to be stuck to the vinyl.

"You are in a better mood today, Tomás."

"Si, es verdad. Yesterday, I was thinking about my last turistas. They were, I am sorry to say, very stupid about Cuba. Always saying how much better everything was in England. The roads, the food, the hotels. Ha, they thought I did not know about English food. About bangers and mash and mush peas. But now I see you are not the same as them."

"I sure hope not."

"You are right, it is hot in here." Tomás begins to unbutton his shirt.

"Yes, uh, in fact, I think I'll go sit outside now. Find some shade," she says quickly, trying not to look at Tomás and his now bare torso. At his belly button surrounded by a little circle of hair which sprouts into a line then blooms across his chest.

"See you," says Thelma, surreptitiously sliding her bra and blouse into Cathy's bag.

"Not if I see you first."

———

FOLLOWING HER OUTSIDE and standing beside her, Tomás asks: "Did you know they call Jorge 'el loco hombre de amor'?"

"The crazy man of love? You don't say."

"Do you like him?"

"That is a rather cheeky question."

"Cheeky?"

"Irreverent."

"Cheeky is my middle name. You should have said to Jorge you wanted a more obedient driver."

"But you're partners aren't you? You're his friend?"

Tomás pulls a cigarette from the package of populares in his shirt pocket, lights it and waves the match out.

"Ah, si, we are all friends in this business."

"What business is that?"

"Turismo."

"Jorge is in the tourist business?"

"In unofficial capacity, yes."

"But I thought he was a...." What the hell did Jorge say he was? Or did he say?

Thelma notices she has carried the incriminating papaya skin with her. She picks it up and wraps it in some dry leaves.

"You like that?"

"What?"

"Fruta bomba?"

"Fruta bomba? Oh, papaya, yes, I like it."

"Where are el loco and Cathy?"

"Gone for a walk. When, exactly, is that mechanic coming, Tomás?"

"Don't worry he will come. Ahorita." He pauses then sings "quizás, quizás, quizás."

"You are alternately charming and annoying you know."

"So I have been told."

———

FINALLY, ROBERTO, the mechanic/pig farmer/rabbit killer arrives on an old Forever bicycle and begins fiddling under the Lada's hood, Tomás chain smoking and making suggestions.

The sun is an anvil on Thelma's head, weighing her down, squeezing every bit of moisture out of her skin. Why didn't she bring more water? Does Cathy have some hidden away somewhere? And where are Cathy and Jorge? If Roberto ever gets the rust bucket fixed, she wants to leave tout de suite. She has passed through the screened porch, front door, living room, dining room, kitchen, and out the back door of frustration. She is beyond wanting to scream at Wally for running off with a famous gold finding profesora. Or with Rosa. Or both. For ruining her vacation. His vacation, his research trip, but hers, too. And said vacation wasn't supposed to involve being stuck in a heat wave beyond the back of beyond.

Thelma lifts her arms to let a little air circulate, fans herself with the top sights of Cuba pamphlet. It's so hot she's tempted to take off the blouse she managed to slip on when Tomás went to greet Roberto. But there's the problem of the incriminating teddy and the possibility of Cathy's return.

"You are happy I found a mechanic?" asks Tomás who has snuck up on her from behind.

"I'd be happier if he fixed the car."

"He will."

"When?"

"By tonight."

"Tonight?"

"By this afternoon."

"It's already afternoon."

"There is afternoon left."

"If he can't fix it, what will we do?"

"Spend the night."

"I am not spending another night here!"

"It will be nice, the moon and the stars, just the..."

"Four of us, yes. Where do you think Jorge and Cathy went? They've been gone for ages."

"Someplace private? His nickname is el loco hombre de amor, remember."

"Um hm. Are you sure the car can even be fixed?"

"I think so."

"You think so? I thought it was a small problem. I thought Cubans could resolve any problem. How are we going to get to Cienfuegos and find Wally and the profesora? I'm running out of patience, Tomás. It's burning hot and I'm starving, I'm thirsty, I'm filthy, my ankle hurts, this is supposed to be my vacation and..."

He puts his hand on her arm. "I am kidding, Thelma. Calm yourself. In Cuba, we are resourceful. We will fix the car. I will carry you to Cienfuegos on my back, if necessary."

"I'm sorry. If I could just cool off..."

"Would you like to swim?"

"You know a place to swim?"

"Si."

"Here?"

"Yes, I just said. It is not too far."

"We are near the ocean?"

"Yes."

She could have been swimming instead of sweating like a pig. Of course, the ocean. She should have smelled it. She would have figured out they were near the ocean if heat, pain and frustration hadn't scrambled her brains.

———

"Do you like to swim?"

"I love to swim in the sea."

"Not the sea."

"I thought you said we were near the ocean."

"We are. But I am going to take you to a cenote."

"A cenote? Where?"

"Over there." Tomás points toward a row of trees.

"Why didn't you tell me about it before?"

"I had to go to get help, remember. You didn't ask. And I am not the guide, Thelma. Only the diver."

"Driver."

She imagines Tomás as a winged diving God floated down a temple archway at Tulum.

"And also the driver," he confirms.

# CHAPTER 24

*Cuba*

THE WALK TO THE cenote is taking forever. He said it was close, but they've been walking under a heavy sun for fifteen minutes now. Walking, apparently, on limestone riddled with faults. This is the Zapata peninsula, an area that was sparsely populated until Fidel Castro caught wind of the planned Bay of Pigs invasion and gathered the carboneros, charcoal burners, and students, gave them Czech rifles and Stalinist tanks to repel the U.S. invaders, Cuban exiles. Well, Tomás doesn't tell her all of this, she knows some of it from her guidebook.

"I can't believe Cathy and Jorge didn't want to come swimming. It's so beautiful here, this white road, the screen of trees behind us," says Thelma.

"As beautiful as a painting."

"Or perhaps more so, being the real thing and all, Tomás."

"A talented painter could make it more beautiful, brighten the browns and soften the blues."

"A talented painter such as yourself, sir?"

"Perhaps."

"Where did you learn to paint?"

"At ISA, the Instituto Superior de Arte in Havana. It's near the Palco, where I picked you up. When I was six, the principal of the school I was attending told my parents I had a talent for drawing and painting, so I was sent to ISA. When I was eighteen, I got a scholarship to study artes plasticas, fine art I think you say, in Leningrado. The snow and cold pierced my body, stabbing into my bones. As it does in your country, perhaps." He gives a mock shiver.

"Yes."

"I studied, I drew and painted and made sculpture. I met Olga in a, how do you call it, life drawing class."

"Olga?"

"My wife."

Her stomach tightens. He's married. Of course, Thelma. He's your age. Why wouldn't he be?

"She was the model for life drawing class. I painted her as an angel in ice," Tomás draws the form in the air. His fingers are long, slightly thickened at the ends.

"Sounds interesting."

"Professor Illych denounced it as too religious and fanciful. But Olga was my angel. She helped me with my Russian. She was the only thing that kept me warm that first winter. After my degree, we got married and came to Cuba to teach."

He has a wife. She glances at his hand. But he doesn't wear a ring.

———

WATER HAS DONE this. Collapsed the limestone ceiling, scooped out this large rounded pool, and smoothed its chalky walls. Water seeped up from underground rivers, down from the sky. The surface is a milky-blue that deepens into royal blue. Pavonine. A word Wally once used in a poem, to describe what? Eyes, the sky, a piece of clothing? Not her eyes. Her eyes are hazel. Witch hazel, Wally used call them, they put a spell on him, he used to say.

"You are changing now."

Can he read her mind? "Pardon me?"

"Or you are swimming in your clothes?"

Oh, that kind of changing. She opens her purse, as if a bathing suit and towel might miraculously appear there, but all she finds is her guidebook, a Cuba map with the cover half ripped off, and Cathy's pamphlet. Her suit is in the suitcase in the trunk of the bruised orange. Why didn't she bring it? What is happening to her head that she remembers the past clear as day but can't seem to remember the simplest thing in the here and now?

"Yes, I mean no."

"You are taking them off?"

"Nice try."

She could swim in her clothes and let them dry on the way back to the car, dripping water like Gretel with her forest crumbs: like the picture in the book her father bought her, Gretel wore a puffy sleeved blouse and dirndl skirt, like the uniform Thelma wore at the Gasthaus by the river where she waitressed her last year in high school. Ron was the dishwasher, got her the job, they used to sneak outside to the mud-leaf smell of the Thompson, fish-lipped smoke rings into each other's mouths.

"You are shy. Not like other women."

"Which other women?"

"Tourists: Swedish, Danish, French, German."

"Well, Canadian women don't remove their clothes at the drop of a hat."

"Why?"

"It's a cold country."

"So is Sweden."

"You are a brat."

"Am I?" he asks, unzipping his pants and stepping out of them. His briefs are just that. Navy blue. He walks to the lip of the cenote. His bum, she has to admit, is quite nice, high and just a little round. He stands surveying the water.

She wants to be in that water. Cathy and Jorge are obviously not coming. She'll wait until Tomás goes in. The teddy will dry off; she'll put it in her purse, wash it and later sneak it back into Cathy's bag.

Tomás raises himself on his toes, then dives in.

She counts to ten. She counts to twenty. Where the hell is he? Does he even know how deep it is under the surface?

He's been under half a minute.

"Tomás!"

Can the guy even swim? Maybe the pool leads to an underground cave, maybe he's trapped, can't find his way out. She strips off her blouse and skirt.

Forty-five seconds.

She dives in. Breaststrokes furiously down but it's dark, she can't see. Her breath gone, she plunges up into air.

He's floating on his back, a few feet to her right.

"Christ," she splutters. "I thought you were drowning."

"I told you I was a diver."

"Well you scared me half to death!"

She turns on her back, gulps in great draughts of air. Relax, Thelma. Enjoy the water cooling your back, the thin clouds running across the sky. She wonders if the cenote leads into a tunnel and out to the sea. Wonders if the diving gods at Tulum ever swim over here from the Yucatan peninsula, through the turquoise water of the Caribbean Sea. Setting out from that little cove there where she found herself swimming one drunken morning, many, many years ago.

Saved when she didn't need saving.

She flips over and dives under the cool water, feeling it stream through her hair, frustration and sweat slipping off like a layer of skin. How long can she hold her breath? Can she swim from one side of the cenote to the other without stopping? When she was a girl, she could swim the length of the pool in Riverside Park. A water baby, her dad called her.

She used to pretend to be a mermaid. When her dad called her out of the water, she'd say she had no legs, she couldn't walk on land. And he said, too bad, he guessed mermaids couldn't eat fudgesicles. He was going to the concession to fetch one for himself, so if she wanted one, she'd have to grow legs quickly.

"Yoo hoo, Thelma! Tomás!"

Cathy and Jorge are standing at the cenote's edge. Cathy has removed her t-shirt, revealing a bra and bikini underpants the same colour as the teddy Thelma's nicked. Cathy is curvy, a Mayan Goddess, the young Ixchel. She raises her hands over her head and arcs gracefully into the water, legs together, toes pointed. Jorge dives after her. Waves bounce off the cenote walls.

———

IN THE SUN. Tomás beside her. The hair on his chest looks soft and springy, like a little baby's. She can feel the heat radiating off his skin.

"What is that?" she points to a bag beside him.

"Clay. I found it in a bank by a stream."

"A stream? Where?" She sits up.

"Near the caserio. I brought some back."

"What are you going to do with it?"

"I could make a mask of your face."

She laughs. "I don't think so."

Water drips from Thelma's hair onto her shoulders, trickles down her breasts. She thinks to pull the teddy away from her body but doesn't.

"It seems that Canadian women do remove their clothes."

"I haven't removed them all."

"And the pieces still on are very nice."

"Thank you."

"You know Frida Kahlo?"

"Yes."

"Each portrait she painted was a mask."

"A mask?"

"Of her own face."

"Oh."

"Look at this clay," he says, taking some from the bag. "It is the perfect consistency for your mask. May I try?"

She doesn't say no.

Gently but firmly, he strokes the cool clay onto her cheeks, around her chin, her nose, her mouth, his fingers smooth and firm.

In Mexican folklore, Professor Smythe said, people who die in childbirth go to the House of the Sun. People who die by drowning go to the paradise in the east, ruled by the rain god.

People who die of natural causes go to Mictlan—the place where heaven and the underworld join—and wear their ideal face. And into eternity, the chosen wear their own face.

Which one did her father wear? Which will she?

———

In Mexico, they found a cenote. The girls slathered themselves in baby oil and lay baking on the grass, while the boys passed beers back and forth and then dared each other to dive in. Dr. Smythe read under a ceiba tree. Thelma sat near him, reading her notes from that morning's supplementary lecture about the paddler Gods who piloted canoes containing the souls of the dead across the Milky Way then steered them down a waterfall and into the depths of the watery underworld.

———

WHY DOES HE want to make a mask for me? He could just like you, Thelma. He could be looking for a Canadian girlfriend. A sugar mama. No, he's married.

The mask finished, she takes a small mirror out of her purse. Her nose is a bit big, true, but her teeth are good, white and straight and she does have a nice smile. She spies some postcards she bought in Havana. Fishes one out, a bare-chested man holding up a marlin on a beach at sunset, above him the slogan: Cuba: a paradise you'll remember.

*Dear Gisela,* she writes,

*You probably think I've forgotten all about you. But I haven't, of course, mi amiga. Wish you were here. I've met a woman named Cathy, from Calgary. She's a talker. Funny the people you meet, in foreign places. Right now we're in...*

Where exactly are we, Thelma wonders. Somewhere on the Zapata peninsula?

*...near the Bay of Pigs. Enroute to Cienfuegos. I hope the girls aren't giving you any trouble about the dusting. If so, get their names and I'll talk to them! I ho...*

Her pen scratches to a halt. She shakes it then scribbles on the corner of the postcard but the ink is finished. She puts the pen and postcard down, continues the message in her head:

*How is the bunny? Wally is making progress on...*Why mention Wally at all?

"Thelma."

Tomás is back from a jaunt to the car to check on Roberto, wearing clothes now. His jeans brush her thigh as he sits down beside her.

"Is the car ready?"

"Ahorita."

"How soon?"

"Quite soon."

"Aha. That clarifies things."

"You liked the water?"

"Yes."

"And now you are drying up?"

"One might say that."

"It is not a good thing to be drying up?"

"Not for a woman of my age."

"Why is that?"

"It means I'm getting old, becoming like a raisin, an old prune."

"But you are not an old prune. You are young and red like a new grape."

"Red?"

"Your skin."

"I'm burning!"

"Si, you are on fire. Perhaps you should go back in the water."

But the teddy is almost dry and she doesn't want to get it wet again. And she still needs to figure out how to wash it and get it back into Cathy's bag.

"Brat."

He smiles. White teeth, that wolfish grin.

# CHAPTER 25

*Cuba*

THEIR LEGS DANGLE in space, over the cenote.

"What colour would you call the sky, Thelma?" She looks up at it. "Hm. Maybe cornflower blue."

"There is a painting by Alexander Deineka, *Sleeping Child with Cornflowers.* He painted it in 1932. It is a beautiful painting of a naked child asleep in front of a vase full of these flowers. Maybe I will do a painting of you and call it: *Lady with Cornflowers.*"

"Flattery will get you everywhere. How long did you study art in Leningrad?"

"Four frozen years."

"Were your parents artists?"

"No. My parents came from a little town near Santiago in Oriente province, Dos Caminos. My mamá was a teacher."

"And your father?"

"He was a hero of the revolution."

"Impressive."

"Yes. My papá was the oldest of seven children. He was smart, although he only had a grade three education. He left school to work at the sugar mill. My mamá helped him with his reading and writing; she introduced him to Zola and Voltaire in Spanish translation though she could also read and write French. They got married and two months after I was born, my father went into the Sierra Maestras."

"To fight?"

"Yes. When los guerilleros came down from the mountains, they came through the main street of our town, some on mules, some on carts, some walking. A dirty man with a long beard, who smelled of smoke and sweat, picked me up and hugged all the air out of me, calling me Tomásito."

"Your father?"

He nods. "We moved to Havana where my papa worked in the Ministry of Agricultura and my mama taught school until she died in 1967."

"You were young when you lost your mother."

"Yes."

"That must have been hard."

"Si. That is just what Olga, my wife, my ex-wife said when I told her this."

"So you're, uh, divorced? From Olga?"

"Yes. In 1988, she went back to Leningrado on a teacher exchange. It was supposed to be for six months. After five, I received a letter. She'd met a Russian man, she was pregnant, and they wanted to be married."

"I'm sorry."

He closes his eyes, shakes his head. "Yes, I am sorry, also."

"So do you still paint? I mean, when you're not driving an underground taxi."

She's heard professionals like teachers make only about twelve dollars a month. She assumes he's taken up taxi driving because it's more lucrative.

"I do."

"What happened after Olga left?"

"This part maybe you don't want to hear."

"Well, if you don't want to tell me..."

"Do you want to hear it?"

"Sure, yes, I do," she says, looking over at him. He's staring vacantly across the cenote.

"After Olga deserted me my life went into a spiral. When I got the letter from her, I drank two bottles of rum. The next day I drank two more. And two more and two more. You see where I'm going. Straight to hell. I kept teaching, though I could hardly string a coherent sentence together. Finally, I lost my teaching job, but because my father was a hero of the revolution, my chief gave me a job as groundskeeper at the institute. He saved me art supplies; paper and tubes of paint and brushes left by visiting foreign artists. He encouraged me to paint myself out of whatever torture I was in. Instead, I slept with his wife. I got fired. One morning I woke up in the cárcel, the jail. I couldn't remember how I got there. I thought, one morning I won't wake up at all. I went home and poured my bottles into the toilet."

Oh. Jesus. Poor man. She touches his arm. "I'm sorry, Tomás."

"I haven't had a drink since then."

"That took a lot of courage."

"Yes," Tomás says bitterly. "Hurray for me. Brave Tomás, battling his demonios. Just like our national hero, Martí."

"Battling them through art, you mean?"

"No. Señor Martí is rumoured to have enjoyed his rum, his whiskey, though you won't, of course, find this in any Cuban history book."

"Why?"

"Is a rumour."

Below them, Jorge and Cathy splash water at each other.

"How did you meet Jorge?"

"El loco is an old friend from primary school. He became an English teacher but it is hard to survive on what the government pays us. So he applied for a license to drive cab. I mean, a nice, Japanese tourist cab. A Nissan. Not the cacharra naranja."

"Oh? A nice, Japanese tourist cab? With a suspension, air conditioning, comfy seats, springs that stay buried?"

He laughs. "You wonder, where is this nice tourist cab? Jorge lost his license because his sister, who is a pediatrician, went to a medical conference in Mexico and didn't come back. So Jorge came to me with a proposal to use my cacharra naranja as an unofficial tourist taxi."

"La naranja is yours? I thought that most Cubans couldn't have cars."

"In the 1980s, the government brought in some Ladas to sell to 'upstanding' professional people: doctors, military men, professors. I bought her for 300 pesos. This was before Olga left, before my disgrace."

"Oh."

"Olga was so excited when I got the car. 'Now we can go everywhere,' she said. And we did. On summer weekends, we'd drive out to Playas del Este, Santa Maria, Guanabo. Olgita would put on her best summer dress, a green chiffon scarf to protect her blond hair. We'd drive to the beach, or to Soroa to look at the orchids, to Pinar del Rio, to Matanzas to swim, and eat paella by the sea. I treated her like a baby and she ran beautifully. The car, I mean. Olga, too. After Olga left, the car she started to become cranky, refused to start, farted black smoke. I couldn't find parts, didn't even want to drive her. I put her up on blocks, in the alley behind my apartment."

"Why didn't you sell her?"

"That is illegal."

"So she sat in the back alley rusting into la cacharra naranja?"

"Yes."

"She wasn't always la cacharra naranja."

"No. Her first name, the one Olga christened her with, was el sueño naranja, the orange dream."

"The orange dream," Thelma repeats. "Lovely."

———

"Now," he says when they are settled in the shade under a huge banyan tree, away from the cenote because he insisted she was getting sunburned, "it is your turn."

"My turn for what?"

"To tell me the story of your life."

"What do you want to know?"

"The usual things in a story. The setting, the characters, the rising action, the climax though perhaps the climax hasn't happened yet."

She laughs. "OK first the setting. I was born and grew up in Kamloops, a little town in British Columbia where two rivers come together. I think I told you my dad was a geologist and my mom was a nurse. My dad was born there, too. His dad, my grandpa, worked as a logger."

"A town where two rivers come together. Very poetic. And what is your first memory of that town?"

"My first memory." Thelma pauses. She remembers walking to school, her hair in bouncy curls, wearing a red velvet dress with a white lace collar and a white bow in the back. She walked past the hospital with its *quiet* sign, recalls that she tried to walk more silently there. But there is an earlier memory...

"I'm not sure, even, if this is true, if my mother told me about it or if I imagined it, but I remember being in the river, the Thompson River. My dad was there, too, but he wasn't close, he was standing far away from me, holding out his hands. I remember him saying, 'come on, Thelma, swim to daddy.' I was trying to swim to him but the river was fighting me, the current kept pulling me further and further away from him, I couldn't reach him, though I tried and tried."

"How old were you?"

"Five maybe. I think I remember the panicky sound of my mom's voice when she yelled at my dad to get me."

"Were you drowning?"

"I don't think so."

"Were you afraid?"

"Yes. That's probably why it's my first memory."

"Your father is a hard man?"

"No. He wasn't."

"Wasn't?"

"He left me when I was young."

"Why?"

"He died."

"Like my mamá."

"Yes. I was eleven. But my father wasn't hard. He just wanted to make me tough." She sees her little girl self, wrapped in a towel, teeth chattering, shivering against her mother, trying to suck up her warmth.

"And are you tough, Thelma?"

"Yes, I am."

He picks a large, black seedpod from the ground. "I think you are like this seed. It is hard on the outside but if I break it, seed how soft the inside is."

"You think so."

"Yes, I think. And then?"

"I grew up, my mom remarried; I went to university, met Wally, studied archeology."

"So you are a detective of the past."

"No, actually, I'm a manager for the city of Calgary."

"You also studied management?"

"I took some night courses."

"So you are an archeologist working as a manager. A business woman."

"Listen, I'm not an archeologist. I, I didn't finish my degree. I dropped out of school."

Tomás frowns. "You had bad marks?"

"No, I had excellent marks."

"Then why?"

Why has she told him this when she hasn't told anyone else about not finishing her degree? Not her mom, Peter, or even Wally.

"I can't answer that, Tomás. I really don't know."

———

SOMETHING IS DRIPPING. She opens her eyes. Cathy.

"I can't believe it!" Cathy kneels down.

"What?"

"I have the same one. The Bay? Mid-winter sale?"

What is she going on about? Oh, Jesus, she's forgotten to put her blouse back over the teddy. She quickly sits up and wraps herself in Tomás' towel.

"Um, yes."

"Did you buy the matching bra and undies?"

"Uh, no. Just the teddy."

"It looks good on you."

"Thanks."

Cathy stretches her hands over her head. Her stomach is flat as a girl's.

"Isn't it glorious here? Next time I am definitely bringing my baby."

"You have a baby?" You left your baby at home? Thelma would never do that.

"No I mean Sara. She hates that I still call her baby. I love her to death. I guess I just love kids. I'd have ten of them, Thelma, if I could. I absolutely adore their soft little faces, how they smell, their sense of wonder about everything. If Sara were here, she'd be peppering me with questions about this cenote. How it was made. What geological period it's from. I couldn't answer that one. The only geological period I can remember is cretaceous. Do you remember any?"

"Precambrian, Paleozoic, Mesozoic, Cenozoic, those are the eras. The cretaceous is in the Mesozoic era, after Jurassic and Triassic, I believe."

"Wow, where did you learn that?"

"My dad."

"He taught you well."

"Your daughter would have fun in Cuba."

"Oh, she would! She'd play with the Cuban kids. Aren't they darling, the little girls especially, with those wiggly braids all over their heads? Did you ever want them, Thelma?"

"Wiggly braids all over my head?" She giggles.

"Kids."

"Yes, I did."

"Oh. But you..."

"Couldn't," Thelma finishes for her. "Yes, that's right."

How old would he be, her boy who didn't get to be born? Twenty-three?

Would he be filling out grad school applications and scholarship forms? Working evenings at a coffee shop? Perhaps he'd be an alternative, 'save the rainforest' kind of kid. Would he have her temper, her bullshit detector, her ability to make and concede a well-argued point? Would he dye his hair platinum blonde, the roots shouting *don't be thinking this is natural?* And what color would those roots be? Wally's strawberry blond, the white-blond of her young girlhood?

Thelma used to dream that she was living on her own in a basement apartment, the same apartment, in fact, that her friend Marianne rented on the bottom floor of the house on Battle Street owned by a widow: what was her name, Mrs. Canelli? Mrs. Costanza? The widow couldn't speak much English, but grew Roma tomatoes, which she left in brown paper bags on Marianne's bottom step. The apartment had one window where light seeped in, grudgingly, between the hours of ten and two. In the dream, Thelma was sleeping on a futon mattress on the concrete floor. Then she woke up with the feeling that something was wrong with the baby. She rushed over to the crib where he lay, still and blue, under the afghan she'd crocheted in high school for Marianne's baby, put her hand on his belly, her ear to his tiny mouth, felt nothing. Picked him up and kissed his tiny face until he opened his mouth and wailed.

"Do you think he's finished?"

"Finished?"

"Fixing the car, silly."

"Oh. I don't know."

She hasn't thought of that dream in years. She had it every few months from the age of 21 until when? Her late thirties? She'd never dreamed her baby older than three or four months. She'd always dreamed him in Marianne's baby's white crib, under the lilac-coloured afghan. She didn't dream his first word, his first step. Didn't dream his first day of school, her boy scared and clinging to her leg, refusing to let go. Didn't dream him into grade two or three or four, reading the books she loved as a child: *Charlotte's Web, Ramona the Pest, the Narnia Chronicles.* Didn't dream him checking to see if the green tomatoes on the windowsill had turned red yet. Didn't dream him helping her to make sourdough bread, drawing the starter out from its dark hiding place in the back of the fridge.

Didn't dream him as a twelve-year-old redheaded boy with freckles and scabby knees, asking about his dead grandpa.

"Hey, Thelm, are you OK?"

"Fine."

She fumbles in her purse for sunglasses. Cathy pats her shoulder.

"Don't worry, everything will work out. Tomás said Cuban mechanics are geniuses, they can fix anything. We can probably be in Cienfuegos by evening. Maybe we'll even find Wally tonight."

She nods.

"Roberto will come and get us the minute the car is ready. Listen, I hear something, it sounds like an engine."

This is the way Cathy would comfort a child in her class or her own daughter.

She sniffs. "It's not Wally. It's not the car."

Cathy's puts her arm around Thelma. "What is it then?"

When did she finally put her childlessness down? On her fortieth birthday? Her forty-first? Or did she lay it down gradually, waking up at forty-four and realizing that it was too late.

"Nothing."

"Not nothing."

"I was thinking about a little boy. A skinny, redheaded boy with freckled arms."

"A real boy?"

"Real to me."

———

THIS MEMORY: a sweating avocado. The pieces on the orange plastic plate have a delicate layer of water on their tops like the moustache of wet above Thelma's lip. She sits across from her father at a picnic table, watching his hands fast-shuffle the cards, deal her a lightning seven. He turns over the crib board, slides open the metal piece that holds the pegs and takes out two blue for him, two red for her.

Her mother puts a plate of crackers beside the avocado. Thelma can smell sausages grilling, hear them hissing in the black-bottomed camping pan on the grate over the fire. A kid rides by their campsite on a banana seat bike, ringing his bell. Light pencils through the willow branches above the picnic table. Bathing suit elastic hurts where it rubs against her sunburned legs.

A shout from someone down by the lake. Help! More voices, help me! They run down a grassy hill. There's a blue baby on a blanket in the sand.

Her dad drops to his knees beside the baby. His mouth on the baby's, blowing, then pressing the tiny chest with his fingertips. Blowing, pressing. The baby coughs. The baby cries. The baby comes back to life.

**3**

# CHAPTER 26

*Cuba*

THE FIRST THING she does after the rust bucket has burped down the hill in the dark and farted to a stop outside the Rancho Luna Hotel, after she and Cathy have checked in and rolled their suitcases up to their respective rooms, is call Gisela.

"Digame."

"Gisela, it's me Thelma." The line crackles.

"Thelma, que tal? I was just thinking of you and Wally, we are buried in snow here, how you doing? How is Cuba? Where are you now?"

"We're—I'm in Cienfuegos. Can you hear me?"

"Mas o menos, amiga. More or less. You said you are in Cienfuegos?"

"Yes," Thelma yells.

"It is a beautiful city. I went when I was thirteen. We were doing volunteer work at the botanical gardens. Have you been to José Martí park, the Terry Tomás theatre?"

"No, we, we just arrived."

"Oh, I wish I could be there. When I have my Canadian passport, for sure I will go. It has been snowing for so many days; it is so cold my car won't start."

"Well, the cars here don't start either, my dear. Or, like a pirate taxi, they start but they don't finish."

Gisela laughs. "Si, you are learning about Cuba very fast." She sighs. "I hope you are taking many pictures so I can indulge my nostalgia when you return." She pronounces it nost-al- he-a.

"Um hm," Thelma says, though she hasn't taken a single picture. Wally has the damn camera.

"Listen, Gisela, I need to ask you. Have you seen Rosa?"

"No."

"Do you know where she is?"

"Not at this moment."

"I mean, is she in Canada? In Calgary?"

Gisela doesn't answer. Thelma's air stops somewhere in her upper chest, refusing to move.

"Please just tell me, Gisela."

"Sorry, I was distracted. I saw someone walking to my door but they didn't give a knock. Is that right? Give a knock?"

"Knock. They didn't knock. Gisela, this is very important. When is the last time you saw Rosa?"

"Sunday. We went to see a movie, it was very sad and..."

Wally left Wednesday, she left Friday. "You saw her on Sunday? This past Sunday?"

"Yes. She was very excited to have finished her collection of poemas. She is excited to show Wally..."

There is a long static-y hiss and in that hiss Thelma can feel her body easing: her shoulders release, her chest relaxes. He is not with Rosa.

"Thelma, are you still there?"

"I am here."

"Do you have a message for Rosa?"

"No, uh, yes, tell her, tell her I'm glad she's in Calgary. I mean I'm happy she's there and has finished her book."

"OK"

"And thank you, my friend."

"For what?"

"For everything. I have to go. I will talk to you soon."

He is with a woman. Who may be a beautiful profesora. But who is not Rosa.

———

"GOOD MORNING, Thelma. Did you enjoy the down?"

"Pardon me, Tomás?"

"You enjoyed the down."

"The down-stairs bar?"

"The sunrise."

"Yes. No. I didn't see it."

"How was your sleep?"

"Fine. How was yours?"

"Not so fine. Jorge's cousin owns very lumpy beds."

"That's too bad."

He touches her shoulder. "You got burned yesterday. You should put some cream on that."

His hand lingers, flushing heat down her arm.

"Yoo hoo, Tomás, Thelma, there you guys are!" Cathy swoops across the marble floor, wearing a daffodil covered sundress.

"Hi," says Thelma. "I love your dress. Yellow suits you."

"Thanks! I made it. A matching one for Sara, too. Good morning, Tomás. Where's Jorge?" Cathy asks, looking around.

"He's getting petrol," says Tomás.

"He told me last night we should enquire about the professor at the university here, if that's what you want to do, Thelma?"

"Of course. That's why we came here. To find my husband." She slides her shoulder out from under Tomás hand.

"Well let's get some brekkie first. Do you want to join us, Tomás?"

"No, thank you. I have eaten already."

Has he or is he just embarrassed because they will be paying? Or perhaps he's not allowed in the dining room. She will sneak him some food: ham, bacon, links of sausages.

Gisela said meat is rarely on the Cuban ration card.

———

A TOUR GROUP have arrived en masse, and insinuated themselves into the buffet line-up. A large woman butts in front of Thelma. The woman's two companions wedge themselves between Cathy and the hot table. A disembodied arm reaches in front of her.

"Only I need eggs," the arm's owner mutters.

"Only I need eggs, too," Thelma mutters back, moving closer to the large woman so no one else can jump the queue. She fills her plate with eggs, several helpings of a spam-like substance labeled jamon/prosciutto/jambon/schinken/ham, several buns, tomatoes and orange slices and follows Cathy to a table by the window, away from the hordes.

A trio of musicians, with small tres guitars, launch into a rousing version of *Yolanda*.

Eternamente Yolanda.

"I love how this country is so full of music! Don't you, Thelma?"

Thelma nods. The spam is rubbery and gelatinous and the eggs dry. Completely ravenous, Cathy's papaya of yesterday having been long since digested, and the only thing she could get when they arrived late last night was a ham and cheese sandwich, she chows down.

"You're hungry, eh, Thelm?"

"Aren't you?"

"Not really. I lose my appetite in the heat. So, did you do anything last night after I retired. I mean, did you guys go to the disco or anything?"

"Please, I haven't been to a disco since the 80s."

Cathy smiles coyly. Is she imagining it or is Cathy humming *Ring my Bell*.

"Well, have you, Cathy?"

"What?"

"Been to a disco lately?"

"Oh. No. But I think you're avoiding my question, Thelm. What did you and Tomás do last night?"

"I went for a swim in the pool. I watched an interpretive ballet about the sugar harvest. I called a friend. I have no idea what Tomás did."

Cathy smiles. "Just asking, sweetie."

———

JORGE IS HIS USUAL solicitous self, holding the door to the front seat of the bruised orange open for her.

"Como estás, Thelma?"

"Bien, Jorge. Y tu?"

"Tambien. I have been making enquiries, Thelma, about your husband."

"Wonderful. Thank you. I am very anxious to find him."

"There is a history lecture at the university today. Your husband and the profesora may attend. We will go to this lecture, also."

"We'll be learning Cuban history from a real Cuban historian."

"But it will be in Spanish, Cathy."

"Oh. That's right."

"We should find him today, your husband," says Jorge.

"If he is here," adds Tomás.

"And you will be happy, Thelma?" asks Jorge.

"Of course."

The spring pokes her bum. Tomás turns the key, the engine coughs then dies. He pulls the choke, turns the key again. Nothing. Pumps the gas pedal, turns, the engine finally sputters to life.

Thelma pulls two napkins of food from her bag and hands one to Jorge.

"Breakfast."

"I have eaten but...." He unfolds the napkin. "Jamon! Thank you, Thelma."

Tomás shifts into first and they roar up the hill, trailing plumes of black smoke. Whatever Roberto did to repair the beast, it doesn't look like the fixing will last for very long.

"And for me, Thelma? Do you have some food for your favorite diver?" He steers the car around a large pothole.

"Because that's the first pothole you've missed, yes, I have some food for you." She hands him the napkin.

"I can't eat and drive, Thelma. Can you feed me?"

"No! Put the napkin in your lap."

"But I can't shift, avoid potholes and eat at the same time."

She takes a piece of ham from the napkin, raises her fingers to his lips. He nibbles her fingers.

"Take it," she mutters.

———

THEY WAIT BESIDE a cement bust of José Martí while Jorge takes Cathy to find a bathroom. Thelma stares at Martí's prominent forehead, receding hairline, thick-waxed moustache and far- away looking eyes.

"He died for love," says Tomás.

"Martí did?"

"Yes."

"For love of his country, for Cuba?"

"Certainly. But perhaps for a woman's love, also."

"A woman?"

"They say he was in love with a girl from Guatemala. Her name was Maria Garcia Tomayo Granados. Her father was a hero of the Guatemalan revolution. Martí went to Guatemala in 1877, during his exile from Cuba, to teach. He and Maria fell in love but he was already betrothed to a wealthy Cuban woman."

"So they couldn't get married?"

"No. It is said he went to his arranged marriage as to a funeral. Years later, in New York, Martí wrote a famous love poem about Maria called *La Niña de Guatemala. Como de bronce cadente/al beso de despedida/era su frente la frente/que mas he amado en mi vida!*"

"I got *kiss, goodbye* and *life*. You'll have to translate the rest."

"Like burning bronze, the kiss of goodbye, was her face, the face I've loved the most in my life."

Whose face has she loved most? Her father's? Her mom's? Wally's?

"What happened to Maria?"

"She died."

"Of what?"

"Of love."

"You can't actually die of love."

"No? Maybe what we mean by love is something, something that happens in the body. Many deaths we attribute to other things: a heart attack, a stroke, a miscarriage. But how can the blood keep flowing through our arteries, keep moving through this thing we call this body, if there is no heart to keep it pumping?"

Shaghaf: love that nests in the chambers of the heart.

———

SHE IS LYING on Tomás' jacket, on the grass near the statue. He is beside her. A gentle sun beats down on them. She stretches her arms above her head. Tomás sighs and she turns toward him. His hand is on his thigh. The other moves slowly to her throat, her shoulder, chest. Buttons slip from their moorings.

Her body's a puzzle, sun and shade, brown and red and white. Wind and fingers whispering across her arm, breast, belly. Burning.

The rough trunk of palm. Slippery.

"Thelm? Are you sleeping?"

Tomás' hands on the grass, where they've always been. Cathy, squatting beside her.

"Sorry we took so long. It's a maze in there but we found the bathroom and Jorge found the lecture hall, too. Let's go."

———

THE HEAVY WOODEN door creaks shut behind them. The basement hall is cool like a cave. Rows of metal chairs full of chattering students face the lectern. They sit in the empty back row. At the front, a small woman stands behind the podium, arranging papers. Her hair is short, and dyed a strange purple colour. Aubergine? Glasses hang from a chain around her neck. The woman's nose is long and thin, her cheekbones high, her lips an improbable carmine. Well, not that improbable given her hair colour. She wears a blue blazer and white blouse and appears to be in her mid to late fifties, though it's hard to tell, the only light provided by a single naked bulb and a thin ribbon of sun slanting through a high window.

The woman clears her throat. The hubbub dies down. She begins speaking quickly but clearly, her voice echoing off the cement walls. Thelma wonders how it is possible for the woman to be able to speak so rapidly yet distinctly, allowing Thelma to pick out words that she knows: viaje, nave, reina. Travel, ship, queen.

She searches the sea of heads in front of her. Brown, black, blond heads, large heads, round heads, small heads, long heads. But no reddish blond head. No husband shaped head.

Plata, trabajo, hidalgo. Money, work. The son of someone: a conquistador, a rural Spaniard with an exaggerated lineage. Hernando.

Outside a radio is being tuned. A woman's voice sings mi amor, mi vida. A tired fan circles the dusty air. Above the woman's head are Fidel and Che overseeing the class. Below their portraits, a slogan, black letters on a white banner, reads: El primer deber de un revolucionario es ser educado. The first duty of a revolutionary is to be educated.

Wally, she tells herself, look for Wally. She scans the rows. There. At the end of the first row, a strawberry-blond head.

But the hair on that head is shorter than her husband keeps his. Would Wally's Spanish be up to understanding this fast talking woman whose voice fills the room-cave?

Tomás knee grazes hers, lingering then moving away.

More words she knows: Paraíso y tierra. Heaven and earth. Oro and fuego. Gold and fire. But she can't make sense of what the lecture is about.

Then, as suddenly as she started, the profesora stops speaking. Students close their books, stand. The room fills with chatter. The strawberry-blond head bends to retrieve something from the ground. The head turns and she sees he is a young man, not Wally. Still, she watches the student's back as he makes his way down the cement stairs towards the profesora.

Cathy leans over. "Do you see Wally, Thelma? Is he here?"

"I'm looking."

"What about that guy, going up the stairs?"

She shakes her head. She wills her knee to move away from Tomás', but her knee doesn't listen.

"There," Jorge gestures to a pale man across the room.

"Uh uh."

"Behind you? The guy in the baseball cap?" asks Cathy.

"No."

She turns back to the podium and sees that the profesora has disappeared.

———

THELMA DOES NOT believe in fate. Does not believe that there is a man for every woman, a woman for every man, that things happen for a reason. Otherwise why would her father—who walked through the bush, over the Coast mountains with a backpack full of rocks, a Brunton compass, some dried food, a rock hammer, maps, hand lens, hydrochloric acid, water bottle; who could build a lean-to, a snow shelter; make fire from the sun and a mirror; navigate through a snowstorm—have died?

She doesn't believe in fate.

Yet she is she lying on a chaise lounge on the hotel's beach and wondering whether Wally was fated to have met the profesora, she Tomás?

Her father used to sing a song to her: *Cast your Fate to the Wind.* How did it go? A month of nights/a year of days/Octobers drifting into Mays.

Wally cast his fate to the wind. Maybe that's what Thelma's doing. Because she hasn't called the Palco to see if he's back there. Hasn't called his mother or her mom or their answering service to see if he's left a message.

She didn't move her knee.

A wind springs up, carrying the smell of fish. Beside her, Cathy pulls her chaise into a sitting position.

"I had the most marvelous dream last night, Thelma! I was here, in Cuba, in a yellow schoolroom with camellias on my desk that the children had brought for me and the class was full of beautiful boys and girls, including my Sara. They stood up and began reading the poems of José Martí, the ones Tomás recited to us. Outside the classroom window, I could see the ocean and the cacharra naranja. You and Jorge and Tomás were inside, you were waiting for me to finish teaching, waiting to take me on an adventure!"

"Interesting."

"Yeah. It was so vivid, so real. When I'm having such a good dream, I just hate to wake up. Do you ever feel like that, Thelma?"

"Yes."

"I wonder if Jorge and Tomás will know to look for us out here."

"They probably won't be allowed here."

"Why?"

"The beach is for 'guests only', I'll go inside in a second to check for them."

"You're right about the beach Thelma. You're absolutely right." She pauses. "Can I tell you something about yourself?"

"Depends what it is."

"Don't worry. It's something good."

She shrugs. "Sure. If you want."

"I admire you."

"Why's that?"

"Because you're a realist. You see how things work."

"Well, thanks."

"You're welcome."

"Aren't you a realist, Cathy?"

"No. Not at all. I make up my life. It's wonderful in my head. But it can be disappointing when it doesn't work out the way I've imagined it."

"If you don't hope for much, you won't get disappointed."

"Do you truly believe that, Thelma?" Cathy sounds shocked.

"No, of course not. I was just kidding."

"Oh. Well. Good. Because I think that would be a very hard way to live. Not hoping for anything."

"Maybe. Yes. It would be." It is. But Thelma has hope. Sometimes, she does.

"Thelm."

"Um hm."

"I, uh, well, I was just wondering, do you think we'll find Wally and the profesora?"

"I don't know."

"Do you want us to?"

Thelma looks out to where the horizon and ocean meet.

"Of course you do! That was a stupid question. I talk sometimes before I think. Sorry."

"It's OK"

"Listen, I was thinking, about Jorge and Tomás. They've been so good to us, why don't we take them out for a fancy dinner tonight at a paladar. We could have lobster and shrimp, that rice and beans dish, what's it called?"

"Moros and christianos."

"Moors and Christians. That's it. We could order yucca and those delicious fried green bananas?"

"Platanos."

"Platanos, yes. We'll have a feast. What do you think?"

She's not sure. It would be nice way to thank Jorge and Tomás. But it would also mean their journey is ending.

"If you don't want to..."

"No, I want to."

"OK, then, it's settled."

Cathy picks up her novel. Carol Shield's *The Republic of Love*, about a single woman, a mermaid researcher and her thrice married boyfriend. It's a lovely book, Thelma recalls, full of sweetness and heartache. A book with a happy ending.

Thelma stands and walks down to the water's edge, her toes sinking into the hot, black sand. She stands in the water watching a ship sail out toward the horizon and thinks of Isabel watching Hernando's ship until it disappeared.

A cool wind stirs the water, sends goose pimples coursing along Thelma's arms. Did Isabel believe in fate? In happy endings?

Does she?

———

THE PALADAR HAS high pressed tin ceilings and four tables covered in white linen tablecloths. Heavy armoires from another century loom out from the walls. The linoleum floor is covered by a faded and threadbare Persian rug. They're seated in a corner, away from the other table of tourists whose table is filled with beer bottles and who are speaking in loud, Teutonic voices.

Thelma is wearing a short turquoise sundress with spaghetti straps that Cathy said was smashing. Cathy sports a pink, lace-trimmed dress with an empire waist and cap sleeves. Jorge and Tomás are neat and handsome in short sleeved shirts and dark dress pants.

The waiter brings three Hatuey beers and a Tropicola for Tomás. Music, *Dos Gardenias Para Ti*, slides in from the kitchen. She remembers dancing to it at home while trying to coerce Wally to prepare something scrumptious for dinner. He did, as she recalls. Pork tenderloin with mango sauce.

"Any news?" Cathy asks.

Jorge grins. "We have succeeded."

"You have?" Thelma asks, almost knocking over her beer.

"So? Tell us!" Cathy exclaims.

"We have found the profesora," Jorge announces.

"Where? Was she the woman giving the lecture?"

"No."

"You've seen her?"

"No, not seen her, Cathy," Tomás admits. "But we know where she is staying. We went there and she had gone away for the day, but we left a message that we will go back tomorrow."

"And Wally? Have you seen him?"

"Pardon me, Thelma?"

She clears her throat. "Have you seen Wally?"

"No. But Tomás and I have a lead, an important lead. We will go to the La Cueva tonight. It is a disco in a cave in the town of Trinidad. A man who may be Wally was seen there last night. Trinidad is seventy-two kilometres from here but I think it is worth it to go, to follow the lead."

"Yes, let's go, Thelm," says Cathy.

"To a cave? We might find my husband in a cave disco? My husband who hates loud music, who doesn't like to dance, who gets claustrophobic in confined places?"

There's a ruckus at the next table. "Carvacas. Mas carvacas!" a voice demands.

"Cows, sir? Meat?" the confused waiter asks.

Tomás hisses the waiter over. "Oyé, compañero, ellos quieren cervecas." Listen, they want beer.

"Claro, gracias."

"Yes, we might find him at La Cueva, but if we don't..." Jorge pauses for dramatic effect. "If we don't find him there, he will be visiting the botanical garden here in Cienfuegos tomorrow."

"Wow, you're amazing, Jorge." Cathy pats his arm.

"How did you find this out?"

"Radio bemba, Thelma. Lip radio, I think you say in English."

Thelma stares at her knife and fork. Wally's been seen at a disco. Dancing.

With a woman. No, Jorge didn't say that. He didn't say anything about women and dancing.

Fingers graze her hand. "Are you alright?"

"Fine, Tomás."

"You are very white."

"I'm OK"

"You are more than OK. But are you ill"?

She shakes her head, blinks. Don't cry. He's found, he's safe. He was out dancing last night. Dancing when he should have been calling you. Maybe he was calling you. You weren't where you were supposed to be either Thelma.

Tomás slides something into her hand. A silk handkerchief. She takes it, dabs at the corner of her eyes.

"Camarones," says the waiter, placing a sizzling plate of them at Thelma's elbow.

"Thank you," she says, whether to the waiter or Tomás and Jorge, she isn't sure. She picks up her water, puts it down. Sits on her hand to stop it from shaking.

Is she grateful? Or has that fate-carrying wind changed direction?

## CHAPTER 27

*Kamloops, 1972*

BREATHING. A SHADOW above her bed, bending down, touching her shoulder.

"Wake up, sweetie. We have to go." Her mom's voice, but not. High and panicky.

"Why?"

"The hospital called."

"Did dad wake up?"

"No."

"What happened?"

"Get up, honey. Quickly. Let's go."

In the sliver light from the hallway, the glow from the white owl night light at the foot of her bed, her mother's face a black and white jigsaw puzzle.

Thelma still in pajamas, wrapped in her mom's wool sweater because they can't find Thelma's coat because Thelma didn't hang it up because they have to hurry.

The car speeding past black houses, tires shushing over wet pavement, down Columbia street. Her mom whispering, "wait, wait my love, hold on," but not to Thelma.

Through a red light.

They park behind a yellow cab, its driver sleeping against the seat, street lamp shining on his bald head.

Blinding lights in the corridor, her mother's icy hand. Pulling.

"Hurry up, Thelma Marie."

The tube is in his nose. His eyes are open; his body grey. They should turn the lights off, how can he sleep with them on?

Her mother puts her ear to his mouth, his chest.

"Careful, mom, don't hurt him. You're pulling on the nose tube."

Her mom is crying.

"Don't cry mom. He's just sleeping."

Blue lips.

"Tell the nurse, mama, he's cold."

His arm twitches.

"See, he's waking up."

Thelma leans forward. "Hi daddy, are you cold? Look your blanket slipped off, I'll get it for you, there, is that better? Are you feeling warmer now? It'll be OK, Mama will get the nurse; she'll turn the lights off for you and get you another blanket. There, you're all tucked in now. That's funny how you're sleeping with your eyes open. Night night, sleep tight, don't let the bed bugs bite. Papa? Dad? Mom said it's hard for you to talk. You don't have to talk. Just nod your head if you can hear me. OK? OK, dad. OK?"

"Thelma, sweetie..."

"I'm talking to dad!"

"He's..."

"Cold, I know. Get the nurse. Tell her, please. Tell her!"

———

The coffin was lowered by ropes, down, down, deep into the ground. Thelma didn't cry. Mom squished her fingers hard, too hard, wouldn't let go. Mom's kleenex floated to the ground like a white carnation.

"Don't cry mom," she whispered fiercely. "Don't!"

The priest talked about ashes and dust. Behind her Aunt Mary kept touching her on the head. Pat pat pat.

Her gran didn't cry either. She knew, too. That he wasn't gone. That he was coming back.

———

"I'M SORRY your dad had a heart attack and died." Tommy Fedowski was shuffling his feet in front of her desk.

"It wasn't a heart attack, it was a stroke."

"But he died, right?"

"No." Boys are so stupid. "He made a full recovery. He's on a field trip for work, in the Yukon; he's going to bring me back some gold."

"Real gold?"

"Yes, real gold. The streams up north are full of it. He found some last time."

"But my mom said she saw in the paper. Are you sure he didn't, uh, kick the bucket?"

"Don't you think I would know if my own father was dead, Tommy?"

———

"THELMA, HONEY, I need to talk to you."

"What about?"

"Come and sit beside me."

"Why?"

"We need to talk about your dad."

"What about him?"

"Honey, I know how hard this is for you, with dad gone. It's hard for me, too."

"He's been gone before, mom. We..." What did her mom always say when dad asked how things were while he was gone. "We managed."

Her mom starts petting Thelma's hair like she's a tiny kid or a dog or something.

"Sweetie, he's not coming back."

She pulls her head away. Her mother's hand hangs in the air.

"He died, Thelma."

"Liar," she says, is about to yell pants on fire when his voice comes into her head. Not the happy voice he uses when Thelma's moping around and saying things like other dads don't disappear for months at a time, and he says I'll be back soon, kitten. The time will race like a fire through August grass and before you know it I'll be back.

This voice is stern. This voice says stop.

———

She's lying on her bed in her room where she's been sent for being insubordinate which is a word for when you call your mother a liar, she guesses. Her dresser with the black holes burned into the top where she and Marianne burned incense and then forgot about it looms out of the dark. The curtains move. But her window isn't open. And there's no heat vent there. There's something at the end of her bed.

"Papa?"

"Your mom is sad."

"I know."

"Really sad."

"I know."

"Could you do me a favour? Could you swallow your pride?"

She does a gulp-y swallow like she always does when he says that. "Could you apologize tomorrow?"

———

SHE DOES.

But then her mother does more irritating things. Like leaving her dad's rock collection in Thelma's room.

Feldspar, mica, fool's gold, quartz, lavender coloured crystals, ammonites and agates.

Thelma puts it back where it belongs, where he likes it kept, on the table in the corner of the basement, beside his saws and drills, hammers and wrenches hanging on the wall above it.

Her mother packs up his clothes, puts the boxes in the garage.

Thelma takes them back to the house, unpacks them and puts them away. One day when she comes home from school, the tools are gone.

"You hate him," she screams at her mom.

It snows. The plane can't land to pick him up. But he'll be OK There's enough food at camp for another month.

Her mom takes her to a counselor. But not like the ones in junior high who help kids pick electives and stuff. He gives her crayons and paper and asks her to draw how she feels.

She asks for felts, pastels, pencil crayons. He doesn't have these. She won't draw with crayons. She hasn't used crayons since grade three!

———

DOC K WEARS JEANS, jean shirts and red earth shoes, she knows they are earth shoes because her dad has a pair just like them but not red, red is a spazzy colour.

Thelma brings her own pastels.

She draws a rainbow with a stream full of gold nuggets at one end. That ought to satisfy him.

Doc K examines it carefully, scratching his bushy sideburns, taking off his little round glasses.

"A rainbow. And what is this?"

Is he serious or just stupid?

"That would be the pot of gold at the end of the rainbow. Are you familiar with the Irish legend, sir?"

"Remember, there are no sirs here."

"Are you, Doc K?"

"That's better. Yes I am. Do you like rocks, Thelma?"

"Um hm."

"I understand your father left you his collection."

"He left it for me to look after while he's..."

"While he's?"

"I mean he left it for me."

"And does he have any gold in this collection?"

"Fool's gold. And other kinds of rocks, sir."

"Doc..."

"Doc K sir."

"So this pot of gold is your father's gold?"

"No. It's just a picture, sir, uh, Doc K. I can draw you another one if you want."

"No, no, that's fine, Thelma. When I asked you to tell me how you were feeling, why did you draw a rainbow?"

"I dunno." Cause it rained yesterday and I saw one at the end of our street.

"In the sky?"

Where else would a rainbow be?

"Yes."

"Is there anything else in that picture? In the sky?"

"No, sir, Doc K. Not that I know of. Well I could draw some birds or an angel if you want."

"An angel."

"Sure, if you want."

He smiles. She said the right thing.

# CHAPTER 28

*Cuba*

THE PATHWAY to the cave disco is paved with rocks and illuminated by colored lanterns.

Thelma and Tomás walk behind Jorge and Cathy, Thelma taking small steps so as not to snag a heel.

"You look lovely tonight, Thelma," says Tomás.

"Thank you. You look nice, too."

"Only nice. Not lovely or handsome or beautiful?"

She laughs.

"Maybe is not good for a man to be lovely or beautiful."

"No, a man can be beautiful. Have you ever seen Brad Pitt?"

"Yes, in *Seven Years in Tibet*."

"And you agree he is beautiful."

"Por supuesto." Of course.

Thelma stops to adjust her sandal strap. Tomás waits beside her. She wishes he weren't so attentive. No, maybe it's a good thing. It would serve Wally right to see a man paying attention to her. Now that he's practically found, not kidnapped or in imminent danger, she feels more entitled to her anger.

Couples stream around her: tourists, Cubans, Cubans and tourists together. She starts walking again but her sandal strap still rubs painfully against her sunburned heel.

"Darn shoes."

"May I carry them for you? Or perhaps I could carry you."

"I am hardly carrying size."

"I could try."

"I believe the appropriate response is 'you are a mere wisp of a thing,

I could carry you easily, with one hand tied behind my back.'"

"What is a mere wisp?"

"Tiny, petite."

"But I do not like tiny girls. There is nothing there to hold."

She smiles and loosens her wrap.

Cathy and Jorge wait for them at the cave's entrance where chalky white stalagmites grow on either side of a steep stone staircase.

Thelma's hand grazes the damp wall, touches something round and smooth. A shell? She hears the sound of water, dripping. The air gets hotter as they descend into the cave, music rises to meet them.

They enter a large cavern. At one end is a DJ on a platform. Below him is a wooden dance floor, ringed by tables and filled with people. A mirror ball dapples the floor, ripples off stalactites. She follows Tomás, Jorge and Cathy to a table beside the dance floor, slips into the chair Tomás holds out for her.

Music bounces off the walls, a song she's heard before, about a man who's been cuckolded. Or maybe it was a woman. The place is crowded with cubanas in short dresses and high heels; Cubanos in pressed dress shirts and pants; sunburned tourists in wrinkled cotton shirts and walking shorts, women in loose summer dresses salsa alone, or else dance freestyle with wild flinging of arms and legs. A Cuban man pulls a mickey from his pocket, drinks, wipes the top and hands the bottle to his partner.

A waiter appears, bends his ear to Jorge's mouth, disappears. Soon a bottle of rum, glasses and cans of Tropicola arrive, the cans glinting red and silver in the light from the mirror ball. Jorge pours generous measures of rum in two glasses, adds thin layers of cola and passes them to Cathy and Thelma. He pours Tropicola for Tomás, and straight rum for himself. She nods and smiles her thanks. Hard to hear and talk when it's so loud.

Sweat drips down Thelma's forehead. She wipes it with the back of her hand then looks around the tables for Wally. Too dark. If Wally is here, she'll have to spot him on the dance floor.

"Bienvenido compañeros y compañeras," the DJ booms. "Y un muy feliz cumpleaños a Berta, Berta de Alemania." A tall woman in a t-shirt and jeans stands and bows as the Cuban happy birthday song plays.

Thelma blows hair from her damp forehead, takes a long drink. The rum is sweet and cold. There are ice cubes in her glass. She shouldn't have ice, but she's too hot and thirsty to care. She takes another gulp, sucks the ice cubes, tonguing and rolling them around in her mouth. A new song begins, *Quizás*,

*Quizás, Quizás.* Jorge pours more rum in her glass and Thelma obediently drinks again, holding the sweet liquid in her mouth before letting it slide smoothly down her throat.

The temperature in the cave must be 35 degrees. She wants to ask Jorge to order them some water. But she'd have to shout across the table and that would be too much effort. She stares at the bottle of golden rum. Havana Club. Picks it up and squints at the picture above the red and white logo. It is La Giraldilla. Her Isabel wearing a crown, her scepter held out from her body. Still waiting. She must have had the patience of a saint. She was a saint. She should be canonized or whatever it is they do with saints. And her husband should have been thrown to the wolves. Or whatever wolf-like animal existed in Cuba at the time.

Thelma takes another long sip of her drink. Did this ambrosial liquid ever touch Isabel's mouth? This concoction of cane and sun? Enough musing, Thelma, she tells herself. Look for Wally.

On the dance floor a strobe light illuminates a body here, there. That man could be Wally she thinks, just as he's strobed into darkness. The man is flashed again. Not Wally. From across the table, Cathy says something she can't hear. Thelma shrugs her shoulders. Cathy yells and points to the bottle, Thelma nods and Tomás takes it and refills her glass. Then Jorge and Cathy stand up and disappear into the crowd on the dance floor.

She smiles at Tomás and he smiles back, his straight white teeth shining in the darkness. Stop staring, she chides herself. Watch the dance floor. She does. But she can't find Wally. Her glass of rum, that she can find. I'd rather have a bottle in front of me, than have to have a frontal lobotomy, ha-ha, she thinks.

"What are you grinning at?"

"Nothing."

Tomás puts a hand on her arm, how can his hand be so cool when it is so hot here?

"Would you care to dance?"

"I can't," she says. Meaning she's a bit tipsy already from the rum.

"I can teach you."

"No."

"Porque no?"

"OK, yes."

Hand on her back, Tomás guides her through the maze of tables and onto the floor. He puts his arm behind her back, takes her right hand.

"It goes like this: uno dos tres, uno dos tres," he says.

"Like this?"

"Si, bien, eso es, eso es." They dance slowly until she has a feel for the steps. "OK, now we try something else." He pushes her away, brings her back in, uno, dos, tres. He spins her around and around. Thelma feels light, like she's floating and she is suddenly, he's picked her up, she's off the ground watching her own ankles circling by. Then she's down and dizzy.

"I told you I could."

"Could what?"

"Teach you to dance."

She giggles. "Yes."

The music stops and he turns to leave. No. She wants to keep dancing. But he's not taking her back to the table; he's only leading her to a spot where there are fewer people.

The music begins again. Tomás pulls her toward him then pushes her gently away, she's meant to twirl, and somehow her body does, she's back, so close she can smell his aftershave, feel his heart, then she's away again, spinning, around and around and around she goes, where she stops nobody knows. Wally couldn't lead; when they danced, she couldn't tell what she was supposed to do, where he wanted her to go. What a pleasure to dance with a man who knows how to do move, who makes her graceful. Tomás spins her again. She's on a swing, winding up, unravelling.

When the song ends, Tomás leads her to the roped off edge of the dance floor. He slides under the rope and holds it up for her. Then he takes her hand and they walk across the stony ground, away from their table.

"Where are we going?"

"To a cave."

She giggles. "We're already in a cave."

"Another cave. Keep your head down," he says and she stoops and follows him into the dark.

"We can sit over here." He pulls her down to a stone bench. Sits beside her. Hot in this small cave. Her dress sticks to her stomach, sweat pours down her forehead. Thelma leans back against the rock.

"Oh, that feels good."

"What?"

"The rock, it's cool."

"Limestone."

"Yes. I think I had too much to drink."

"Pardon?"

"Nothing. Shhh." She puts a finger to his lips.

He smells different in here, like cloves, but also like thyme, the wild mountain thyme her father showed her or was that a song he sang. About wild mountain thyme. She's crouching beside a braided river, fingers fumbling moss and rock as she searches for it.

Tomás' hand on her cheek.

"You look very beautiful tonight, Thelma."

"But you can't see me."

"In my mind I can."

"Flattery will get you everywhere," she says and before she can say anything else, he is kissing her. Be careful, she thinks. But Thelma is not being careful, she's turning her body to his, pressing herself into his chest, she's kissing him back.

Footsteps.

"There's someone here."

"There's no one Thelma."

She pulls away.

"Que pasa, Thelma?"

"Hello?"

*"Hello. Quiet in here."*

She sits up straight.

"Come back here."

*"My daughter insisted on my coming to this disco."*

"Really?"

*"Though I'm too old for this sort of thing."*

"Yes really, Thelma. Ven aca."

*"Are you enjoying yourself?"*

"Yes."

*"Have you noticed the rock formation? Very interesting, these stalactites. Formed by the dripping of percolating calcareous water. They're over here, at the edge of the cave."*

"Thelma, why are you standing?"

"Shh, Tomás. Where are the stalactites?"

Dripping water. The braided river.

*"Tomás?"*

"My friend."

"Si I am your friend, I am your lover, whatever you want. Come here."

*"Your friend?"*

"Thelma, you are killing me."

"Yes."

"You agree you're killing me, so sit down."

*"And Wally?"*

"He's gone away, left me, what am I supposed to do?"

"What are you saying, I am here with you. You don't have to do anything."

He is beside her, trying to pull her body down. But she can't sit, she can't.

*"What are you doing here?"*

"I don't know, I'm sorry, I..."

"Don't be sorry, just sit, Thelma and..."

Water. The braided river. She's balancing on the slippery stones. She's crossing over to the other side.

———

THERE IS SOMETHING lovely about watching a man sleep. The soft, slack face, the rising of shoulders, chest, the flow of breath in and out, in and out. When she and Wally were first married and Thelma couldn't sleep, she used to get up in the night, wrap herself in a blanket and sit in the wicker chair by the bed, watching her new husband sleep. He twitched sometimes, called out, gibberish mostly, but occasionally she could make out some words: 'I'm coming' and 'bring the beer'. One time he said 'pancakes' and she imagined him making them.

But Wally sleeping looks nothing like this man. Tomás has his arms flung out, the full moon illuminating his face, long eyelashes, prickles of whisker on his chin, that lovely, luxuriant moustache.

She knows it will come later, the guilt, the justification for what she is about to do. But now she is content to be with him on this stretch of beach somewhere between Trinidad and Cienfuegos where they've stopped in the early morning, the madrugada, because Tomás was too tired to drive anymore and Jorge too drunk to take over.

She stares at Tomás' shoulders, at the small hollows beside the collarbones. His arm twitches and she puts her hand out, to still it, then trails her fingers over his chest.

He gives a little moan. "Thelma?"

"Yes?"

"Come down here where I can see you."

She giggles and lies down beside him. Runs a finger around his mouth, his nose, leans over and kisses his damp eyebrows that taste like salt, his cheeks, the tip of his nose, his mouth. He kisses her back, softly at first and then more urgently, his hands sliding under her dress.

Laughter. Cathy and Jorge coming back from their walk down the beach? She sits up quickly, pulls down her dress, combs her fingers through her hair. Takes out her mirror and stares into her own eyes. In the moon's light, Thelma thinks she might see a hint of what Tomás sees in her face: a spark in her eyes, a hint of sweetness in the lift of her mouth. Something a little bit beautiful.

———

TOMÁS DROPS THEM outside the Rancho Luna, promising to return to take her to the Botanical Gardens at noon. Cathy stumbles up to bed, but Thelma knows she won't be able to sleep. She wanders out to the beach. A breeze chops the waves. Ixchel, baby rabbit dimming her light, rides the edge of the sky. Thelma slides her bare feet across the sand. In the distance, a fisherman pushes a boat into deeper water, looking like a kid running his bike down the street before hopping on.

Thelma watches the boat heading out to sea. When she can no longer see it, she turns and walks down the beach. Wonders if Tomás is watching the same sky. Or is he lying on a lumpy bed in Jorge's cousin's house, tossing and turning and trying to sleep. She imagines herself sliding in behind him, wrapping her arms around his wide back.

Perhaps he's just got out of the shower, his body wet and gleaming. Or maybe he's just finished shaving, is wiping water from his face. Which she imagines touching, for its softness, for its...

*For its what, Thelma? Do you think I want to know the details of your affair?*

*Affair, Wally? Don't be ridiculous. Besides, you're the one who ran off. I thought you were with Rosa.*

*With Rosa? Are you mad?*

*What about Deirdre then?*

*Jesus, Thelma, that's ancient history.*

*Is it?*

180

*We've been through this how many times? She was the one who kept calling me, wanting help with her Riel paper; I mean she was crying, begging me...*

*To have sex with her?*

*To help her. What was I supposed to do?*

*You were supposed to help her, Wally, not sleep with her.*

*Her boyfriend just broke up with her, she kept saying, 'am I ugly? I must be ugly, I...'*

*Spare me the details. Now go on, get out of my head. I'm trying to enjoy the morning, if you don't mind.*

*My pleasure!*

Thelma stretches her arms above her head, trying to recreate that purring feeling she had in her body on the beach with Tomás. The wind tries to lift her dress. Clouds run across the sky.

Down the beach at the ocean's edge an elderly man, his pants rolled up to his knees, walks into the water. He carries a book in one hand and shoes in the other, wears a battered Tilly hat. The man stops, puts his binoculars to his eyes, scans the ocean, then drops them and walks back toward shore. When he reaches the sand, he turns and walks toward a headland. There is something about the way he walks, quickly but purposefully. His hat disappears around a bend. She follows it.

In Thelma's favourite movie *Contact*, Ellie Arroway, an astrophysicist, travels through space in a machine built from blueprints sent by an extraterrestrial civilization. She wakes to find herself on a Florida beach at dawn. Her father, who died of a heart attack when she was a young girl, is walking toward her. He calls her Sparks, her childhood nickname. He reveals himself to be an alien who has stolen Ellie's thoughts and memories in order to take her father's form. Ellie and her alien father walk together along the beach through a pink dawn. And then he is gone and she is back in her spaceship, hurtling toward earth. According to the scientists, her rocket malfunctioned and Ellie didn't leave earth. But she knew she had. That she'd gone to the future and found the past.

———

HER MOTHER SAYS she has carried Long Beach home. There is sand everywhere. It sifts out of her bathing suit bottom, falls away from patches on her back and chest. Her mom insists on a bath. Thelma watches the tub water swirl down the drain, leaving behind a layer of fine, golden sand.

On a table in the rented cottage, her father is arranging the shells they have found: blue-black California mussel, caramel-coloured razor clam.

He takes her hand and they go outside to join her mom on the deck.

Look, her father says, pointing to a cormorant swooping low over the water. He holds his binoculars to her eyes. Thelma looks and looks but the thing she could see with her naked eye, she now can't see at all.

———

A SHELL, A ROCK, a wisp of moss hanging from a tree. It wasn't until she grew up that she realized not all parents explained everything to their children. Not all parents taught their children to recognize feldspar and mica, cedar waxwings and orioles, juncos and snowy owls and ruby-throated thrushes. Many parents did not search old rock beds for signs of ancient life, leaves and grasses and tiny footprints in stone; did not collect petrified wood and fossils, dinosaur bones and geodes, argillite and arrowheads.

Not all parents kept the encyclopedia in close proximity to the dinner table for easy access should an interesting or perplexing question arise during a meal. 'Whenever I asked my old man a question,' Wally told her, 'for example, what is alchemy, he'd say something like, Al Kemmie, don't think I've had the pleasure.'

———

SHE CATCHES UP to the man. He lifts his hand, waves.

"Hello," he says.

"Good morning."

"Beautiful sunrise isn't it?"

"It is."

"Are you staying at the Rancho Luna?"

"Yes. And you?" she asks loudly, though he gives no evidence of a hearing problem, not turning his head to the right to listen with his good ear as Dr. Smythe did sometimes, when there was too much noise or people spoke too softly.

"Yes. I just spent five wonderful days with a group in the Zapata swamp, bird watching. I'm covered in bites but it was worth it. Have you visited the swamp?"

"No. But I'd like to go."

"If you do, keep your eyes peeled for the bee hummingbird. Tiniest hummer in the world. You know, even some Canadian birds winter in the swamp. We met a couple who saw a flock of Sandhill cranes flying overhead. Imagine. They'd flown all the way from the Cariboo in B.C. apparently."

"Such a long journey."

"Indeed," he agrees, nodding his head vigorously. "And every year they return to the swamp. The first nip of winter in the air, and their bodies tell them it's time to go. Not unlike we tourists."

Thelma laughs.

"Well, I'd better get back and rouse my daughter. She likes to sleep late."

"Oh."

"You have yourself a wonderful trip, young lady."

Young lady?

"You too, sir."

She can imagine her father on that bird watching trip, searching the trees for a glimpse of the elusive tocoroco. But not her father as he would be now. Her young father, her frozen-in-time father, her extraterrestrial father.

———

THE TRAVEL ALARM buzzes, jangling Thelma awake. She can't remember setting it but she must have when she got home from the beach. Light pours through the gap in the curtains. The beginnings of a headache pulse dully in her frontal lobes. She's thirsty and constipated.

Struggling out from between the damp sheets, she trudges to the bathroom, gulps water from the bottle, fumbles through her toiletry bag for the ibuprofen. It's not there and she's too foggy to think where it might be.

She stumbles back into the room, pulls the heavy black-out curtains tight together. Shapes and edges disappear into blackness. Slips back into bed and pulls up the sheet, settles on her side. Just a few more minutes sleep.

But there's someone in the room. Someone moving between the door and the bed.

She sits up, reaching for the bedside lamp. She finds it, twists. Nothing.

"Who's there?"

The moving stops.

"Papa?"

"*Where you expecting someone else? The Cuban gentleman from last night, perhaps?*"

"I'm all grown up now, dad." Her voice comes out high, like a little girl.

"Have you found Wally?"

"No."

"You will."

"Maybe. Papa, listen. About the cave. And Tomás, I..."

She stops. She's a grown woman. She doesn't need to explain.

"Papa? Are you still there?"

"Yes."

"I have a question for you."

"Alright."

"I want to know, papa, I need to know. Why did you abandon me?"

"I beg your pardon?"

"Why did you stop coming after I met Wally?"

"You didn't ask me to come."

"But last night, in the cave, I didn't ask you to come."

"You did."

"Did I? My mind was so addled by rum and that beautiful man, I could hardly think. And if thinking about you was all it took, you should've come every day, papa. Because I've thought about you every single day since you left me."

"I know. Listen, my girl, I need to tell you something. About yourself."

"Oh, OK"

"You've been a disappointment..."

"I know. I didn't do anything you wanted me to do. I didn't finish university. I didn't become a geologist or an archeologist. I got married too young. I'm wasting my life in a dead- end job."

"No..."

"I can be hard on Wally and he's extremely sensitive"

"Wally loves you."

"I should have been a better daughter to mom, I should call and visit more often, I..."

"No."

"I've been such a disappointment to you."

"Not to me."

"I was only eleven when you died, papa, remember. I became disappointing later."

"You are not a disappointment to me. You are smart, tough, funny, curious, independent, stubborn. Never disappointing."

"C'mon, papa, look at my life. You know, when I was little I used to worry about you and mom dying. But then I'd tell myself, they're only thirty, they still have more than half their lives left. But half my life is gone, papa. More than half. It's too late to go back to school, I have too much seniority at the city, I have a good benefit package and pension plan, Wally can't support us, it's too late for me to change, I..."

"*Is it?*"

"What?"

"*Is it too late?*"

"Papa, do you remember that night in the hospital? When mom and I came?"

"*Yes.*"

"I held your hand. I thought if I held it hard enough you couldn't leave us, you could get warm again. I squeezed and squeezed but you didn't squeeze back."

"*Yes.*"

'You didn't squeeze back, papa!'

"*I couldn't.*"

"I never got to say goodbye to you, papa." She is shivering, shivering badly. Someone knocks at her door, it opens and sunlight slashes across her bed. "Ay, perdón," the maid says, closing the door.

Thelma's bowels clench. She untangles herself from the sheets and blanket, feels along the wall to the bathroom, gropes for the toilet. Sits. Come on, she urges, but nothing comes out. She waits until the cramps have subsided and stumbles back to the bedroom.

"Papa. Are you still here?"

"*Yes.*"

"Who am I a disappointment to? Mom? Dr. Smythe? Wally?"

"*Not to any of them,*" he says in the slow, patient voice he once used to explain things to her. Photosynthesis, volcanic eruptions, combustion engines.

"To whom then?"

"*To yourself, my lovely daughter. Only to yourself.*"

185

CHAPTER 29

*Cuba*

THE JARDÍN BOTANICA SOLEDAD is deserted. Thelma surveys the detritus from last year's hurricane that felled the garden's palms. Surveys piles of palm husks, trunks with roots pointing to the sky, like arms raised in supplication.

A faint path wanders past a grove of palms and into a field; off to the side are huge banyan trees covered in vines, stands of bamboo, and small green leaved trees with orange blossoms. Mimosa? Vanilla smelling sweat trickles around her nose and into her mouth, rum leaking from her body. She drinks from her water bottle then searches the horizon for the library in which Wally may be ensconced, wandering happily through treatises about rare botanical plants, unaware of a thing called wife. Or perhaps he's lumbering down some rutted cart track in muddy boots and filthy shorts, all tuckered out from a day of hiking, surveying what was once De Soto's fiefdom. Though how botanical plants fit in with De Soto and Wally's novel, she hasn't a clue.

There's no one on the path. In the distance a palm leans over, it's fronds brushing the ground. The sky is a milky blue, the colour of a puffy ski jacket she once owned. Around her is an insect-y buzz. She walks through vibrating clusters of bugs, brushing them away from her face. Looks at her watch. 12:30. Jorge, Tomás and Cathy will return at 2:00. She has exactly an hour and a half to find her husband.

Thelma pushes through hot air that pushes back. It's heavy, like water. To her left is an uprooted palm. Beside it, stands another, right side up and unscathed. She leans against this tree, then slides down its smooth bark to the ground, settles on leaf husks. She'll just sit here for a minute and think, make a plan. Why would Wally want to come here, to this wrecked garden, in the hottest part of the day? Fronds wave above her head, striping her legs. Her abdomen feels heavy, like she's going to get her period.

Closing her eyes, Thelma remembers lying under a sleeping bag in the almost dusk, how the campground air smelled of wood smoke, how the sky changed colour from forget-me-not to indigo blue. Remembers her dad with his big mutton chop sideburns, his crinkly brown eyes, the red and green lumberjack shirt he always wore camping. That young father who didn't suffer from failing eyesight, hearing, arthritis, the thousand natural shocks that flesh is heir to. Her body right now: tight hips, sore back, bloated stomach.

"Thelma?"

"Dad?"

"Thelm, is that you?"

She squints into the sun. Sees a shadow. Someone walking toward her. A man. Coming into focus now. He's wear a baseball cap, a faded red t-shirt and a pair of baggy beige shorts. Not papa. Stunned, she stares at him, unable to decide if this man is in fact her errant husband and not some vision of her younger father she has recreated. There's a peculiar smell in the air, her own sweat mixed with something sweet and musky, humus, overturned earth. A wasp flits around her eyes. She bats it away but the buzzing remains. Time seems to be stretching like a Dali clock melting in the sun.

The man stops a few feet in front of her and squats. Sweat from her forehead mixes with her sunscreen and slides stinging drops into her eyes which she rubs, making the stinging worse. Wally. Relief unclenches her shoulder muscles. He's safe. He's alive. He's alone. And she very much wants to kill him.

"Thelma! What are you doing here?"

"What do you think I'm doing here?"

"I, uh, well, right. How are you?"

"You've been gone for days. How do you think I am?"

"You're mad. I know you're mad. But before you say anything, let me explain."

His face is tanned, his nose peeling. He's obviously spent more time on the beach with the profesora than in libraries. Still he's here. He's safe. He sits beside her, close but not too close. She can smell his sweat.

"Listen, Thelma, remember when I told you that I got this grant and that it was for research? Well, that's truly what I wanted to do here. Research De Soto. And then when I met Patricia, I couldn't pass up the opportunity to travel with her. She's a De Soto specialist, in fact she did her thesis on the Cuban encomienda system. And well, Thelm, quite frankly this trip was supposed to be for my research. But I knew you needed a holiday and I didn't want to disappoint...um, Thelm, are you OK?"

She is going to throw up.

"Water."

He thrusts a filthy red plastic bottle at her. She wipes her hand across the top, drinks. Her stomach settles. "Go on."

"I thought when I left with Patricia..."

"You mean Rosa?"

You know he wasn't with Rosa.

Wally's mouth moves, guppy like, but nothing comes out. Finally he manages: "you think I've been with Rosa?"

"It crossed my mind."

"How could you think that?"

"You fucking disappeared, Wally. You have a crush on Rosa. I put two and two together."

"She's half my age for God's sake."

"OK, then explain. What happened?"

He pulls up a handful of grass, throws it at his boot.

"What happened, Wally?"

"I thought I'd be back to meet you but then her, Patricia's, car broke down..."

"Seriously?"

"Yes. The garage took forever to fix it. It was something in the engine, they had to make a part and...."

"Why didn't you just get a bus back to Havana?"

"Have you seen the state of transportation on this island?"

"I believe taxis are widely available."

"They kept promising the car would be fixed and I kept thinking, tomorrow, we'll be back tomorrow, I tried to call."

"Yes and time passed so fast by your time, there was nobody or nothing that could change you."

"You know Cabrera?"

"You put quote in my lunch bag the day you left."

"I did?"

"Yes you bloody well did. And I've spent the last week trying to figure out what the hell it means."

"It doesn't mean anything. It's from a book I was reading. I thought you'd like it..."

He looks at the ground and shakes his head.

"And?"

"I put a quote in your lunch bag, Thelma. It doesn't mean anything."

"Everything we do means something, Wally. How did you meet Patricia?"

"Pardon?"

"How...did...you...meet...her?"

Thelma' stomach cramps. From last night's shrimp? The rum? Her period coming?

Her husband looks away. He rubs a hand across his forehead, takes another sip from the filthy water bottle. If she didn't feel so poorly, she'd stand up and shout at him.

"Well?"

"You have to promise not to be mad."

She narrows her eyes. "Tell me."

"OK I, uh, found her on an internet site."

"An internet site?"

"Not that kind of site. I found her while I was doing research on De Soto at home. Her name was on a paper about early conquistadors. Rosa translated it for me and I wrote to the Spanish journal where she published the article and they gave me an address in Cuba. When I got here, I thought I'd see if I could find her. I went to the address, the apartment, and she was there! She offered to bring me to Cienfuegos to meet a De Soto specialist, Dr. Perez Acuña. Unfortunately, Dr. Perez is out of the country. But we didn't know that and I couldn't pass up the offer, Thelm, a De Soto scholar and she was willing to take me..."

"You didn't think to tell me?"

A call is all it would have taken. A simple call to Canada before she left. Better still, he could have told her all this before he left. Was he afraid to tell her? Didn't he think she'd be happy for him?

"I told you this trip was for my book, you're the one who insisted on coming."

"Why didn't you call me at the Palco?"

"I left messages."

"How many?"

"Quite a few."

"Ten?"

"Uh..."

"Five?"

"I'm not sure, Thelma."

"Two?"

"I..."

"NONE. YOU LEFT NO MESSAGES, WALLY. ZERO. NINGUN. WHAT DID YOU EXPECT ME TO DO WHEN YOU DIDN'T SHOW UP? YOU DIDN'T THINK I'D BE WORRIED?"

"Calm down, Thelma. I left messages. I just don't know how many."

"And you thought these messages would reach me immediately, given the generally acknowledged Cuban efficiency in message taking. Precise and on time, like German trains, or Swiss watches, you thought?"

"I guess. Yeah, I did. I tried to call the hotel. You were never in. The front desk guy said you were sightseeing, that you seemed to be having a good time. So I thought, she's OK, I called yesterday. When the guy said you'd left, were coming to Cienfuegos, I told Patricia I had to find you and she said she'd try to help. A waiter at a paladar we went to, which does an excellent paella by the way, said he'd met your taxi drivers. Patricia and I were looking for you, Thelma, looking for you in Cienfuegos. I didn't want to go back to Havana in case I missed you, and..."

"The front desk guy? What front desk guy? You are full of..."

"What?"

"Nothing."

"I'm full of shit? You don't believe me?"

"Well, for one, the people at the front desk were women."

"Men, women, I can't remember, Thelma."

The air is still, the sun is relentless, her head is pounding, she should have brought a hat, she feels nauseous, she just wants to be somewhere cool, in water, floating in a pool, a cenote, the ocean.

"You phoned Rosa."

His eyes widen. "How do you know?" She didn't.

"I, I just wanted her to know."

"Know what exactly? That you'd abandoned your wife?"

"C'mon Thelma! I was excited. I wanted to tell her that I'd met Patricia. Listen, I'm sorry, it doesn't mean anything. I'll make it up to you."

Just what he said about Deirdre. "Um hm."

"We have five days left, Thelm. We can go back to Havana, see the sights, visit Morro Castle."

"Seen it."

"Tour the José Martí monument?"

"Been there."

"We could go to Regla and take in a santeria ceremony."

"Done that." Well, she hadn't but all's fair in love and war.

"You did those things all by yourself?"

"With Tomás."

"Who's Thomas?"

"It's ToMÁS, actually."

"Who's ToMÁS?"

"A friend."

"A Cuban friend?"

"Um hm."

"Your driver?"

"Sort of."

"Your guide?"

"Sort of."

"Can you qualify sort of?"

"You're the writer. You qualify it."

"Is he your... your lover?"

She picks up some leaves, sifts them through her fingers.

"Jesus, Thelma. He is, isn't he?"

"Don't be ridiculous. So, you and Patricia...." Cramp. She tries to breathe through it.

"Forget about Patricia. I said I was sorry. Let's forget it, OK? Let's just make some plans for the rest of our trip. What do you want to do?"

"Nothing."

"Nothing. Sure, we could just lie on the beach and relax. I've done most of my research. We could go to Playas del Este, Santa Maria beach is supposed to be nice, Pat said. Thelma, what's the matter?"

She swallows but she can't stop it, the rising of rum and shrimp and something else, undigested and raw, that comes pouring out of her.

———

BY THE TIME they get back to Wally's taxi, she is in severe pain. She collapses under a tree beside the taxi, rolls into a ball.

"Thelm, please, get up, get in the car. You are not alright."

No, she is not alright, the rum the shrimp the ice, her guts heaving, more coming up, she can't stop it.

Wally hovers above her with the water bottle. She wipes her mouth and shakes her head.

"No."

"You'll get dehydrated."

"I'm OK now."

"Can you stand?"

"I think so."

"Lean on me, just a few steps. There, slide into the back, lie down, that's good."

"Where to?" the driver asks.

"The Rancho Luna," she says weakly then remembers Cathy is there, maybe Tomás and Jorge, too, she doesn't want to have to introduce them to Wally. She needs to go somewhere else. She needs to lie down in a room that is cool and quiet and dark. "Unless yours is closer, Wall."

"Yes. The Pasacaballo, driver," Wally says.

Another cramp hits her, a wave of nausea, she turn on her side and retches but her stomach is empty. A line of saliva dangles from her mouth. She wipes it away.

The taxi bounces down the rutted road, its shocks and gas smell are worse than the cacharra naranja's.

"Hang on, Thelm. We'll be there soon. I have some medicine back at the room. He lowers his voice. Is it your...?"

"My what?"

"Your uh, your you know?"

"My period?"

"Yeah."

"Maybe. Or food poisoning."

He turns in the seat, reaches an arm back and brushes the hair from her eyes.

"Thanks, hon," she says before she remembers that she's mad at him.

Another wave of pain hits, moving up from deep in her pelvis, tearing her in half. Her husband pats her head. She's too weak to tell him to stop.

WALLY'S ROOM IS cool, quiet and smells like oranges. At first, he perches on the edge of the bed fussing over her, pulling the sheet and blanket around her shoulders when she shivers, pulling them off when she says she's burning up. She tosses and turns, curling into a fetal position when the cramps come. She has to shit but when she staggers to the bathroom, can't. Falls into a deep sleep.

Waking up, Thelma wonders where she is. Then sees Wally sleeping in a rusty iron patio chair beside the bed, his head on his chest, one leg thrown over the arm.

Her body is wet, her head foggy and full. Her pelvis feels heavy but there is no pain. Did she take a Tylenol? Did Wally give her one? She can't remember. She struggles up to a sitting position, looks around the room. It's small, furnished only with the single bed she is lying in, one chair and a rickety table by the door. The walls are painted a light green and covered with scuff marks. Sun slides through the gap in the faded yellow curtains. Wally's suitcase peeks out from the closet.

Thelma slides back under the covers. Exhausted. She didn't know pain could be so tiring. When she wakes again, the sun has disappeared and so has Wally. Her abdomen is rock-hard, she's constipated, she needs some Ex-lax, she needs a drink. Wally has left a bottle of water by the bed. She reaches then drops it as another cramps come, relentless, one after another.

———

SOMEONE IS BENDING over her, saying something, but she can't hear, she can't think, she needs to keep herself rolled up but she can't because someone's trying to open her.

"Thelma, he's a doctor, please co-operate."

She is unrolled. Warm fingers probe her stomach, her pelvis.

"Owww."

"Please, Thelma, he's..."

The doctor bends his head to her stomach then he and Wally withdraw to a corner, whispering.

Wally's above her. His eyes are red.

"We have to go to the hospital, Thelma. They need to take an x-ray to figure out what's going on. Don't worry. Dr. Garcia Tomayo is a specialist."

Wally's trying to be reassuring but he sounds scared as hell.

AN X-RAY HAS been taken, her belly's been probed and prodded and now Thelma is hooked up to an IV, an NG tube running into her nose. Her hospital bed is surrounded by a clean, white curtain. Outside the curtain, someone is snoring. The floors are the colour of diluted pee.

A wave of cramps passes through her, tears squeeze out from under her eyes. When the cramps pass, she breathes slowly, in and out, in and out. Christ. She's never had food poisoning like this before.

She hears footsteps. The curtain is pulled by a man in a white coat, the front covered with tiny spatters of blood, like someone flicked a paintbrush at it. He's followed by a pale Wally, the skin under his eyes the colour of plums.

"Hey," Wally says.

"Hey yourself."

"How are you?"

"As well as one can be with an angry gut."

"It'll be OK". She's not sure what he means by it. Her illness? The rest of their holiday? Their marriage?

"The doctors have read the x-ray. They have to do surgery."

"For food poisoning?"

Wally looks down, takes her hand and squeezes hard then turns to the somber looking doctor beside him. Clean shaven, hazel eyes, wavy brown hair. Surely he's too young to be a proper doctor.

"Hello Señora Dangerfield. I'm Dr. Garcia Tomayo."

"Isn't surgery for food poisoning a little drastic, doctor?"

"Señora, you have a bowel obstruction and an abdominal mass that requires immediate removal."

"Pardon me?"

"An abdominal mass," he says pronouncing every syllable carefully, in case her brain has started to malfunction as well. "That requires removal. We should do the surgery immediately. I do not advise waiting."

"What kind of mass?"

Marianne's mother had an abdominal mass. The doctors opened her up to do surgery and found she was riddled with cancer. They just sewed her back up and she died three months later. Thelma shivers and pulls the sheet up to her throat. She looks at Wally. Wally looks at the floor.

"Its, uh its, well...," Wally begins.

"I want to go back to Canada, Wall, I don't want surgery, not here, just book a flight, get them to pump me full of morphine and off we go."

Cramps. She brings her knees to her chest, rocks back and forth. "Christ," she says when she can breathe again.

A nurse pulls the curtain, whispers to the doctor. He nods. "I am needed elsewhere. I will come back."

Wally stands there, shuffling from foot to foot like a little boy who has to pee.

"For god's sake, Wall, tell me what I have."

He takes her hand. His bottom lip starts vibrating. He closes his eyes.

"For the love of God, Wally, what?"

Wally is squeezing the hell out of her hand. Maybe the cancer has metastasized. She wishes she was a religious woman, that she knew some prayers. A prayer. Something they could say together, so Wally's lip would stop shaking and her heart would stop drum soloing and her body would stop shivering and these cramps would go away.

He pulls the blanket higher. "Do you need more painkillers? Should I call the nurse?"

"No," she gasps when another cramp has passed. "Just tell me what I've got."

"It's not cancer."

"That's a relief."

"It is, it was..."

"What can be worse than cancer? Just tell me."

"Abay."

"Abay. Is that the Spanish word? What is it in English?"

"A bay...."

"For God's Sake, Wally, what? A bay leaf? A bay mare? I'm dying here. No pun intended."

"...bee," he finishes weakly.

"A bee?"

"A baby."

"A baby?"

"Yes."

"No. No. Absolutely not. They're wrong. I would know if I was pregnant, I can't be."

"Maybe you don't remember."

Has he gone mad? "I forgot I was pregnant?"

"The baby is twenty-three years old, Thelm."

———

A DEAD BABY. She has a dead fetus in her, which she's been carrying for twenty-three years. How could she not have known? Surely she would have felt it. Sensed its presence, curled in a ball, in the fetal position, sucking its thumb. She probes her hardened abdomen, her fingers searching for a head, a tiny foot. Can't feel a thing.

The door opens and Dr. Garcia Tomayo enters, sun from the window blinds cutting his body into strips of light and dark.

"How are you?"

"In shock, frankly."

"I understand. You've had upsetting news. Do you recall being pregnant as a young woman, Mrs. Dangerfield?"

She nods.

"When exactly was that pregnancy?"

"When I was twenty one."

"And what happened during that pregnancy?"

"Nothing, I... I dropped out of school; I wandered around the city, trying to decide what to do. I, I miscarried."

"Why do you think you miscarried?" Does he think she's a complete idiot?

"I stopped feeling any movement. I had some bleeding." A little blood. Maybe too little.

"Were you under a doctor's care?"

"No."

Dr. Tomayo raises an eyebrow. "No?"

"I, it...it was..." How to explain that she was ashamed, that she was too smart to be pregnant, that she prayed daily for the baby to be gone, that she prayed daily for the baby to be alright.

"I just wasn't. Please, tell me about the, uh, the, the..."

"The fetus is a lithopedian. A stone baby. It is extra-uterine, that is in your abdomen. It is partially calcified. Adhesions, that is strings of fibrous tissue from the lithopedian, have attached to your abdominal wall and twisted your bowel. That is why you've been having cramps, and have been unable to pass gas and stool. Do you have any questions?"

Does she have any questions? Jesus! A stone baby. A calcified baby that she's been carrying around inside her for twenty-three years.

"Mrs. Dangerfield?"

"Is, is this common?"

"No, extremely rare. There are less than 300 reported cases in the medical literature."

"I guess you'll write me up, eh?" She can't believe she's joking with this doctor who has just told her she has a dead baby inside her.

He smiles.

"Listen, Doctor, could you just give me something for the pain, then once I'm home I'll have the surgery."

"Your bowel is obstructed and if we don't do surgery within the next few hours you could die."

She could die. Here, right now, in this room.

No, she won't die right now. But she could. Sometime soon. If she doesn't have the surgery. She has heard Cuban doctors are good. But do they have the right equipment? The proper drugs?

Thelma touches her belly. How could she have had this stone baby inside her for so long and not know? This calcified skeleton, this day of the dead baby, sending out its deadly white strands, tentacles to wind around her bowel and kill it. This little boy, a boy, she's sure of it, who died twenty-three years ago.

"Mrs. Dangerfield?" She manages a nod.

"Do you have any other questions?"

Another cramp. Breathe, breathe. When it passes, she whispers, "Please, can I have something for the pain?"

"Certainly," he says. "I will tell the nurse. And I will come later to check you."

Deadly white threads wound around her baby suffocating him. No. He died. The calcification came later.

———

THE BOYS IN THE apartment downstairs were partying that night, playing Alice Cooper's *School's Out* at eardrum splitting level. Nineteen eighty-one was the hottest June on record, the radio said. She'd left the front windows open, hoping to cool the baking apartment, hoping that the sound of cars speeding by on Kensington Road combined with her earplugs might drown Alice and the boys out. She fell asleep and then was suddenly awake. Something inside her had loosened. A tap turning on. She felt the wet between her legs. Threw the sheet back. Made her way down the dark hallway, turned on the bathroom light, lifted her hand. It was covered in blood.

Thelma remembers sitting on the bathroom floor. Remembers hearing a police siren, remembers looking at the cracked blue lino and trying to decide what to do: yell, scream, bang on the floor until one of boys came upstairs? Crawl to the phone and call an ambulance? She couldn't call Wally because Wally was at his sister's commune somewhere north of Comox, helping to build a new kitchen. And because Wally didn't know she was pregnant. She couldn't tell her mom because her mom and Peter were on a wine tour of France.

She couldn't call a girlfriend because she didn't have any girlfriends.

So Thelma lay in a ball on the cool floor, a line of blood trickling down her leg, onto the lino, and cried.

———

She lies in the dark, thinking of her young self, getting up finally, wiping the blood from the floor, getting a pad and a new pair of panties and putting the stained ones to soak in cold water, closing the window.

Alice sang *Only Women Bleed*. Did the boys play it that night?

She lay on her bed in that stifling apartment, thinking she should be happy that the baby was gone, that she should go to sleep, that the blood would soon stop, that she couldn't bleed forever.

Near dawn, it started to rain, a hard summer rain that drummed on the roof, and pounded at the windows trying to get in. Thelma stumbled back to bed, slept, and when she woke up, the bleeding had stopped, the sun was up, and the emptiness inside her was as big as that summer's day, as big as the prairie sky, as big as the world.

———

WALLY CAME BACK from the commune with a tan and new muscles.

They sat on his balcony in the sun, Thelma listening while he talked about which Master's program to attend. Three wanted him. Really wanted him. He was leaning toward UVIC, because it was closer to his sister, and the commune.

"I need to work, Wall. I need to pay off my loans".

"You could work in Victoria, then apply to grad school next year."

"I've got a good, cheap apartment here and..."

"And?"

"Nothing."

"Don't you want to go Grad School? I'm sure Dr. Smith..."

"Smythe."

"...Smythe would help you; give you a letter of reference."

"I did."

"Did what?"

"Did want to go to Grad school."

"But you don't anymore?"

"What kind of jobs are there in archeology anyway? I'm making good money now, Wall. Ten dollars an hour and I can apply for other union positions with the city, work my way up the ladder."

"Are you serious?"

"Yes."

"Geez, Thelma, I thought you had ambitions."

"Yeah, well, I did, until I got pre..."

"What?"

"Until you got?"

"Nothing."

"Pre what?"

"Pregnant."

"You're pregnant?"

"No."

"You just said..."

"I miscarried."

"When?"

"This summer."

"Oh my God, Thelma, why didn't you tell me?"

"You were incommunicado, remember."

"I, I gave you the number to the closest store on the island. Oh Christ. I can't believe it. Were you, did you go to the hospital?"

"No."

"Jesus, Thelm, what happened?"

"I bled a bit. The baby obviously died."

"I'm sorry. I, we, oh shit. That's terrible."

"Yeah, well, it's over now."

"I thought you were on the pill."

"I went off it after we broke up."

"Can you get on it again? The pill, I mean."

Why would he say that? When sex was the last thing in the world she wanted. All she wanted was to be cuddled and held, to be rocked like a baby to sleep.

# CHAPTER 30

*Cuba*

THE DRUGS THEY'VE injected seem to be helping. Are very nice, actually, though they seem to cause a little trouble with her words. Her cramps have gone, or maybe she just can't feel them. Everything seems very far away but detailed, too. Like Wally, sitting in a wooden chair beside the bed, wearing a t-shirt the exact colour of his sunburnt nose.

"Have you got the flight changed? I want to leave tomorrow."

"Listen, Thelm, Gisela said Cuban doctors are very well-trained."

"Gisela's here?"

"No. I called her. She said the Cuban government exports their doctors all over the world."

"All over the communist world you mean?"

"What communist world?"

"North Korea? And um, and um. That big country. And China."

"Um hm. Listen, Thelma, they'll be coming to prep you soon."

"For my final exam?"

"Ha, ha."

"I'm not having surgery here. I told that doctor, what's his name, Garcia Tamale."

"Tomayo. Listen to me, Thelma, your bowel is twisted from the adhesions. It's not getting oxygen. The doctors say if they don't do the surgery soon you'll have a complete bowel obstruction, you could, you could die."

"Oh. He did say that."

"Don't I have to sign some papers if I'm having surgery?"

"You signed the papers."

"I did?"

"Listen, Thelma. Dr. Tomayo will be doing the surgery. He'll be assisted by a gynecologist, Dr. Santamaria Beltrán. They may need to remove a piece of the bowel, or untangle it, but they assured me that pelvic surgery isn't so difficult. The anatomy is fairly easy to deal with. Of course they have to make sure they don't cut the ureter, and..."

"Ureter. Isn't that what I pee through?"

"I think so."

"I don't want a cut ureter."

"I didn't say they'd cut it."

"I don't want to go around with one of those bags."

"They won't cut it."

"You inspired it."

"Inspired it?"

"You know what I mean. Implied."

"Sorry."

"What about the others?"

"There are only two doctors."

"No. My friends. Tomás, Cathy, Jorge."

"They're going back to Havana. They've probably already left."

"They're gone?"

"I think so."

"They didn't say goodbye."

"They left you a letter."

"Can I see it?"

"It's at the hotel."

"Did you read it?"

"No."

"Is it seeded?"

"Seeded?"

"Closed."

"Yes, it's sealed."

Then he wouldn't have opened it. She hopes. She opened Wally's diary. But it wasn't seeded. Sealed.

"Who is it from? Is it from Tom....?"

No, she can't ask that. Thelma closes her eyes. Carmine and tangerine swim up out of the darkness, aquamarine, lavender, colours that fade then resolve into Tomás lying under a full moon in the still warm sand. If she hadn't put her face above his, she wouldn't have felt the air; she wouldn't have known he was breathing at all Buttercup yellow, emerald. Cinnamon water in a pothole, Tomás splashing through.

He was going to paint her with flowers in her hair. Which ones? Bluebells? Cockle shells?

Easy, ivy, over.

The cave. The sound of dripping water. He's kissing her. She's kissing him back.

Then he's gone and Thelma's lying on her back in a room trying not to cry.

———

"WALLY?"

"What?"

"What's the stone baby called again?"

"A lithopedian."

"It could kill me?"

"A bowel obstruction is very serious."

"My baby could kill me."

"Thelm, please it's not a baby, it's a, it's a..."

"A what?"

"I don't know. A mass, a tumour."

"It's not a tumour!"

"Listen, the nurses will be here soon, why don't we do some breathing, that yoga breathing thing you learned, how does it go, in for four out for six?"

"Does it look like a baby?"

"Ready? In 2, 3, 4, out 2, 3, 4."

"The doctor said it's carbonized, I mean calcified. Maybe it's all tucked up like you see in pictures, its tiny thumb in its mouth."

"Thelma, please, just breathe."

"It's calcified. Calcite is in everything. Those things in caves – stalagmites and the other one."

"I'm breathing now. Nice and slow in 2, 3, 4, out 2, 3, 4."

"What is the other one?"

He doesn't answer.

"What is it?"

"Stalactites."

"Stalactites are coated with it. Cenotes are covered with it."

"Breathe."

"No. This is important. My dad used to put hydrochloric acid on rock to check for calcite. It's a miner, no, not a miner. What's the word?"

"Try to calm down Thelm."

"Why isn't he helping her?"

"A mineral, Wall. It's in limestone; it's on limestone, where does limestone come from?"

"I don't know, Thelma."

"This island, it's made of limestone. It's from the ocean, that's right, I remember dad telling me, heat and pressure change it, limestone, it's made of, it's made of little animals, the skeletal remains of tiny little sea animals."

"Um hm."

"Tiny little sea animals that have died and settled to the bottom. From the ocean, Wall. That's where calcite's from. The bottom of the sea".

Her baby covered in milky white calcite.

She sees him swimming in her stomach, aloft on foaming waves, in the wide turbulent sea. She is singing him a lullaby, one of her father's songs:

*My father was the keeper of the Eddystone light*

*And he slept with a mermaid one fine night.*
*And from that union there came three*
*My momma and my poppa and the other was me*

*Yo ho ho, let the winds blow free.*
*Oh for the life on the rolling sea.*

———

SHE PROBES HER stomach. Where is it? There, just there, is that a little calcified foot? A tiny skull? How could she have had this thing, this fetus, this baby in her for twenty-three years and not have known?

She wants to sleep and wake up and know it's gone, this baby. No, not baby, fossil.

This calcified fossil inside her.

Her father had the most beautiful geodes with crystals: lavender, amber, sea green.

He told her, 'calcite is one of the common minerals. It's in the chalk your teacher uses. And the fertilizer I put on the lawn and the lime I put down the outhouse at that cabin we rented at Shuswap Lake last year.'

It's in our bones. In my body. In this thing that's inside me. Not thing, Thelma, baby. She shivers. Feels her stomach rising, swallows, she can't be sick with all these tubes.

Will they show her baby to her? Take a picture? No. She doesn't want to see it.

The curtains open. The big orderly looks like a wrestler with a shaved head and droopy moustache. He picks her up and lays her gently on a gurney, wheels her and her IV pole down narrow corridors. Wally is beside her, his face the colour of calcite.

"It will be over soon," Wally whispers, squeezing her hand.

The wrestler stops outside a room with swinging doors. Thelma lashes her fingers together: here's the church, here's the steeple, open the doors and see all the people.

———

THE BABY THELMA thought she lost that hot August night would have been a boy. She felt in those early stirrings his need to run and jump and hang upside down from tree branches. She would have dressed him in tiny sleepers. She would have taken him swimming, to the mom and tots class, watch him float. She wouldn't have been one of those fretful mothers, holding him every second, seeing danger everywhere.

He would have been good in science. Like his grandpa. She would have given him his grandpa's rock and mineral collection, taken him on camping trips, snuggled his hot little body between her and Wally at night. Woken and listened for his breathing.

Wally would have taught him how to cook, corrected his grammar, helped him with his book reports.

They'd have read him stories. All kinds of stories. *Curious George; The Cat in the Hat, Green Eggs and Ham, The Snowy Day, Where the Wild Things Are.*

They'd have taken him to lakes to swim, waited with a dry towel as he ran, skinny freckled arms and legs and protruding little boy belly, into the her arms.

Now, he'd be grown.

She remembers a movie she once saw. *My Dinner with Andre.* Andre, the theatre director and the playwright, Wallace Shawn, have dinner in a fancy New York restaurant. Andre tells Wally about making a movie in Poland, with satyrs and images of bacchanalia and the devil and mass graves from the war, and Wally, the playwright, talks about the pleasures of domesticity: a good cup of coffee in the morning, dinner with his girlfriend, an electric blanket to stave off the winter cold. Andre does most of the talking and Wally the most listening, and then Wally walks home alone through the dark, empty New York streets and this is what he was thinking, what the voice over said: "people hold onto these images father, wife, mother, son, because they seem to provide some firm ground. But there's no wife there. What does that mean? A husband, a son? A baby holds your hands and then suddenly there's this big man lifting you off the ground and then he's gone."

———

THELMA WAKES UP in the dark, alone. The cramps have disappeared. The NG tube is in, the IV still attached to her arm.

She is in a different room. A bigger room with a window. Outside a full moon, Ixchel, goddess of fertility, sits on the horizon.

While she, goddess of infertility, struggles to sit up.

"It's gone papa," she whispers. "I'm OK, now. Don't you want to say anything?

Something profound? Something soothing? Anything papa?"

She listens. But there is only the sound of footsteps in the hallway.

"Do you remember when you saved that drowning baby?" A door creaks open, closes.

"Papa?" Nothing.

"Are you here?" Silence.

"You couldn't save this baby, this drowned boy."

She pulls up her gown, touches the railroad track of black stitches running across her abdomen. The baby is gone, leaving what. Space to be filled. But with what? With what?

She sees the dark entrance to a cave, a cave that goes on and on, down into the bowels of the earth, into the underworld.

She thinks that grief is a thing. A thing you can carry in your body. For years. Twenty- three years. No, longer than that. That you can carry in your body since you were a stoic, dry-eyed eleven-year old girl holding your father's cold hand. Watching your father's coffin being lowered, your mother's sodden Kleenexes falling like carnations, the scrape of shovel, the sound of dirt hitting the wood, with a dull thud, thud, thud.

Something rises from the very bottom of her, a feeling of loss so profound she pushes her mouth into the pillow to try to stop it, but it doesn't stop, it comes rushing up from her gut, into her lungs, her windpipe, her throat, she pushes her head into the pillow to stop the moan that emerges, the sound of an animal in pain the sound of a woman holding her dead son, father, husband, lover, in her arms, rocking, keening. Great sobs shake her; shake her hard like a dog with a bone, a black hound that is holding on to that bone for dear life, shaking it in her angry mouth, unwilling to just let it go.

# CHAPTER 31

*Cuba*

WALLY WALKS INTO her room. "You're awake."

"Yeah."

"Sorry, I had to go get something to eat. I was starving. Hey, Thelma, what's the matter? Does it hurt a lot?" He strokes the hair from her face.

"Not too much. I was just thinking."

"About the ba, the fetus?"

"About my dad."

"Oh."

She wipes her eyes with the sheet.

"Did the operation go alright?"

"Yes. They decompressed your bowel but it wasn't damaged, thank God. They didn't have to cut any pieces of it out."

"When can I get these tubes out?"

"As soon as your bowel starts working. In a day or two."

"When can we leave?"

"In about a week."

"A whole week"

"You just had major surgery."

"Where's your profesora?"

"She went back to Havana with Cathy and the taxi drivers."

"Did you meet them?"

"I met Cathy when I went to your hotel to get your suitcase. There was a message under your door asking you to go to her room immediately. So I went."

"What did she say?"

"She was worried about you. When they came back to the garden to get you, the ticket seller told her you left with a man in a taxi and that you were very sick. I told her you were having emergency surgery. She asked if she and the taxi drivers could visit before they left but I said it probably wasn't a good idea, you were kind of out of it. She gave me some letters. Do you want me to read them to you?"

"No. I'll read them later."

"OK." He drops an envelope on the bedside table.

"So you didn't meet Tomás? And, and Jorge?"

"No, oh and also, I phoned your mom and Peter to let them know what was happening."

"You didn't tell them about the baby, did you?"

"I said you had an obstructed bowel and had to have surgery. That's all. I thought you could tell them yourself if you want to. They're worried. They send their love."

"What happened with Patricia's car?"

"It still isn't fixed. Apparently the mechanic went off to visit his girlfriend in Playa Larga. Pat's arthritis was acting up and she needed to see her doctor in Havana. A friend will drive it back when it's..."

"She has arthritis?"

"Yeah."

"She's old?"

"Sixty-five, give or take a few years."

Old enough to be Wally's mother.

"Tomás and Jorge, I owe them, I didn't pay them."

"Cathy said she'd take care of it. I changed our flights. Everything's under control, Thelm, don't worry. You don't have to do anything except heal. Now, why don't you try to get some sleep?"

———

SHE WAKES TO A FAINT, pink dawn. Alone. The light from the half-open door to the hallway falls across her bed. Someone coughs. She lifts her sore body up, reaches over to the bedside table, and picks up the envelope Wally has left there. She opens it and takes out the first of several pages of hotel stationary.

*2908 Brentwood Dr. N.W. Calgary 284-6542*

*Dear Thelma,*

*When we couldn't find you in the gardens, we were so worried. And then we heard you were sick. I'm so sorry!*

*Wally said you had to have an operation to remove a growth in your abdomen. But he says it's not cancer and I am so glad it's not. Jorge says that you are in good hands. I'm sorry I couldn't visit but my flight home leaves in two days and by the time you are able to receive visitors, I'll be leaving this beautiful island.*

*I may come down here again in the spring if I can scrape the money together. Jorge says I could stay at his apartment so that would cut down on expenses. I also promised Sara that I'd take her to Disney World during spring break. I'll have to sub a lot to manage both, but maybe. Maybe I can do it.*

*I'm glad we found Wally. He seems like a very nice man. He was so worried about you, Thelma. He said to thank Tomás and Jorge for taking such good care of you.*

*By the way, I looked after the payment for them. It's the least I can do, since you agreed to bring me along and this was one of the best vacations ever. It was life changing. And I have you to thank for introducing me to Jorge. Tomás told me that his nickname is 'el loco hombre de amor'. Isn't that cute?*

*I hope everything works out for the best for you. And if you don't mind me saying, dear Thelma, whatever you decide to do, I hope you find a little peace.*

*Love, Cathy*

She sees Cathy in her daffodil dress, her hair swept up in a silver comb. She's the one Tomás should paint with white hibiscus in her hair, in a garden overflowing with tropical flowers: a riot of colours, soft greens and pinks; Cathy's eyes full of wonder

The door squeaks open and a nurse enters.

"How are you feeling?"

"Tired, sore, kind of spacey. Otherwise OK."

"Have you evacuated your bowels?"

"There's nothing to evacuate."

"Have you made any bowel sounds?"

"I think I farted, if that's what you mean."

"Excellent! That means the obstruction is clear." She picks up the chart at the end of Thelma's bed, scribbles something on it. "Doctors will be very happy."

———

THE SECOND LETTER is from Jorge.

> *Dear Thelma*
>
> *I'm glad you found your husband and that Tomás and I could be of service to you in that regard. I hope the surgery is a success and you are soon on the plane back home to your country. I hope, also, that you can visit us again. I enjoyed getting to know you. Thank you for introducing me to your lovely friend.*
>
> *With warmest regards and un abrazo,*
>
> *Jorge de Cruz Ortega*
>
> *Edificio 2, entre Siboney y Constancia La Lira,*
>
> *Havana*

Jorge is such a gentleman. She hopes it works out for him and Cathy. He'll be good to her and her little girl.

She picks up the third page.

> *Dear Thelma*
>
> *I hope your surgery was not too painful and you are healing well.*
>
> *I'm sorry I didn't have the opportunity to paint you but perhaps ojalá as we say or God willing, we will meet again, my beautiful comrade in pain. In the meantime, I will practice painting you from memory, with a little cat on one shoulder and a monkey on the other in a field of cornflowers. Or as you were in the cenote, your hair like wings around your shoulders.*
>
> *I am happy you found your husband. But sorry. Sorry for me. Perhaps I will repaint la cacharra naranja. With a new orange coat and a tuned up engine, perhaps she can be again mi sueño. My dream.*
>
> *Besos y abrazos,*
>
> *Tu conductor, tu buceador, tu Tomás*
>
> *Tomás Fuentes Echevarria*

*Martí Edificio 3, Apto. 9, entre 5ta y 6ta Rpto. Eléctrico*
*Arroyo Naranja Havana*
*44-86-29 (aunt)*

Your diver, your driver. Your Tomás.

She pictures him swimming in the cenote, doing a lazy backstroke. Swims over to him, but just as she reaches him, before Thelma can touch him, Tomás disappears beneath the surface.

Outside her window, the sky is streaked tangerine, peach, the faintest, softest wild rose. If you are out there, Tomás, on a lonely, potholed road by the airport, watching an airplane descend out of this magnificent sky, Tomás. Paint it. Paint it for me.

———

SHE AND WALLY have one day together. One day at Santa Maria beach before they fly home.

Thelma surveys the postcards she has bought. A cigar smoking guitar player sitting on an upturned box on a Havana street; smiling children in red uniforms waving from a bus; El Castillo de la Real Fuerza, with Isabel, La Giraldilla, just visible at the top; a woman in a long gown posed against a tropical sunset; a group of tuxedo clad musicians in a park; a bride and groom in a pink De Soto, her veil blowing back in the wind.

On the back of El Castillo de la Real Fuerza she writes:

> *Dear Señor De Soto,*
> *Sorry to hear you perished in the wilds of America, on the Mississippi*
> *river, which you "discovered." Maybe you should have kept your gold*
> *and remained in Spain. Though I can understand how bored you must*
> *have been there after your "adventures" in the slave and gold trade and*
> *such.*
>
> *History has remembered you, Mr. De Soto. Wally found 10,000 hits*
> *when searching your name on the internet though many have to do with*
> *places named after you: hotels, diners, cars, a Floridian swamp or two.*
>
> *Wally found only three mentions of Isabel. One described her beauty*
> *though she was apparently no longer in her first youth when she*
> *married you; one her relationship with Beatriz de Bobadilla, confidant*
> *of Queen Isabel of Spain; and the last her governorship of Cuba for*

*which she is immortalized in a weathervane and on a rum bottle. She waited for you, Hernando, waited and watched the seas for signs of your ships. Did she curse the day she married you? Did she pray fervently for your safe return? Did she dream of adventures of her own? Did she take a lover who removed her shoes, rolled down her stockings, slowly slipped off petticoat after petticoat, unlaced her bodice stays with his teeth? Something you didn't think to imagine, perhaps.*

*Though I'm sure you thought of her watching the watery horizon. Watching and waiting. How could you not have?*

*Sincerely,*

*Thelma Dangerfield*

On the one of the woman, she writes:

*Dear Isabel,*

*When your husband disappeared, did you:*

*Curse your fate?*

*Accept your lot?*

*Celebrate your freedom?*

*Send ships in search of him?*

*Decide you were better off without him?*

*Worry about your future?*

*Give him up for dead?*

*Soak the bedclothes with your weeping?*

*Did you find comfort in your faith?*

*Did you take a lover? Did you keep him? Or did you let him go?*

*Whatever you did, I know you are a good and strong woman.*

*Thank you for helping me.*

*Love,*

*Thelma Dangerfield (nee Roberts)*

The musicians are for Jorge:

*Dear Jorge,*

*You are the perfect gentleman! Thanks for your many kindnesses and your diplomacy.*

*My surgery went fine and I am recovering well. I hope everything*

*works out for you and Cathy. I hope to see you again, my friend.*
*Thelma*

The bride and groom is for her friend, Cathy.

*Dear Cathy,*
*Muchas gracias for looking after the payment for Tomás and Jorge. I'm*
*glad we could travel together. I apologize for my abruptness with you.*
*I know I can be a little short with people. I appreciated your*
*enthusiasm and sense of wonder. Don't ever lose them.*
*Hope things work out for you and Jorge.*
*I look forward to seeing you again in Calgary. Your friend,*
*Thelma*

She picks up the last postcard. The one she has chosen for him. It is a reproduction of a print by the Cuban artist Eduardo Guerra, a study in blue of two nudes. A bearded man stands behind a woman with wild hair and dreamy eyes, one hand on her belly and the other on her thigh. In profile, the same woman smelling a red flower.

*Dear Tomás,*
*If I could paint, I would paint as you were the first time I truly looked*
*at you. Leaning against la cacharra naranja, looking out to sea, your*
*eyes a little sad, a wry smile on your face. I would paint the car the way*
*it was when you first got it, a brilliant tangerine orange.*
  *But I can't paint. So I will have to imagine you. Which will be easy.*
*You are etched in my mind, diamond sharp.*
  *My physical pain is gone, mostly. It is the other I have to deal with*
*now. Harder, I think.*
  *I would love to pose for you one day. No romantic pose, in*
*cornflowers or with monkey. Just me, the real Thelma, with my real*
*face.*
*With love.*
*Thelma Roberts Dangerfield*
*1827 Westmount Rd. N.W.*
*Calgary, AB*
*T2N 0G7*

She puts the postcards in an envelope in her purse and looks over at Wally. He is asleep under the beach umbrella, one arm thrown out into the sun, freckled white. A defenseless, boyish arm. She picks it up gently, places it back under the umbrella.

Waves crash against the shore. The sun creeps down the horizon. She will leave him to go and buy stamps for her postcards. When she returns, she will wake Wally and they will sit together in the fading light, watching the sky change colour, the sun sinking and the moon, Ixchel without her baby, rising.

———

THEIR PLANE HAS pulled out from the gate, and, for some as yet unexplained reason, stopped.

"Wall?"

"Umm?" He looks up from his book on conquistadors.

"I kind of butted in on this trip, didn't I?"

"Kind of."

"I'm sorry."

"It's OK, I should have left you more than a note at the hotel."

"You should have."

He returns to his book. Outside her window, two men with orange batons guide a plane into the gate beside them.

"How many times did you try to phone me, Wally?"

"At least twice."

The flight attendant offers headsets. Wally takes one. Thelma declines.

"I wanted very much to work down here, Thelma. I should have just told you about Patricia."

"Yes, you should have. Then I wouldn't have had to picture you with the lovely Rosa."

"But why? She's going out with Alvin."

"She is?"

"Yes."

"I didn't know that. For how long?"

"Since our dinner party."

"Oh. So we were successful. But why didn't you tell me you didn't want me to come to Cuba with you?"

"I tried to but you got this idea about coming. And you're a hard person to dissuade. Listen, you've been through a lot, Thelma. Why don't you rest?"

Thelma puts her hand on her abdomen. She can feel the stitches, the tenderness there.

"I found your diary in my suitcase."

"What?"

"I read it."

"Oh."

"I know, I shouldn't have, but I thought there might be a clue in it about where you were. I did think you ran off with Rosa, at first. I was kind of desperate. I'm sorry about the guy on the bike."

"Jerk."

"Do I honestly make you use only one bowl?"

"Well yeah, sometimes. But I was in a bad mood when I wrote that."

She looks over at her husband. His nose is red and peeling. The hair at his temples seems greyer than it was a few days ago.

"Did you mean for me to find the diary, Wally?"

He moves his head. A nod? A shake?

"You went off with Patricia."

She stops. He went off with a retired professor. You went off with a man who you fell in love with, Thelma.

"Yeah, I...listen, Thelma, I know you haven't been happy lately and, well, and I haven't been happy either. I mean, look at me, an aspiring writer. Aspiring for what, twenty some years? So when I got the grant and I found Pat and she wanted to help me, I was over the moon. And I wanted this trip to be mine, something I accomplished on my own. But I should have been straight with you."

"You should have."

This tangled web. Hers and Wally's. Full of holes, tiny rents. Can they be mended? Or is the fabric too tired? Too old and thin to take all the stitches required?

Is their thin picture spread of years together, as Cabrera says, enough? Is habit? Is comfort? Is knowing what someone's going to say before he says it, is that enough?

Outside the gate's window, pale tourists in bright clothes walk to the airport entrance. Are they inhaling the fragrant island air, feeling the humidity that springs hair into curls, sloughs away winter skin? Are their thoughts full of plans for adventure, romance, escape? Or are they just hoping for sun, a quiet beach, cool water to wash away their troubles?

Thelma turns from the window, puts her hands over her empty belly. There is a heaviness there, an ache.

"Water?"

"No thanks, Wally."

An emptiness. But emptiness can also hold possibility.

"You need to drink lots of fluids. Remember what Dr. Garcia Tomayo said." Wally hands her the water bottle and she takes a sip.

"OK. There." She hands it back to him.

"Thelm?"

"Uh huh?"

"I've got all the information I need to finish my book. And I was thinking. Maybe I could do some editing work. Alvin knows a guy at U of C Press who's looking for a copy editor. I mean it's not full time but it would help with expenses. Then maybe you could work four days a week, instead of five. Take that archeology course you were interested in."

He rests his hand on his knee. This hand that is so familiar, the line of freckles across his wrist, the piece of lead he jabbed into his palm in grade two, that lies just below the surface of his skin.

"Yes, Wall, a job would help."

The plane turns and taxis down the runway. Thelma holds her breath until they are up in the hazy air. The plane climbs over a scrubby field, a few skinny cows. Or are they bulls? Over an empty road. No, not empty. There's a car racing along below them, as if trying to keep pace. Then the plane banks sharply and heads out to sea.

What were those Arabic words? Walah: love that carries sorrow within it. Gharam: love that is willing to pay the price.

*Thank you* to all of my writing group buddies over the years for your helpful critical feedback, most recently JoAnn McCaig, J.Jill Robinson, Joan Crate, and Roberta Rees. To Margaret MacPherson for her faith in Thelma and the book; my childhood friend, Katherin Edwards, for edits and recommending Radiant Press and Judy Millar for the clever title ideas. To Jessie Haynes who encouraged her daughters to write and sent our youthful oeuvres to be published in the young co-operators section of *The Western Producer*. To my sisters Jocelyn and Melissa Haynes for encouragement and Leslie Haynes for her poet's eye.

*Thanks* also to Nancy Sagmeister for exploring Havana with me, to Richard (Ricardo) Ibañez and Mercedes Pupo for teaching me about your amazing country and for your friendship, and Rosita Alvarez for helping me with the Spanish (any errors are mine not hers). To my high school friends, las chicas: Connie Bossert, Michelle Novakowski and Jackie Niblock, for general cheer leading. To Susan Musgrave for the perceptive editing. To Fred Stenson and the Wired Writing Studio at the Banff Centre and most especially Anne Fleming for the rigorous and humourous mentoring. And finally to Debra Bell and the wonderful folks at Radiant Press for taking a chance on me!

Elizabeth Haynes
Calgary, AB
August 1, 2021

Elizabeth has studied writing at the University of Victoria, University of Calgary, Booming Ground (UBC) and the Banff Centre. Her fiction and travel writing have appeared in numerous magazines and anthologies including: *Walk Myself Home; This Place a Stranger* and *Shy: an anthology; Waiting,* and *You Look Good for your Age.* Her short fiction collection, *Speak Mandarin Not Dialect,* was a finalist for the Alberta Book Awards. She has won the Western Magazine Award and the American Heart Award for fiction. She works as a Speech-Language Pathologist, studies Spanish and travels whenever she can. Elizabeth lives in Calgary, Alberta.